Hurricane

STORMY WEATHER
BOOK THREE

BA TORTUGA

Contents

Hurricane

1380 Rio Rancho Blvd #1319

Rio Rancho, NM 87124

Cover illustration by AJ Corza

Published with permission

Second edition.

First electronic edition published 2008 by Torquere Press. Second Printing: Dreamspinner Press, 2017. Third printing: November 2019

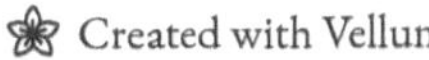 Created with Vellum

Hurricane

Stormy Weather: Book Three

Galen and Shane are back in the final installment of the *Stormy Weather* series, and a tempest of epic proportions is brewing. Once they couldn't get enough of each other, but now Galen's long hours are driving a wedge between him and Shane. Lonely and starved for his lover's attention, bartender Shane falls in with a new crowd that doesn't have his best interests at heart, and Galen struggles with a workload he can't manage and an unscrupulous partner who wants to eliminate Shane. He can barely keep his head above water, let alone chart a course home to Shane.

While they're floundering and trying to hold their relationship together, a hurricane heads for the Florida coast—and they're directly in the path of the storm. It's a crisis that will either finally break them apart or remind them how much they stand to lose if they don't hold on to each other.

Also included is the free novella *Bartender Rescue*.

To my wife, just because.

Chapter One

G ALEN THREW the phone across the hotel room and listened to it crack against the wall, pissed as hell he couldn't get Shane on the goddamned line. If he heard his own voice on the answering machine one more time....

Jesus, he hated Chicago. When he'd thrown in with Frank on the whole promotion business, he hadn't planned on being in a cold fucking city for two weeks, listening to the wind blow past the windows of a high-rise hotel.

No, sir. He thought he'd do one or two trips a year, and the rest would be on the phone, wheeling and dealing from the bait shop.

The bait shop. Hey, if Shane wasn't home and wasn't at work, maybe he was there.

His phone was all broken when he dug it out of the pile of suitcases and shit, so Galen dialed from the hotel phone.

It rang and rang, and then, about the time he was fixin' to snarl, he heard barking and laughing and Shane going "'Lo?"

"Hey, babe," he said, sitting back on the bed and breathing a sigh of relief. "Was starting to think you left town."

"Nah, Len. That's your job. I was down here cleaning some shit up."

He could hear Goober barking away, hear the radio in the background. Hell, he could damn near see Shane, whistling and working.

"Ha." His gut clenched up, but he kept it light. "Was missing you, darlin'."

"Yeah? How's the big city? You having fun?"

"It's fucking cold." Growl. Snarl. "Coming home in two days."

"No shit?" Well, that made him feel a little better—the excitement, the way he could hear the happy in Shane's voice. "I'll go get stuff at the grocery and shit."

"Yeah? Get me something to burn on the grill, man." He wanted his deck, his grill, and a naked Shane. Not necessarily in that order.

"I can do that. I'm going out on a boat tomorrow before work. Wade got him a new one and invited me out to see. Goob, lizards are not toys."

"Oh man, no slimy lizard dog toys." *Goddamn it. Fucking Wade. Fucking ass, getting time with Shane.* A not-so-quiet part of him pointed out that Shane had stopped managing the bar so they could spend more time together and he'd fucked that up, well and often. "Well, you be careful. I don't want you all waterlogged."

"Shit, unless he ties my ass to an anchor, I can swim out of anything." Shane just hooted, laugh ringing through the phone.

"Hey, that ass is mine." No one touched Shane's ass but him. Well, him and the cold dog nose.

"Yep." He heard a door open, close. "Miss you, huh?"

"You busy, darlin'? I can call back tonight." Unless Shane was working.... Maybe he should switch his flight to tomorrow.

"No. No, I'm not busy. I'm just fucking around. Pottering. You know."

Yeah, he knew. He kept thinking of Shane, wandering, working the bar, driving that old Jeep all over. Alone. Without him. Lord, he was getting maudlin. "Oh, good. I have a while before my supper meeting. Thought we could chat."

"Sure." Shane started jabbering aimlessly, telling him about the bar, about the bait shop, about the dog.

About Wade.

A knot settled deep in his belly. He didn't know who this guy was, but he was damned sure going to meet him when he got home. Maybe have a little chat.

"So, you gonna be home for a while this time? Should I order supplies for the bait shop?"

"I'll be there a bit, yeah." It was supposed to be two weeks. Galen figured he might have to extend.

"Yeah? Cool! I'll tell Buck down at the marina. They'll be tickled that you'll be here for the summer. Me too. I was thinking we ought to get us one of them big aboveground pools with a little hot tub."

"That sounds good, darlin'." God, did it. Maybe it was time he put his foot down, told the investors they needed another seller.

"Doesn't it? We could get floaties with beer holders and get Goob a little floaty of his own and.... Oh. How do you feel about Rottweilers?"

"Rott.... What did you do, Shane?" He liked Rotties as a rule. But when Shane sounded like that, it could be bad.

"Uh. Nothing?"

Uh-huh. Right. "Darlin', what did you do?" He grinned a little, playing the game of cat and mouse you had to play to get Shane to talk.

"Mmm." That was a happy little sound, all need and sex and his. "I've been good."

"Yeah? Really good? Waiting for me?" He knew. Galen knew Shane didn't cheat any more than he did, but sometimes it niggled at him.

"Well, I mean, I fucked a soccer team from Brazil and these Siamese quintuplets, but besides that? Yeah. I got you a surprise...."

"You little shit." That had him smiling, easing off his tight grip on the phone. "Wanna come home, babe."

"Then come home, Len. I got money in savings. I'll buy you a plane ticket. Come on."

"I'll come home tomorrow. Tonight I have that one last dinner. Fuck the rest of it." There. See him make a decision like he used to before he started fucking dithering.

"Tell me when to pick you up. I'll be there."

"I thought you were going boating?" That wasn't fishing for Wade info. That was Galen honestly wanting to make sure he didn't fuck up Shane's day. Mostly.

"Yeah, well, that's when I wasn't picking you up, wasn't it?"

"It was." Oh, Galen did love that man. "I'll try to make it at three."

"I'll be there with bells on."

"Promise?" Laughing at himself, Galen pulled out his little laptop and started working on a plane ticket. "I'll settle for the nipple rings."

"You got it." Shane chuckled, the sound husky. "Tomorrow, then? For real? I'm ready."

"For real, darlin'. I'm coming home."

Come hell or high water.

Chapter Two

"OKAY, NOW. Here's the deal. Y'all both stay quiet 'til Len gets in the Jeep." Two sets of tails set to wagging—Goob's big long hound dog tail and No Name Puppy's short little stubby tail.

Galen needed a dog.

Shane had thought about it for a while before somebody brought the picture into the bar of that sweet little dark puppy face with the pretty light eyebrow dealies. He'd known when he saw her. She was Galen's, and if Galen hadn't been home enough to pick her out himself, that wasn't his fault. Hell, maybe having a pup to take care of would make Galen want to stay home more.

If nothing else, Goob had a friend now. Had had a friend for three whole days.

He watched the doors, looking for that familiar hat in the crowd.... *Oh. Oh, there.*

"Galen!" He waved from the Jeep, Goober popping up and howling like mad.

Those long legs ate up the ground, Galen looking weird in that suit, but the hat and boots were the same. So was that damned pirate smile. "Hey, darlin'. Hey, Goober. You sound just the same."

Goober was wagging so hard his tail whacked No Name in the face, and she yelped, biting down on Goob's tail.

Hard.

Goob spun around, knocking the puppy down onto the floorboard with those great big ears and just barking away, telling her no.

Galen's head tilted, that hat shadowing half his face. "Who else did you bring, lover?"

"Uh. She's your welcome home surprise. Gimme your suitcase." *La la la.* See him. See him get out of Galen's reach.

The little Rottie leaped right over Goob, landed in Len's arms, and licked that stubbly face. Galen gaped for a minute, then hooted and started giving scritches. "Lord love a duck."

Oh, go him. Dog, meet Len. Len, Dog.

"Hey, you mutt. What's...?" Len peeked under the puppy's belly. "What's her name?"

"I don't know. What's her name? I've been calling her Len's puppy." And periodically, *"Goddamn it, no peeing on the floor."*

The puppy growled, getting a hold of Len's tie and pulling at it ferociously. Galen laughed hard, tugging it away. "We'll have to call her Khan."

"Khan? Cool." Galen was a little weird. "Get that tie, girl. Galen's home. He doesn't need it here."

"No shit. Hold her." That tie went flying, and Len put an arm around him and Goob and the little girl. "Hey, darlin'. I'm home."

"Yeah." Damn, it didn't feel real. Galen. Home.

"Can we go? I want my jeans." Nuzzling in, Len gave him a light kiss before grabbing the pups and hopping in the Jeep.

He nodded and hauled himself into the driver's seat, then

started the engine. It was almost weird, having Galen back in the car again. "How was your flight?"

"Fine. And it's nice, it being warm and all." One big hand landed on his leg, the gold ring on Len's pinky shining. "You okay, Shane?"

"Yeah. Missed you some." He reached out, squeezed Galen's fingers. "Maybe more than some."

"Mmm. Yeah, honey." He could hear that deep growl in Len's voice. That growl that made him understand just how much Len had missed him.

That sound shifted things in him from weird to wanting, just like that. Boom. Goddamn. "Yeah. Yeah."

Home.

Home.

Driving.

"Gonna take the road fast for me, darlin'? Let me feel the wind?" *Look at that smile.* Galen looked fucking happy to be home. He'd almost been worried that Len wouldn't be at all.

"You know it." His own smile popped out, and he stepped on the gas, pushing it, pushing them. "Got your truck detailed."

"Yeah? Get my other boots polished?" Oh, that hand was gonna get them in trouble—it kept sliding up and up his leg.

"Shit, no. They're in the closet. I didn't let the puppy chew on them, though."

"You rock." One long finger traced the seam of his jeans. *Oh. Oh damn.*

"Careful, Len." He gritted his teeth, pushed it to eighty-five.

"What?" *Sure. Uh-huh.* 'Cause innocent worked so well for Len. That man knew what he was doing.

"Don't make me beat you."

"Oh, that ain't how it works." Leaning in, Len nuzzled his shoulder. "Faster, Shane."

"Fuck. Fuck, Len. I need you." So bad it hurt, deep in his belly.

"I know, Shane. Soon. Come on. Come on." Oh, the house was gonna come into view any minute. Their house. Their bed.

He took the corner on three wheels, gravel flying everywhere as he squealed to a halt in front of the house. "Home sweet bait shop."

"Excellent." Len grabbed the little girl puppy and his bag and headed right for the house, leaving him with Goob and an amazing view of that tight ass.

Goob hopped right out and followed Galen, tail just a'wagging. Yeah. Yeah, he sort of got that. He'd be wagging too.

They got the dogs in and shut away, and damned if Len wasn't half-naked by the time they got to the bedroom, that stiff shirt and coat gone.

"You need more time in the sun." Shane was sure of it. He was also pretty damn sure Len needed more time in the bed with him.

"Later. We can lie out on the deck. Get your ass over here."

"Bossy asshole." He pounced, hands sliding right up Galen's belly. Mmm. Fuzzy.

"You know it. Need you." Len kissed him, lips hard and hungry on his, loving on him all over.

Oh hell yes. Galen was hard as a rock, those hands on his ass almost as good. They stumbled a little, slamming against the wall, Galen pressing right into him. Those hands lifted him right up. Oh, someone had been working out at the hotel fitness centers. Like, a lot. So fucking strong.

He'd forgotten how Galen tasted; how could he have fucking forgotten? He was making these noises; he couldn't hold them back for love or money.

"You got too many clothes on, darlin'. What's with that?"

God, that voice. He'd heard it on the phone; Galen always called. But here in their room, it was just too damned much. Too good.

"I dunno. Fuck, missed you." He pinched Galen's nipple, dragged his fingers down along that dark trail to glory.

"Uhn. Oh. Shane. More." Galen pulled back, putting enough room between them that Shane could open those slick suit pants.

"Uh-huh." He fished out Galen's cock, started jacking it good and hard. So fucking *fine*.

"Shane. Yeah." Galen spread, stance wide and solid, and started fucking his fist. Damn.

"Yeah. I just. I need." Shane dropped down, ignoring the scrape all along his back in favor of paying attention to that fat, heavy cock that was waiting for him.

"Darlin'?" Len stared down at him, eyes so dark they were almost black, looking dazed and hungry.

"Uh-huh?" He licked all the way up Galen's cock, tongue sliding around the tip.

"Oh Christ." Those hips pushed forward, sliding that hot prick along his lips, Len begging for it.

"Love you." He took Len all the way to the root, sucking hard.

"Uhn!" Hands cupping the back of his head, Galen started thrusting, babbling all the while. "Love you, Shane. So damned much. Missed you so bad. Remind me next time I start to go...."

Uh-uh. No way. No more going for a while. Len was home now. Damn it. He growled a little, pulling Galen into his throat. That hard belly went even tighter for him, muscles clenching. Yeah. Oh fuck. Galen tasted so damned good. He pulled those slacks down, rolling Galen's balls, pushing a little.

"That's it. That's it, darlin'. Gonna make me.... Fuck!"

That was it. Ping! Galen came for him, hot and salty and bitter-good.

Swallowing every drop down, Shane held on, taking all Galen would give him.

Len stroked his hair, staring down at him like he hung the moon. "That was the best welcome home ever, honey."

"Uh-huh." He rested his head on Galen's hip, rubbing himself hard through his jeans. *Home. Fucking hell.*

"Bed." Staggering, Len lifted him right up and hauled his ass to the bed, then tossed him down and attacked his jeans. Those big square hands closed around his cock when it sprang out of his zipper, pulling at him fist over fist.

"Len! Len!" He arched, hips snapping, needing it so goddamn bad he couldn't bear it.

"I got you. I got you, Shane." He could hear the tiny slur in Len's voice that came with a fine orgasm, but Galen wasn't gonna let him down. No, sir. That amazing mouth dropped on him like a ton of bricks.

That was all she wrote and he came so hard his teeth rattled, every fucking thing he was pouring into Galen's mouth.

Galen stroked his thighs, humming and nodding a little, that sweet mouth cleaning him gently. The tip of his cock got a little sucking kiss before Len scooted up next to him.

"H... hey." He sorta blinked, sorta grinned. "Welcome home."

Len's grin made his heart trip a little. "Hey. Glad to be back, darlin'."

"Uh-huh." He leaned in, licked the corner of Galen's mouth. "Gonna keep you here this time."

"You think?" Curling right around him, Galen pressed close, sweaty and fuzzy and *there*. "Suits me."

Him too. Down to the bone.

Chapter Three

THE DUST was kinda terrifying. Shane used to like to clean. Galen had to wonder what had happened to that. Oh, not that the house was skanky or anything. Just... dusty. The dogs had worn little paths in some of it, though, which was hellacious cute.

Galen rubbed a hand over the back of his leather chair. "Darlin'? Where did you put those dusting cloths?"

"Huh? Oh, they're in the kitchen. Sorry." Shane headed for the drawer, whistling, tiny ass swinging. "Me and Goob've been hanging out with the guys a lot. It's closer than driving home from the club."

"The guys...?" A little spike of jealousy tried to work its way out. Galen squashed it viciously. "Cool. Anyone in particular?"

"Depends on who's available, who wants to hang. Wade— Wade Patterson—you remember him, huh? He's the one with the fancy-assed boat." Shane tossed one cloth over to him, started working away, lean muscles tensing and relaxing like Shane was doing a little dance. God, Shane was cute, ball cap covering his short, short hair, little wire glasses he only wore at home magnifying his pretty blue eyes.

"Yeah. Yeah, I do." Wade. Galen had heard that name from too damned many phone calls. He'd have to tell Wade what was what. Nicely.

"Not today, though." Shane looked over at him, those eyes damn near pinning him to the wall. "Maybe not for a few days."

"Yeah?" *Hello! Hoo yeah.* That was more like it. He took two more swipes with the dust cloth before he let it drop and grabbed for Shane instead.

"I missed you, darlin'. So bad."

"I hear you." Shane came easy, wrapping one hand around his neck and tugging him into a kiss so deep it burned at him.

"Mmm." He grabbed right for that fine ass, pulling Shane up against him so they could keep that kiss going, could forget how to breathe.

Shane hadn't forgotten how to get under his fucking skin, hands pushing into his sweats, wrapping around his cock and giving him what he needed, not giving him a chance to slow down. His skin drew up with chicken skin, his muscles shuddering. Galen spread his thighs, pushing up into Shane's touch.

"You know how long it's been, Len? Since you fucked me? Since I fucked you? I got *plans*, man."

"I like plans. You know that." His cock ached, the thought of him inside Shane's body making him so hard so fast. Jesus.

"I know." Shane grinned for him, eyes all lit up. "You think you remember how, Galen?"

"I think so. Even if it has been a bit." There was no one else for him, but he'd fantasized about it enough to remember. "Bed."

"Too fucking long. I may be a virgin again." Shane kissed his nose, winked. Not a chance.

"Oh, sure. God. Lover. I need." He dragged Shane to the bedroom, caveman style. His whole fucking body was on fire.

Shane managed to get them damned near undressed on the way too, using feet and fingers to push the clothes off.

"Yeah. That's it, darlin'. You still got some lube?" He sure as hell hoped so. They didn't have time to shop.

"You know it." Tubes started flying—raspberry and chocolate and KY and cinnamon and... guava? Who the hell made guava-flavored lube?

Galen went for the tried and true KY, grabbing that wiggling ass and pulling Shane right over. "Got it, babe."

Shane spread for him like butter under a hot knife. "Got me too."

"That's the best part." Shane was warm and sweet under his hands, under his mouth, and wasn't that a thought? Yeah. Before the lube, he needed a taste. Bending, Galen put his mouth right on Shane's skin, tongue sliding right to that tight little hole.

"Galen."

Oh fuck yes. Listen to that sound, all for him. Shane begged for it, rocking into his touch, just fucking on fire.

Humming, Galen fucked that hot hole with his tongue, loving on the man like he had in his dreams for weeks. He could feel Shane shifting, hear the slap and rub of that as Shane jacked off, moving faster, harder.

"You wait for me," he said, backing off and groping for the lube. "You just wait for me, darlin'. That's mine."

"I. Fuck. I'm...." Shane rippled, hips rocking. "Come on, come on, now."

"Now," he agreed, lining his cock up and getting all slick. He knew Shane would need stretching, but damn. He could barely wait to get inside, though. "Ready?"

"Fuck yes. Now, Galen. Need you. I won't break."

"Love." That was all a man could take. Really. Galen

pushed in, feeling like his head might explode, needing more than he could even have, but trying anyway.

"Yeah." Shane pushed back, taking him in, skin going all flushed, muscles rippling. "Yeah. Again."

"Again." Galen pushed in again, his muscles screaming, his breath coming in hard pants. He reached down and palmed Shane's stiff cock, feeling it wet and hot for him, loving that he did that.

"Missed this. Need it. You." Shane grabbed the headboard, adding his strength to the thrusts.

"Darlin'. Oh. I...." He was gonna lose it. Just boom. Galen worked harder, hips snapping, hand working hard on Shane's prick.

They were giving that old bed one hell of a workout, the springs singing "The Star Spangled Banner" as Shane jerked, shooting hard. Galen shouted that last note, his whole body shaking as he came, his cock jerking right into Shane's body. They landed together like a felled oak, bouncing and grunting.

"Oh. Better. Fucking better." Shane laughed, that tight ass jerking around his prick.

"Watch it, darlin'. You'll have me going again." Grinning, Galen nuzzled right in, smelling them together, licking Shane's skin.

"And that would so suck." Shane's laughter just did it for him, happy and horny and satisfied to the bone.

"Oh, it would. Mmm sucking." He kissed the back of Shane's neck. "Love you, honey."

"Yeah. Yeah, Len. So much."

"Good." Who cared if the house was dusty? He had what he needed right there in his arms.

Chapter Four

KHAN HAD a hold of Goob's ear and was dragging the hound around the yard, trying to get Galen's attention.

Galen, of course, was sleeping on the deck chair.

Shane thought on it some—if he let Khan pull Goob's ear off, he'd have an unbalanced basset. If he turned the hose on Galen to wake him up, he'd have a wet, bitchy Galen. If he removed Goob's ear from Khan's mouth and set both dogs on Galen's flip-flops, that would be both entertaining and leave Goob with both ears *and* wake Galen up.

Especially since Galen was still in his flip-flops.

He grabbed both dogs, hauled them over to the deck, and pointed out the blue shoes that were moving just a little as Galen snored. "Go get 'em."

Goob actually stared at him a moment, head tilted, but Khan was younger and in love with her man, and she pounced. Hard.

Galen shouted and flailed, almost kicking his pup, but the man was good, even half-asleep. "What the fuck?"

Shane grinned, snorting as Goob got into it, grabbing one shoe and shaking for all he was worth.

"Shit! Shane. Would you—" The whole kit and caboodle went down, Len crashing to the deck, the dogs badgering him.

Shane would have helped, if he could stop hooting, bent over with it. *Oh. Oh fuck. That was. Damn.*

Galen was laughing like a fool too, wiggling and trying to get away, those long legs more of a hindrance than a help. "Damn it, Goob, get off my balls!"

Goob reared back, howling away, the sound cut off when Khan grabbed one poor ear again.

"Khan!" That roar had both pups stopped in their tracks, panting, tongues lolling. Galen sat up, pushing them both off. "No biting."

Goob came running to Shane, ears flopping as Khan groveled at Galen's feet.

"Oh now." Len scritched Khan's ears, making low soothing noises. "That's a girl. Who's a good girl?"

"You are so owned, man." Shane plopped down, got himself an armful of hound dog.

"Uh-huh. Like you aren't." Those dark eyes laughed at him over Khan's head.

"I never claimed not to be, Galen." He grinned and winked. "At least Goob's a boy."

"Hey, I'm a momma's boy. Why wouldn't my dog be a girl?" With a wink, Len got up and went to get both pups a biscuit, giving them a treat.

"She's wanting to come visit. Says she hasn't seen you in forever." Not that he was fishing for news of when Len was leaving....

"Yeah? We should have her down." Stretching, Len showed off for him a little, looking much easier in his bones.

"That would be cool." Look at that man. All heavy muscle and long limbs, dark hair scattered across the wide chest and ridged belly. "I gotta go back to the club tomorrow. You gonna come see what all we've done?"

"Hell yes. I'm not letting you out of my sight for at least a week." Len wandered over and stroked his back, fingers dancing along his spine. The calluses weren't as pronounced now, Len's fingers almost weirdly soft.

"Only a week?" He leaned back into the touch, happy as a pig in shit.

"For a start...."

When Len started rubbing his shoulders? He was even happier. "Oh...." He leaned forward, head down. "More. God, it's good to have you back."

"Mmm-hmm. Sun. Swamp. You." Strong fingers dug in hard, really rolling his muscles.

"Yeah." His phone started ringing, and he ignored it, letting Galen love on him.

Goob went for his phone, growling and pulling, ears flopping like crazy. Which got Khan all fired up too, that Rottie going right for the ears.

"Tell Wade hi, Goob, and that we're real busy."

Goob barked, Galen laughed, and the phone slid off the deck. *Oops.*

"Damn. That's like the third one this year...." He snorted as it sank. Where was Vic when you needed him? Damned gators, never showing when you expected.

"Yeah, well it's not in a chicken...." Leaning down, Len kissed his shoulder, that fuzzy belly rubbing along his back.

"You making steaks for us tonight?" He hadn't felt so settled in....

Weeks.

"I am. Gonna dust off the cobwebs and fire my baby up!" Lord, feel the man bounce. Len was waaaay too excited about his grill.

"Make sure nothing had babies in it." He waited for the slap.

He got a nipple twist instead, Len biting down on his shoulder. "Asshole."

"Man. Len, you've been gone too long." He fought his grin hard. "That is my *nipple.*"

"You're so going down." Those big hands rolled him right out of his chair and across the deck, Len rubbing on him all the way.

That brought the dogs back, and things got messy—with barking and licking and laughing and wagging butts.

Good stuff.

Real stuff.

Chapter Five

GALEN FLIPPED the steaks, making sure they had a nice crosshatch pattern on them. Shane had asked for steaks, and he was gonna do his best to get them right, despite not having grilled in weeks.

Maybe months.

He heard the phone ringing inside, not his cell, but the house phone. He ignored it pretty handily.

"Leave it, darlin'," he said when Shane would have wandered in to answer. "Come help me get the potatoes unstuck."

"'Kay." Shane swerved, leaning against him. "It's just Wade. I told the boys at the club to let him know I'd be out of pocket all week. Fuck, that smells good."

"Yeah? I marinated it in your favorite red.... Honey, what's the deal with this Wade guy? I mean, y'all seem to see each other a hell of a lot." Jealousy was a stone-cold bitch, but every other word out of Shane's mouth was this fucker's name.

"I do. He's a cool guy. You'll like him, if you get to know him. He's from Texas, and he used to run some company with computers, and now he's learning to drive a boat."

"Cool. Nice to have someone to hang out with." *Shit.* He probably would like the guy. Shane had much better taste in friends than he did.

"Yeah. He was real lonely, and I was missing you fierce and getting bitchy. We've been hanging, him and me and Jake and Aaron. There's a new guy at the club, did I tell you? His *cock* is pierced. *Twice!*"

His arm went around Shane's back, squeezing. "How do you know that?"

"He pulled it out and let a magazine guy take pictures of it. He was sharing." Shane leaned a little, smiling and shaking his head. "It was fucked-up, but no one mentions my rings anymore."

"Well, there you go." Magazines. Lord. He was out of the loop in the worst way. "So do I get to meet him too? When I go to the club tomorrow?"

"Yup. You won't like him so much. He's mouthy and shit, and thinks he knows everything." It was fucking hard to be jealous with Shane not hiding a damn thing.

Galen leaned around for a kiss. God, he loved this man. All the way, deep down to his toes. Shane gave it up for him, moaning and laughing into his lips. Look at that man, wanting him. Shit. Sometimes he needed a reminder that he had something so good at home. Sometimes he was fucking stupid. The grill spit at him, seeming to agree.

"Shit! Come on, darlin'. Let's get these steaks resting."

"Mmm. Steaks. I've been dreaming of those."

"See how you are? Nice to know you love me for my steaks." The side of Shane's neck was irresistible, and Galen gnawed a little while he pulled the steaks up.

"I love you for all sorts of.... Oh. Oh, I.... Fuck. Len. Gonna leave a bruise."

"Uh-huh. You know it." That was a challenge, right? He set the steaks down and turned to really suck. Right there. He hadn't heard that raw sound in weeks, hadn't seen that tanned, fine skin covered in his bruises in longer. Goddamn it.

Galen nibbled and licked until Shane was squirming, making happy noises. Then he grinned and backed off. "Want supper?"

"Fucker." Shane shivered, those pretty nipples tight-tight around those little gold rings. "I'm going to kick your ass."

"Yeah? Okay." That could be fun too. Shane all fired up and ready to go. Galen couldn't resist tugging at one little ring. "Be a shame to waste the steaks.... I guess they'll hold."

Shane went up on tiptoe, chin going stubborn. "We'll eat. I can wait."

Was that a challenge?

"You sure?" His fingers toyed with that ring, then went to the other to give it a nice, hard tug.

"Uh... uh-huh." Shane's belly went tight, those nipples begging for his attention.

"If you're sure...." Look at that. Someone had been working out. He stroked Shane's belly before going back to those nipples, pulling. "You need your chain."

"You need to put it on. I only wear it for you." Yeah. Yeah, that was a challenge.

"Let's go, then. Grab the steaks." He'd carry the Shane— his favorite appetizer. Once Shane had the platter, Galen hoisted the man right up, hauling him inside.

"Goddamn, you're strong." Shane held on, muscles shifting in his arms.

"I've had nothing to do but hit the gym in between meetings." He should take Shane with him. Except there were the dogs. And Shane's job....

"It shows." Shane turned his head, bit his bicep.

"Mmm. Now, where is that chain?" They put the steaks in the microwave to keep the bugs and dogs out before Galen started for the bedroom.

"In the top drawer of my dresser."

"Good." That he could reach without putting Shane down. Or Shane could. He walked them right over. "Grab it, darlin'."

Man, Shane had been buying stuff from the 'net. There were some new toys that he barely saw before that little box was grabbed, handed over.

He leaned Shane's ass against the dresser. "You looking forward to playing, honey? No plastic hands, right?"

"No plastic hands. You. I need you." Serious as a heart attack, right there.

"That's all I need to know, Shane. All I need...." The little box seemed to fight him, but he got it open, the chain glinting in the light.

Shane reached out, finger tracing the chain, the gold catching the light. "Had that a long, long time, Len."

"Been a while since we used it, huh?" He let Shane prop himself up so he could attach one end of the chain to the left nipple ring.

"Uh. Uh-huh.... A while." Shane watched, blue eyes staring at his fingers, at that pretty chain.

He got the other side clipped on and let go, letting Shane feel the weight, the pull. "Fucking pretty."

"Feels good." Shane's eyes went heavy-lidded, lips parted on a moan.

"It sure does." Shane was hot and heavy against him, rubbing all along his lower half. Made him crazy.

"Remember when they got done? I was so fucking hot for you."

"Jesus. Yeah. I remember how I was crazy because you didn't let me see the first one...." God, that trip to New Orleans had been one long party. Shane had been... well, fucking amazing.

"I wanted to surprise you. I was aching for it, man."

"You surprised the hell out of me. But it was a good kind of shock." They'd been so hot. Kinda like Galen was now. Rarin' to go. He tugged the chain, wanting Shane to give up on waiting until after supper.

Shane arched, that fine, fine fucking belly rippling for him, going pink. Shit, the things he wanted to do with all that strength. Right now he'd settle for watching Shane shiver and groan, and he'd pull at that little chain again and again. His. This was all his.

"Galen. Galen, I...." Shane humped against him, starting to shake. "More."

"Anything, darlin'. Anything for you." Jesus, he could stand there all day and watch that. Except his legs were shaking, so Galen lifted Shane again and headed for the bed.

He sat down, and Shane shifted, straddling him, hands landing on his shoulders. "Hey. You. Fuck, Len."

"Okay." He grinned, looking right into those pretty blue eyes, needing like crazy. "Hey."

"You're home." Shane pushed him back, following him right down, flat belly slapping against his while Shane wiggled out of his shorts.

"I am." Sprawling, Galen pulled at Shane's chain, watching the man shiver for him, feeling that hot body all along his.

"Do it again." Shane reached back for Galen's cock, fingers wrapped around it. Thank God for easy-access swim trunks. They needed to go, though, so Galen shucked them, twisting, making it even better where Shane touched him.

"What? This?" One more tug at the chain had all that pretty skin goose-bumping up for him, had Shane rolling his hips.

"Yeah. Yeah, Len. That. That." Shane's thumb rubbed right over the tip of his cock, working it hard enough to make his toes curl.

"More." The challenge went right out the window. Galen didn't care a bit about who won anymore. He just wanted Shane.

"More." Shane scooted back, rubbed his prick right against that tight little hole, taking the tip in before sliding off.

"Oh fuck. Shane. I.... Damn." Galen pushed up, trying to get that feeling back.

"Uh-huh." Shane teased him, taking him in and then sliding off, driving him out of his mind.

"God, darlin'. Please." He'd gone beyond being ashamed of begging a long, long time ago.

"Yeah. Yeah, Len." Just like that, Shane sank down on him, taking him to the root and squeezing him tight.

His eyes rolled, a shout pushing right out of his throat. His hips rocked up, his hands clenching on Shane's skin, just enough to bruise.

"Do it again." Shane pulled up, staring down at him. "Come on."

"Oh yeah." Yanking hard, Galen gave it to Shane, every little thing. Every big thing too. He chuckled, bucking harder with each thrust. Shane bounced on his cock, riding him hard, not backing off one bit. The chain shifted with every bounce, tugging those hard bits of flesh.

Galen reached up with one hand, the other staying right where it was to keep the rhythm going. He tugged at that pretty chain, knowing it would drive Shane wild.

"Galen! Galen, fuck!" Oh hell yes. Shane bucked, ass like a goddamn fist around him.

Arching, his muscles straining, Galen fucked Shane with everything he had, staring right into those glorious eyes. It had been too fucking long.

"Love." Shane bit the word out, hand reaching down to jack that hard cock.

"Now, darlin'. Come for me now." Galen bit it out

between clenched teeth, teetering on the fucking edge, so close he could *feel* his balls emptying.

"Now." Shane grunted, bit the word out and shot, heat splashing over his belly.

"Now!" His whole body went tight, his cock pushing in and filling Shane deep, wet and hot.

"Mmm." They stayed like that for a minute, and then Shane slumped forward, landing on him with a thud.

He wrapped his arms right around Shane's back, holding on for dear life. They lay skin to skin, just the way he liked it.

"Okay. You're better than steak." He felt Shane's grin on his chest, the soft laughter tickling him.

"Love you, darlin'. You know that, right?" Suddenly it was very important to hear Shane say it.

"I do. I miss you."

"Well, I'm right here." Galen snuggled in tighter, not minding the humidity one bit. So what if they were a little sticky.

"Yep. Where you belong." Shane nodded, patted his ass. Those fingers stayed on his skin, holding on.

"Right where I belong." That was the important thing. Galen was gonna try hard to remember it.

Chapter Six

"DUDE! SHANE!" The guys were hooting and laughing, waving to him like he'd been gone for fucking ever. Man, you'd think he'd never taken a three-day before.

"Hey, guys!" Shane waved, Galen right there. "Look who's home!"

"Dude! We thought you'd died, man. We had a pool going on about whether Shane'd murdered your ass for the insurance!" Jake's laugh rang out, the bar cracking up.

Galen snorted and shook his head, that black hat sitting low over those hot eyes. "Yeah, yeah. Shut up, y'all."

"Oh no way. We haven't messed with you in *weeks*!"

Shane chuckled, headed behind the bar to check inventory. Lord love a duck, the boys did enjoy poking the bear.

Galen didn't seem to mind, really. He just growled for the show. At least Shane thought so. "Can I have a whiskey, darlin'?"

"Sure, Len." Shane grabbed a bottle, a glass.

"Shane. Dude." Wade grinned from his corner of the bar, blond hair all in his face. "You disappeared on me!"

"My guy came home. What do you expect?"

"Oh. Man. Shot down by the steady." Wade grabbed his heart, wobbled on the chair like a big old dork.

"Hey, he's been a little busy." Oh, that was almost a growl, but Galen smiled and held out one big square hand. "You must be Wade."

"I am. You must be Galen. I've heard a shitload about you, man. Real nice to meet you. Real nice. You got yourself a good man there."

Shane beamed a little, poured Len's whiskey, and grabbed Wade a beer. "Yeah, yeah. You just hush."

"I do." The smile Len shot him was brighter, more real. Sitting at the bar, Galen tossed back his shot, their fingers brushing when he got the glass back.

Oh.

Oh now.

That felt sweet as fuck.

He was bouncing as he got back to work, sporting a little happy, jonesing on the lights and the crowd and the music. The shift seemed to fly by, and it looked like Len was being a sweetheart, talking to all the guys, including Wade. Mostly about football, but that was okay.

"You want to dance one, Len?" Maybe two. He hadn't danced in a while.

"Hell, yes." Winking, Galen hopped up and held out a hand. Man, Len never said no when he wanted to dance. Not anymore.

Shane was grinning so hard it hurt. He hopped over the bar, to the amusement of the whole goddamn bar, and let Galen lead him out onto the little dance floor. He loved how they fit, hand in glove, Galen's muscles against him. That big body slid alongside his, feeling like heaven. Well, maybe more like someplace naughty, as hot as it was. But still, it was too fun to stop for a little sweat.

The music kept on and on, Galen's hands on his ass, moving them in little circles together. The guys hooted and hollered some more, but Len wouldn't let him pay them any mind. Those eyes stayed right on his, that low, rumbly voice humming along with the music.

The bar slowly emptied out, and they were still fucking dancing, and Shane was on cloud nine—possibly cloud eleven. Goddamn.

Galen's lips slid down the side of Shane's neck. "Getting hornier all the time, darlin'."

"Uh-huh. Feels good, letting it build up."

"You think?" Grinning, Galen rubbed them together, then pushed back away.

Damn. Oh damn. "I do." Fuck him, that was nice.

"I can go there. 'Course, I like the hot and fast and dirty too. Remember that first time out by my truck?"

"God, yes." He looked up, caught in those dark eyes for a second. "You blew my mind, Len. I swear. And then that night. I'd never let anybody mark me like that before."

"You have a little bruise on your neck right now," Galen whispered, giving him a wicked grin. "I could do better, though."

Fuck. His belly rippled, muscles going tight as his cock jerked. "Yeah? You think?"

"Oh hell yes. I think a lot. Jack off to you at night in those nasty hotel rooms, thinking of leaving a trail of bruises on your belly...." Galen had that... growl thing going.

Shane was going to fucking die from pure overload. "It's still there. Just waiting for you."

"Then we'll work on it tonight, huh? Jesus, Shane." Yeah. Galen was hard against him, the zipper of those tight jeans straining.

"Uh-huh. Tonight works. Tell me you're done dancing." Please, God, before he creamed his jeans.

"I'm done. Can you leave now?" Those hard hands slid right up to his shoulders, squeezing.

"Fuck, yes. Now is good for me." Now so worked.

"Cool. Come on, darlin'. Say goodbye to the boys...."

"Bye, y'all. Going home." He didn't even look back at the few patrons and bartenders that were left; he just walked, Galen's hand on the small of his back.

That big body threw off so much heat he thought he might burst into flame. Galen was all but vibrating, pushing him faster and faster. His cock was leaking, hips moving in little jerks with every step. Shit. He hadn't needed so bad in months. Years.

"Where the hell did we park?" Len turned full circle, rumbling. Look at that man. Just look. All muscle and need.

"Toward the back." He trailed his hands along Galen's belly, teasing the ridges of muscle.

"Darlin', you're gonna make it hard to wait...." One big hand closed over his, yanking him along.

"Home." He followed, damn near humping Galen's legs as they fought to get the truck open.

The door finally sprang open on the passenger side, and his ass hit the seat, Len muscling in between his legs. He got a kiss that felt like it burned his tongue, all fire and need. He wrapped his legs around Galen's waist, tugging him in close. Their chests slapped together, the need between them burning.

"God, yeah." Nuzzling right against his throat, Galen pushed his T-shirt aside and bit down.

"Galen!" He was going to fucking crawl inside Galen's skin and rub. So fucking hot.

"Need you so damned bad." Those hands moved lightning quick, shoving his shirt up so Len could twist the rings in his nipples.

"Got. Got me. Fuck. Len. So good." That burned so fucking bright.

"Want everything." Sweet. Galen humped against him, cock rubbing his through their jeans, making him grit his teeth.

"Uh-huh. Want." He got one hand on the small of Galen's back, pushing them harder together.

"Need skin. More skin." Chuckling, Len moved back a little, fighting his hands to get at their zippers.

"Perv. In the parking lot." He spread, leaning back so Galen could have more.

"Some things don't change." His cock slapped right into Len's palm, and the man went to town, stroking him up and down.

"No. No, some things...." Shane couldn't quite get his hands to move, couldn't quite figure his shit *out*, man.

"Love the way you move for me, the way you feel." Galen licked at his throat, squeezing him.

"Love you. Come on. Come on." He humped up, ass sliding on the seat.

"Shane. Darlin'." Oh, look at the flush on those cheeks, that tanned throat. Len rubbed harder, pulled harder, eyes right there, holding his in that hot gaze.

What was he supposed to do but come so hard his teeth chattered? Nothing. Nothing at all.

"Oh fuck." That was it. Galen came for him too, big body shaking where it pressed up against him, hot as fire.

"Yeah. Home. Home and we'll tear it up." He licked Galen's lips, panting, still half-hard.

"You know we will." Groaning, Galen lifted off of him, bending to press one hard kiss to his lips. God, the man was good.

Good thing the man was his.

Chapter Seven

"NO, FRANK. I got plans." Galen resisted the urge to throw the phone at the wall. His accountant was gonna stop accepting receipts for new phones. "I have to.... What? Yes, I bought that laptop you recommended. Shit, Frank, I don't have time."

Pacing back and forth from the kitchen to the front room, Galen sucked down the warm dregs of his root beer. He had plans for Shane, and he didn't want to be all wilty, so he was skipping the beer.

"No. Look.... Khan, don't chew that. No, I was talking to the dog." *Damn it.* Shane would be out of the shower soon, rarin' to go to supper. He had to get rid of Frank. "Okay, okay, I'll think on it, all right? I got to go."

He hung up on the man who had dragged him into the fucking promotional business, then rubbed the back of his neck. Jesus, he needed an antacid.

Warm hands landed on his shoulders, thumbs working the back of his neck. Shane didn't say a goddamn thing, just rubbed some, working the tense spots. Galen let his head fall forward, let Shane take some of the grrr out of his spine. God, that felt good. Reaching back with one hand, he found Shane's hip, touching a little himself.

"You ready to go to that shrimp boil, darlin'?"

"You know it." Shane was wearing soft, loose little draw-string pants and a big old shirt that just hinted at those little rings. Goddamn.

That was one of his favorite looks.

Right behind naked Shane bouncing on his cock.

Grinning, Galen turned and pulled Shane closer, leaning down to press his mouth to Shane's open lips for a moment. "We'd best go, then, or I won't want to."

"Mmm. Nope. Wade's coming. Jake and them. There's a whole party of folks. Dancing. You fill up the cooler?" Shane had been bouncing about this thing for days.

"I did." The little flashbulb of jealousy that went off at Wade's name snuffed out just as quick as it came. Shane would have stayed home with him, even if he'd had to work. Shane didn't lie about shit.

"Cool." He got another quick kiss, and then Shane corralled the beasts and grabbed a bag of random shit—brats and chips and grapes—to bring. Lord, someone was looking forward to the beach and all that being social. Shaking his head, Galen slipped his cell phone out of his pocket and left it sitting on the kitchen counter as they left.

The sun was just setting, the spring not yet warming up to miserable as they drove out to the beach. There were a zillion fucking cars and a bonfire and music and.... Lord, somebody was already in the green. He was just there to carry the cooler and smile and wait for his chance to dance with Shane. They could get a heck of a lot nastier on the beach than they could at the bar.

"Shane! Dude!" The swarm hit as soon as Shane slid out of the truck, a half-dozen guys taking the cooler, pushing a beer in Galen's hand, and dragging Shane off to look and see and do. Wade came up, nodded.

"Hey, man. How's it going?"

"Not bad. How're you?" It was hard not to like Wade. He obviously worshipped Shane, and God knew, Galen could relate to that.

"I'm good. The decent beer's in the black coolers over there." Those eyes never left Shane, who was immediately drawn over to the makeshift bar, laughing at the little wannabe trying to spin bottles.

"Thanks. You know he's off-limits, right?" He just had to. Lord love him, he just had to.

"I know." Wade looked at him, gave him a grin. "You know if you ever turn him loose, I'll be there waiting, right?"

"Not gonna happen, but I can't blame you for trying." He gave the grin back, not really wanting to pop the guy in the nose, which was kind of a surprise.

"Cool. You're into football, huh? You look it. I played quarterback at Tennessee." They started walking, heading toward the crowd.

"No shit? Yeah, I played semipro. Never made first string for more than one season, though." Galen was watching Shane too, jonesing on the smile, the easy body language.

"Shit, the way Buster goes on about you, I thought you'd have a Super Bowl ring." Buster, damn. He hadn't heard folks call Shane that in a long damn time.

That kinda put his back up, which was unexpected. That was something he thought Shane had left behind in his party days. "Nah. I mean, I was just as good as the next guy, but the first-string guys were better than that." He wanted a shot of Jack all of a sudden.

"Bullshit." Shane was at his elbow, hand wrapping around his arm. "You rock. Hey, Wade."

"Hey, man."

"Hey, darlin'," Galen chimed in, patting Shane's hand with is free one. "You done with the hello and howdy?"

"You know it. I'm not getting stuck slinging suds. You hungry?"

"Am I awake?" His stomach growled, echoing the words. "Come on, darlin'. Let's get some meat."

"You man. You eat meat." Shane hooted, waved at another group of men tumbled together on a pile of blankets. "Steak? Hot dog? There's some chicken somewhere...."

"You know, I would kill for one of those brats we brought. Beer and onions? I'll grill." He wasn't letting Shane out of his sight, though.

"Somebody took those to add to the others...." Shane looked around, up on tiptoe, stretching out. Pretty, pretty.

"I think it's over there, man. By the fire." Wade shook his head, waved toward the beach. "Gonna get wet, y'all. See you."

They both waved him off, wandering arm in arm until they found the grill with the bratwurst and some onions. Yeah, that was the ticket. Shane fucking knew everybody, talking and waving. They found a spot to perch, a little out of the way, and settled, Shane damn near on his lap. Wrapping his arms around that lean, square body, Galen nuzzled against the back of Shane's neck, enjoying the salt air and slight breeze.

"Mmm. This is good." Shane hummed along to the music from somebody's radio, leaning into him with a sweet grin.

"Very good." They were both having onions, so that was okay, and Wade was nowhere to be seen....

Just like Shane knew, that face turned, lips offered over. "Hey, Len."

"Hey," he returned, letting his mouth find Shane's, a wet, sweet melding.

It was the applause and whistling that broke the kiss, Shane not pulling away as much as laughing into his lips. "They're jealous."

"You know it, babe." Who wouldn't be, with Shane right there, all tanned skin and bright blue eyes?

Shane stayed right where he was, waving idly behind him, shooing the guys away. "Busy, y'all. Happy. Go... do stuff."

Now look at that. It made Galen's heart glad. He hummed, nuzzling against Shane's temple, arms squeezing a little. "They're not gonna break out a guitar and sing, right?"

"Fuck, I hope not. None of these assholes can sing worth a damn."

Snorting, he reached out and snagged a Coke someone offered, letting Shane grab the beer. Then he sat back and listened to the idle chatter, feeling Shane breathe against his chest. It was getting dark before they saw Wade again, leaning on some twink, drunk as hell. Shane chuckled. "Maybe he'll get lucky, huh? If he doesn't pass out."

"Yeah. I figured sober I'd have a better chance with you, darlin'."

"Mmm. You get all sorts of chances with me, sober or otherwise."

"You're gonna give me a swelled head." In more ways than one, he figured. Galen pulled Shane a little closer, a little more fully into his lap.

"Promises, promises." He could just see a nipple ring, the chain catching the shirt. "You get enough to eat?"

"I did. I might could use something sweet here in a bit." Not that Shane wasn't sweet enough for him. God, he was a sap.

"Yeah. There's a rum-soaked watermelon, and somebody had banana pudding...." The sun got lower, the music got louder.

A small group of guys wandered over, heads together, laughing. "Buster, dude. You want some green?"

Shane shook his head. "No, man. I got Galen."

"Aw, come on, man. You're gettin' old and stodgy." The

guys were hooting again, giving him and Shane no end of shit, but Galen was floating on that one little no.

"Yeah, yeah, yeah. That's me. Stodgy." Shane was fucking tickled, he could tell. Tickled and not moving a bit.

Stroking Shane's belly, Galen nodded at the boys. "He has to catch up with his old man. Y'all go play."

"Mmm." Shane hummed, that thin, gauzy shirt not hiding a thing. "This is way better with you home, Len. Swear to God."

"Yeah?" He kissed Shane's temple, tasting sweat and a little grit. "Love you, darlin'."

"Yeah. You doing okay? Missing work yet?"

"No. In fact I hung up on Frank today...." They'd have to have a conference call soon, but he could put it off a little longer.

"And I missed it? Damn, Len. You know I love that." Shane hooted, reaching down to pinch his leg a little. "Shit, I usually get laid from it."

"It was right before we left. Didn't want to ruin the fun." And he was having fun. Lord above, he was.

"Ah. Yeah, we don't get out enough." Shane nodded, fingers sliding on his leg. "You ever think about what you're gonna do after you're tired of the sports thing?"

"I don't know...." He hadn't thought about it because he really hadn't planned on the sports thing.

"I been thinking about Wade a lot—he quit working and bought a boat and just wants to sail. I don't think the dogs would like that."

"No. No, I think we got a good place. Are you bored, honey? You want to come with me on the road?" His fingers stilled low on Shane's stomach, and he kinda held his breath.

"And what? Sit in a room and wait? What would we do with the pups? I can't do that. I got a job and shit. 'Sides, you don't have time for me on the road." Shane sighed a little, leaned harder.

Damn. Galen turned Shane's head, kissed that sweet mouth. "Well, I figure sooner or later I need to go back to the bait shop."

"Yeah. Yeah, that's what I'm thinking. You told me I didn't have to work but another five-ten years, right? Then I could have enough saved?" Galen grinned, kissed Shane again. Shane didn't have the slightest clue, just turned the lion's share of the cash over for Galen to invest.

"It might be less than that, darlin'." Sweet, goofy man. Galen took another kiss, then another, warming to the task of distracting Shane from the whole work thing. It wasn't a hard job either, Shane sliding full into his lap, humming into his kisses.

He slid one arm around Shane's back, turning that sturdy body into his so they were chest to chest. They both moaned, rubbing hard. Yum.

Hot. Shane's cock was like a fucking brand against him, obvious as fuck in those thin pants. "You... you want to dance?"

"I do. Maybe we could dance a little behind those rocks, huh?" Maybe they could get out of sight....

"Works for me." Shane stood up, the firelight just making all those edges glow.

Fuck, he all but drooled. Maybe he did a little. Galen climbed to his feet. Yeah. He could dance, for sure.

Shane waited for him to slide his boots off and then grabbed his hand, encouraging him to slide off, head behind the stones.

They wandered around a couple of dunes, but then they stood right at the water's edge, their toes sinking into the sand. The tinny little radio sounded awfully far away, but Galen heard it enough to get the beat. That was all he needed.

It was different, dancing like this—still out in the open enough that it wasn't straight-up foreplay, private enough that they were both loose and easy, focused on nothing but the moment.

He slid his hands up and down Shane's back, his hips moving to the music. All Galen had to do was brace his legs and sway, holding Shane close. He could smell the ocean, smell Shane's soap and that scent that they made together. Shane's lips mapped his jaw, his chin, the touch easy and soft. His cock was hard as could be, but Galen wasn't rushing, didn't feel like they needed to get any busier right now. He just wanted to dance the night away.

"I think we should do this more often. Just come to the beach. Touch. Dance."

"We should...." God, how long had it been since they watched a storm come in? "Next storm we ought to take the Jeep."

"Oh yeah. Yeah." Shane's lips brushed his earlobe. "The Jeep. Those little black ties...."

"Uh-huh. Oh, darlin', what I'm gonna do to you...."

"Mmm-hmm. I'll wear the vinyl pants, the white ones." Christ. Those pants made Galen incoherent. Like babbling monkey idiot incoherent. With no shirt, just the little nipple rings and chain.... Shane was fucking irresistible. "Yeah. Yeah, you like those." His earlobe got a good, hard tug, Shane panting a little now.

"I do. I like all the parts of that equation." Galen pulled Shane up on tiptoe, really getting them fitting together.

The ground slid and slipped under their feet, both of them having to fight to stay up, together. It got him to laughing.

Finally the crowd spilled over into their little dance floor, a bunch of half-naked coeds making a rush for the water. Galen laughed, shaking his head. "You ready to take your old man home?"

"You know it." Shane chuckled, gave him another quick kiss. "Let's go, Len."

"Yeah." Steering with an arm around Shane's back, he started toward the truck. "Let's go home and do what we can't on a public beach."

"You got it. I'm ready."

Shane never looked back to say goodbye.

Sometimes it hurt, deep in his chest, how much Shane loved him. Hell, most of the time Galen didn't think he deserved it.

But he was gonna take it anyway.

Chapter Eight

T HE URGE to ask if Galen really had to go was fucking huge.

Really.

He didn't do it, because it wouldn't do a bit of good.

Fucking football.

Fucking Frank.

"You know when you'll be home?"

"I think about two weeks." Those broad shoulders were set tight, and so was Galen's fine mouth. "I put it off as long as I could."

"Yeah. Well, we'll have to go see the fireworks together. Wade says we can all go on the boat." If Shane got enough coverage at the bar....

"There you go." Galen gave him a bit of a smile. "That will be fun."

"Yeah." He nodded and wandered off to get a beer, get them both a sandwich or something. Maybe he ought to see if the guys wanted to go out tomorrow night, get fucked-up.

Galen came right up behind him, arms sliding around his waist. "You okay?"

"Yeah. Yeah, I'm cool." He leaned back, let Galen hold him a minute. "Just being a pouty asshole. I got used to having you home."

"I know, darlin'." Soft kisses landed on his neck. "I'm sorry."

"Gotta work, huh?" *But not yet. Not 'til the morning. Not yet.*

"Tomorrow." Turning him, Galen took his mouth hard, tongue pushing right in.

Oh. Oh fuck yes. Please.

Shane did his best to just let go, let it go. Galen cupped his head, tilted him to get more, and God it was hot. Burning him alive. He kept his eyes open, kept looking, eating it up. Eating Galen up.

They stood in the damned kitchen for an eternity, swaying, lips and tongues moving, before Galen picked him up and hauled his ass to the bedroom. They didn't say a fucking word, slamming the door behind them and both heading down to the mattress.

Len landed on top of him, then pulled back long enough to tear their clothes off before sitting between his thighs and rubbing hard. He pushed back, wanting to feel it, to have Galen leave something for him to remember tomorrow.

"Love...." That was what he wanted to hear. That and "I'm staying."

"Uh-huh." He knew. He did. "More."

"Yes." Licking down his throat, Galen stroked one hand along his side, fingers finally digging into his hip. So strong. He grunted, thigh muscles going taut. Yeah. Yeah, come on. More. Galen rocked, finally getting them right together where they needed to be, cock sliding along cock. Fuck. Good.

He didn't want it to stop, didn't want to come, damn it. He gasped, balls drawing up.

"Mmm." That growl was what sent him over, just... yeah.

Shane grunted, his head snapping back, Galen biting down on his shoulder. He came so hard his bones rattled, his eyes rolling back in his head.

"Shane! Jesus. Fuck...." Len came for him too, all up on his belly, making the way all slick.

He held on tight, shaking for a second, shaking with it.

Len kissed him, easy, gentle, rubbing noses. "We'll go again in a minute, huh?"

"Yeah. Yeah." He could hold on a second. Maybe longer.

He thought maybe Len could too, the way that big body curled around his, the way Len's arms went all tight and squeezy.

"Khan's gonna miss you. Bad." Khan. Goob. Him.

"Yeah? She's a good girl. But she has Goober, huh?"

"Yeah. They're a pair." He was glad to have them, have someone waiting on him after work and stuff.

"I won't be gone long, darlin'. I just have to do a couple of meetings, one appearance." He wasn't sure who Len was trying harder to convince.

"Yeah. I know. It'll fly by, and we'll go have the Fourth. You can cook on the grill. Maybe Vic'll show back up."

"There you go, honey." Yeah, that made Galen smile. He could see why, thinking about their first encounter with the big alligator.

He found a smile, even if he didn't feel it. Man, he needed to grow the fuck up and cope.

"That's it, darlin'." Maybe Len needed him to be cool and supportive and shit, but he thought Len needed to be missed too.

He kissed Galen's chin, the whiskers tickling him. He'd do whatever it took.

Whatever he had to.

Chapter Nine

THE PHONE rang. And rang. And rang. Galen bit a hangnail off his thumb. Damn it. Where the hell was Shane?

He was just about to hang up when Shane picked up. "'Lo?"

Oh damn. That was just what he needed. "Hey, darlin'. How's it going?"

"Okay. I was cleaning the grill for the Fourth. How's you?"

"I'm hanging in. Just ready to come home."

"I hear that. When should I pick you up?" He could hear the dogs barking, going to town.

"Well, I'm not sure. Frank needs me to stay one more day, but I swear I'll be home for the Fourth." He would if it killed him.

"Okay. You just let me know. I bought steaks and some fireworks for the deck, if we decided not to hang with Wade."

"Oh, you're a lover. That sounds fine." He'd much rather spend his time with Shane. Just Shane.

"Yeah. I think so too. Khan, put Goob's leg down. Goob is not a chew toy."

"She still teething? You know that baby gum stuff works on her." Of course, it was a messy, messy proposition.

"I just gave her your boots. They worked fine." *Oh. Shithead.*

"You did not. I'll beat your ass, and not in the fun way." The fun way was so much better.

"I'm terrified." Shane laughed, and he heard a bottle opening. "Shaking in my flip-flops."

"I can tell. I swear, I can't get any respect." That was true enough, if not of Shane. Frank overrode every decision he made, until he was ready to pop the man in the nose.

"Man, that sounded almost serious. Shit going bad there?" He had to say, Shane had the bartender knack for hearing problems.

"Oh, you know Frank. I'm the brawn, as far as he's concerned. The face."

He could almost *hear* Shane frown. "Galen? You're a smart guy. Real smart. He knows that, right?"

"I... yeah. Sure, honey." Shit. Frank thought he was an idiot. Good thing he'd thought to make some contract arrangements on his own with the lawyer.

"I don't like him, Galen." Well, now. That was new.

"What's up, darlin'?" Honest to God, if Frank had been dogging Shane about something, Galen *would* clock the man.

"I just don't, Galen. I don't think... I mean, I think he's not good for you."

Shit. That wasn't like Shane at all, to sound so worried about business. "Why don't we talk on it when I come home, darlin'? I want to hear what you're thinking, okay?"

"Okay. Sure. Your momma called this morning. You should call her. She's got a summer cold."

"Oh damn. She's okay, though, right?" Galen got the little

hotel pad and a pen, making a note to call and to send some flowers.... Huh. Maybe he ought to send Shane some too.

"Yeah. She's just sniffly and sneezy. She wants to meet Khan."

"Of course she does." Wandering, he wrinkled his nose at the hotel bedspread. Even in the nicer place, the thing looked damned foul. "We should have her down before hurricane season starts."

"Okay. I'll see when she wants to come. What're you doing tonight? Anything fun?"

"Nope. I'm staying in. Fixing to get to work, but I wanted to hear your voice, darlin'." He had data entry from hell to do. All those business cards and figures and shit.

"Well, then. You can talk a while. Where are you? You seen anything cool?" Shane jabbered on a little, the sound familiar, warm.

"Michigan. I don't much like Michigan." You know, he was a whiny bastard. If he hadn't gotten himself into this mess, he'd have more right to bitch and moan.

"Never been there. Is it hot? Goddamn it, Goober, quit teasing her!"

"It's not bad, I guess. I'm sorry, honey, I should be there to help." Okay. Okay, he was getting downright girly and shit, sounding like his momma.

"Yep. Come home. Control your dog." Shane chuckled, and Galen could hear the sound of the Milk-Bones in the box.

"I will. I just have to take that extra day." Giving up, he flopped on the bed. "But I could take the red eye."

"I'll be wherever you need me, Len. Just name it."

"You rock, darlin'. How's work?" Why did they always talk about him? Maybe Shane felt like he was the one away from home, but man, he wanted to hear about Shane's day.

"Same old, same old. Me and the boys are still recovering from Pride. You should've seen the crowd."

"What was the best costume?" Lord, he got a little pissy at Pride, with all those people, but Shane seemed to like it.

"Wade looked fucking great—he came in rainbow liquid latex. I thought he was gonna get mauled at the bar. My favorite was this dude dressed like Reba McIntire, though. His hair was taller than me."

"That Wade is something else." What something, he didn't know. It was hard to dislike the guy, but it pissed Galen off that he was always around.

"Yeah. He's a good guy. You wouldn't have had fun, but it was still cool. Me and the pups spent the night on the deck, a bunch of us just fucking off."

"I'm sorry I missed that part...." He loved to hang out. Jesus. What the fuck was wrong with him? He would talk to Frank in the morning, make sure the man knew he was going home for the holiday. Period.

"Me too, Len, but it'll happen again, huh? Over and over."

"Yeah. Yeah, just think of the hurricane parties we can have." That was something they could so do together. "I miss you."

"I hear that, Len. I told the storms, none of 'em can hit 'til you're home with me."

"There you go." His little laptop pinged, telling him he had an email, reminding him of all he had to do if he really wanted to cut and run for home. "I have to go, darlin'. I'll be home soon."

"'Kay, Len. Sleep well." Shane was locking doors, locking up for the night. He could see it in his head.

"You too, lover. Dream of me." He would be dreaming of Shane, no doubt.

"I do." The line went dead, leaving him with his computer, room service, and basic cable.

Chapter Ten

S HANE WAS having a fabulous fucking day.

He'd picked Galen up at the airport. They'd picked up a watermelon and a bottle of whiskey. The grill was going. The beer was cold. The sun was shining.

He dangled his feel off the pier, swaying along to the music from the radio. Fourth of July and his happy ass wasn't at the bar.

Sometimes it was good to be boss. Sucked to be bored, so he had the best of both worlds.

Galen wandered over, Coke in hand, and plopped down next to him. The man looked worn-out, but he was there and smiling.

"Hey." He leaned a little, one hand sliding over Galen's bare knee. "You need a nap before the fireworks start?"

"Huh? Oh. Maybe." Len leaned right back, warm and heavy. "This okay?"

"Yep." Better than. Of course, Khan was stalking her favorite human, crouched down, broad little butt in the air as she prepared to pounce.

"Ooph." The little girl jumped right on Len, who laughed

and scritched her ears and shit, all but tipping them right off the dock.

Goob came wandering, jealous as anything as that big beast settled in his lap with a grunt. "Hey, Goob. You going to teach Khan about fireworks?"

"Oh man. Do we have a leash if she freaks out?" That was his Len. Always worrying.

"Yeah. We got her crate too." He was getting good at this dog stuff.

"Cool." One shoulder pressed against him while Len petted the dogs, laughing at the chewing and romping.

"I haven't seen Vic yet. I'm getting kinda worried. Although with Khan, she'd bite him."

"Well, maybe he got him a girl, huh?"

Oh, that would be cute. Little baby Vics.

"I'm not sure our freezer's big enough to feed an entire family of gators, Len." No, in fact, he'd have to get a part-time job just for the chickens.

"We could get one of them chest freezers. Stock up on turkeys at Thanksgiving." Long fingers slid against his thigh, petting him too.

That tickled him, got him to laughing hard. Goob started howling, and Khan started barking, which got Galen going, and they were all rolling with it. When they sorted it all out, he was on top of Galen, Goob was on his feet, and Khan was licking their faces. "Jesus, Shane. Gonna kill me."

"Nah. Nah, it's good. Good to laugh." They needed to laugh more. Together.

"It is. C'mere." The kiss was a little Khan heavy, but they were all family, right?

"Mmm." He scooted closer, grinning as Khan tried to push between them.

"Jealous girl. As bad as Goob." They finally got a dog on each side, both of them chuckling and reaching for a drink.

"Happy Fourth, man." This was better than the boat. Any day. Wade might have been a little disappointed, but they'd decided that was okay. Him and Galen wanted to be alone.

"Yeah. Same to you, darlin'. I missed Memorial Day and Easter and all, but this I made." Galen seemed *tickled*.

"You did." He might've gone and beaten that asshole Frank's ass if Galen hadn't.

"So, what do you want to do tomorrow?" Head tipped back, Galen watched the sky, his eye wrinkles all showing smile.

"Fuck a lot. Go to the grocery store. Take a long bath." All those worked for him. So long as they were together.

"Sounds good. Maybe we can go Vic hunting...." Oh, tromping through the swamps with the dogs. Yeah.

"Cool. Oh man. We could take the little boat out." That was actually as cool as Wade's yacht.

"Oh, that's a good idea. You. Me. Boat." Cave Galen was in the house. Woo.

"Yup. Beer. Fish. Hot dogs in case of gators." He leaned down, kissed Galen's shoulder.

"Mmm. Do that again." That arm wrapped even tighter around him, holding him up close.

He grinned, tongue sliding on Galen's skin, the taste perfect.

"Oh yeah. Gonna have me for dessert?" That grin was pure-D wicked. So was Galen's hand on his back, stroking down to his butt.

"You on the menu, Len?" He could so appreciate that smile.

"I am. Only for you. Not so much the gators. Did you know they eat marshmallows?" Galen was nibbling on him too, giving him what for.

"No. No, I ain't sharing with Vic." Marshmallows? He wasn't sharing Len with anyone these days.

"Good." That hand slipped right into his baggy shorts, stroking his bare skin.

"Mmm...." That made him shiver and stretch a little, butt shifting on the deck, feet dipping in the water. "Yeah. Yeah, good."

Nodding, Len licked at the corner of his lips, rubbing up good, pushing Khan away with the other hand. Shane rolled closer, bringing their lips together, moaning at the flavor of Galen's mouth. Giving it right back, Len pushed into his mouth, that hot tongue tracing every bit of him. They were setting off some fireworks of their own.

Oh now. That was better than any boat trip. Ever.

They were still kissing happily when the actual fireworks started, breaking out just above the tree line. Oh, look at that.

"Oh dude. Len. Look." He shifted a little so they could both see, the pups pushing in close, Khan shaking like a leaf.

"Shh. S'all right, girl." Len pulled Khan into the curve of his free arm, but the other stayed right there, holding on to him. "God, I'm glad I made it home."

Goob leaned hard, head pushed into his hand. "Me too, Len. This was just what I needed."

They sort of oohed and aahed and petted the pups until it was all over, the sound of the booms fading away on the last of the smoke. Then Galen grinned over at him, nudging.

"You ready to head in?"

"Yeah. Yeah, I am. That was damn fine, wasn't it? All the colors?" Better than DC or New York or wherever that damned Frank was.

"It was perfect." Climbing to his feet, Galen hauled Shane up too, calling the dogs right along. "We'll put the pups to bed and then do a little more celebrating."

"You got it." He was right there, hand on one of those fine, tight buttcheeks. Galen wiggled for him, really giving him something to hold on to. That man had an ass to die for.

"Mmm... shake it, baby!" They chuckled at that, both tickled.

"I can really put on a show for you inside, darlin'." Oh, Len the stripper.

"Yeah?" Now that sounded fun.

"Uh-huh. You just tell me what you want." Listen to that. Him, getting to choose.

"I want you." He shut the door behind them, eyes dragging down Galen's body. "I want to see you smile." He wanted Galen to look rested and happy again. And where the *hell* did that come from?

"You make me smile, Shane." Of course, Galen wasn't smiling when he said it, was he? Nope, he was doing that laser-stare thing, that oh, you now, thing.

He sorta stopped, caught, his heart pounding in his chest. Oh shit. He loved that man.

"Okay, darlin'. Put the dogs in the kitchen and come on to the bedroom." Turning, Galen headed down the hall, ass *moving*.

"Uh-huh." Dogs. Kitchen. Moving. Look at that ass. He was sorta dazed.

Being run over by the Galen truck always did that to him. The only thing that kept his legs moving was knowing that ass was waiting for him. He had damn near shaken it off by the time he got to the bedroom. Almost felt back in control of his brain again. Of course, that was when he saw Galen, leaning against the footboard of the big bed, arms folded, legs stretched out and out.

Oh.

His fucking mouth went dry, and he stood there a second. Watching. "Hey."

"Hey, you." Galen grinned, slow and hot and all his. "Been waiting."

"I. Yeah." His cock was trying to beat its way out of his shorts.

"So what goes first? Shirt? Jeans? Your choice." That man looked like the cat who ate the canary.

"Shirt. You got the prettiest belly." It was. Fuzzy. Hard. Tanned. Ripped.

His.

Jesus.

"You got it." Slowly, inch by agonizing inch, Galen bared that heavy chest and flat belly to his eyes, peeling the shirt down off his arms, then tossing it away.

"Look at you." He just.

Just.

God *damn*.

His cock hurt, it was so fucking hard, and he yanked down his zipper, setting it free.

"You like?" Shit, Galen knew he did. Knew it so well that those big hands moved over skin, touching all of his favorite places to touch.

"Uh-huh. You.... You're fucking hot, Len. Make me...." He motioned down to his cock, already wet-tipped and dark.

"I can see that. So jeans next, huh?" Winking, Galen worked the button and zipper. "Unless you want me to do something else first...."

"Jeans are good." He licked his lips, his knees buckling a little.

"Oh, that's good. They're gettin' tight." Those jeans worked down over one hip, then the other, and Len turned for him, just like some hot peepshow stud, pushing them down over that bounce-a-quarter-off-it ass.

Shane stepped forward, hands reaching, needing to slide over that pretty ass. The jeans hit the floor, and Galen bent, holding on to the footboard, pushing right at him. Those muscled cheeks fucking begged for his hands.

"Jesus fuck." Stumbling forward, he dropped to his knees, getting a double handful, licking right up along the crease.

"Shane!" Going right up on his tiptoes, Galen groaned, hips already starting to rock. "Damn, darlin'. Yeah."

Hot, musky, his. Shane whimpered and went to town, licking and kissing, pushing into Galen's body, fucking his man.

"Good. Shane. Feels so good." He loved it when Galen growled for him, when that voice went all big bad wolf and gonna eat you up and yeah, more. One of his hands moved between Galen's legs, fingers wrapped around those heavy balls, tugging and rolling them.

"Harder." Oh, someone was wanting to play. Galen had been so fucking serious since he started working. Not relaxed enough to really get going like this. It was fucking hot.

"Mmm-hmm." He pushed into Galen's ass with his tongue, fingers tugging good and hard on those sensitive balls. More. He could do more. Hell, he could do damn near anything right now.

Len was moaning for him, low, deep sounds that slid right down his spine. That big body was tight and hard all over, every muscle clenched for him. Galen's cock was leaking and hot as a two-dollar pistol when it slapped into his fist, Galen grunting and bucking back against him with it.

"Lover. Need... need your mouth or your ass or something." Yeah. Galen fucking loved to do the doing, and Shane loved the taking.

"Anything." He spun Galen around, mouth dropping over that heavy cock like a ton of bricks.

"Fuck!" The way that pretty belly pushed in and those hips tipped up was the basis for about a thousand wet dreams. And now Len could touch him too, hand on his head, petting and stroking. Galen tasted like no one else, ever, rich and male, salty enough that his mouth watered for more. Tilting his chin, Galen gave him more, pressing into his mouth, rubbing along his tongue. "Fucking love the way you love me, darlin'."

Damn, that heated him up, balls-deep. He wrapped his lips around the base of Galen's cock, sucking nice and hard. Hips circling and pumping, Galen took his mouth, going for it. Those hands dropped to his shoulders, rubbing and squeezing, then cupped the back of his neck, holding him still so Len could take more.

Shane started shaking, hips fucking the air, hurting with it, he needed so bad.

"Come on, darlin'. Come on up here." Len finally pulled him off, just when he thought the man would shoot for him. He blinked, his lips wet and swollen, and Len yanked him to his feet to kiss him deep.

"Need." His fucking head was spinning, hips rocking furiously, cock rubbing against that flat belly.

"Me too. Want to be with you. Right with you." Their cocks rubbed when Len lifted him, pulling him up and up to get a hand around them both. They made this crazy noise, their skin sliding and catching.

"Galen." His thighs went tight, toes curling so hard his feet tried to cramp. Fuck. Fuck. He. Now.

"Yeah, Shane. Yeah. Come on." Len squeezed. Hard.

He shot so hard his back cracked, his cry winging out.

"Fuck!" That big body shuddered against him, Galen's skin hot and damp, those hips pushing hard enough to rock the bed behind him. Galen's come hit his belly, his thighs, shooting right across his skin.

Oh. Oh fuck. "Better than fireworks. Any day."

"Mnh." Saggy Len was too fucking cute. The man pressed a lazy kiss to his mouth, humming his approval.

Oh. Oh, happy Galen.

Happy Galen.

He was a fan.

"Bed." One-word sentences meant even happier Galen. They danced a little around the side of the bed before flopping, Len giving him a bouncy, hot mattress.

"Ooh." He settled in, kissing one nipple before settling down for a championship snuggle.

"We'll play some more, later, darlin'. Yeah? Right now I'm good." Long arms wrapped around him, one leg curling around his.

"Just fine, Galen. You rest." He'd just do the same, listen to Len's heart beat for a little bit.

Chapter Eleven

"GALEN! MAN, come on. We've got that great flaming cheese thing going!" Luke Pallance was calling to him, waving one beefy arm, and Galen waved back.

"In a minute, man. I'm trying to make a call...."

Trying, and not having much luck. Damn it, Shane wasn't answering his cell, and the house phone was ringing and ringing and....

"Hey. Leave us a message," his own voice told him, making him grit his teeth, the answering machine just not what he wanted.

"Shane? Come on, darlin'. If you're there, pick up."

He waited, wanting to talk to the man, not a recording. When Shane didn't appear on the other end of the line, Galen sighed. "Gonna call you back in half an hour and sing loud. It will make the dogs howl, I swear."

"Lenny! Come on!"

Jesus, they just never let up. "Love you, darlin'," he finally said, just before he hung up.

Then he plastered a grim smile on his face and went to eat

greasy, flaming cheese with a bunch of worse has-beens than him. Even if some of them were nice guys, they weren't Shane. Frank was there, trying to stare him down with that disapproving glare, and the sight of all that food made his stomach turn.

Fuck, he wanted to go home.

Soon.

"YOU FINALLY GETTING SOME INK, BUSTER?"

Shane nodded through the green haze that surrounded him. Dude, whatever that was that Aaron'd given him was *cool*. "Yeah. I want it. A tattoo."

The guys all hooted and slapped his back, but Nemo just watched, lips quirked, waiting to set up the ink and the needles. "You know what you want?"

"Yeah. Yeah, I want a *G* and an *S* all caught up together."

"Well, isn't that precious?" He was going to hit Wade with a hammer. For real.

"Don't be an asshole, Wade. You didn't have to come." Wade stood from the doorframe and headed over with a hangdog look.

"I'm just teasing, man. You're good. Where're you gonna put it?" Wade's hand slid down his back and landed right above his ass, fingers moving and leaving little light trails that he couldn't see but could imagine.

"On my shoulder." Higher. Where he could see it in the mirror.

"What's it stand for? Great Sumbitch?"

"Fuck you." Great sumbitch, asshole.

"Just asking, honey. You want me to hold your hand?"

"You gonna hold my prick when I piss too?"

Wade grasped his chest, all the guys hooting. "Oh man! Will you let me? The poor thing needs a snuggle!"

They all laughed, and Shane thought he could see it, see the laughter in blues and greens and pinks, bouncing on the air, unreal as fuck.

"Come on, Nemo. Let's do this."

"SHANE? HONEY? YOU OKAY?" WADE'S HAND SLID down his arm, fingers squeezing his elbow.

"Yeah. Sure I am." No. No, Galen and him had just had another fucking snarl about whether or not Galen got to be pitiful about missing his birthday. He was thirty-two. Thirty-two. Old. Jesus.

Thirty-two with a lover who remembered because the fucking Blackberry beeped at him in a restaurant where Galen was having steak with a bunch of biggie wows.

He'd just come out to the club, the guys hooting and hollering and pouring him drinks from the time he'd walked in. They'd remembered. Hell, they were all celebrating.

Go him.

"I got you something...." Wade handed him a little box that reminded him a lot of the box Galen'd given him his chain in.

"Oh. Oh dude. I." *Shit.*

"Open it." Wade bumped his shoulder, grinning a little, so he did.

What else was he supposed to do?

Oh. Fucking *cool*. It was a beer opener, all gold-plated and shit, on a heavy chain. "Dude, that's wicked neat!"

He hopped up, hugged Wade tight. Wade's arms wrapped right around him, squeezing the breath out of him.

Squeezing him up against a happy that wouldn't quit.

Shane let go, took a deep breath. Man, bodies were stupid things. "Thanks, buddy. This is too cool."

"I thought you could use it." Wade nodded, clapped him on the shoulder. "Come on. I'll buy you a round or two, and then we can go to the boat, have a little private celebration."

That didn't sound like the best.... "Perv."

"Nah. Nah. I'm just talking about sharing some green. We'll invite Will and Jake, okay? It's cool."

"Yeah? Cool. Yeah. Yeah, I can."

He could.

He didn't want to, but he could.

"Happy birthday, honey."

"Thanks, Wade. Come on. I need that beer."

Chapter Twelve

"Hey, Frank." Galen grabbed his erstwhile business partner by the arm when they passed in the hall of the convention center. "I can't get any reception on my phone. Would you mind calling Diane?"

"Huh?" Frank jerked to a stop, eyeing him like a shark eyed a seal. It always made Galen a little uneasy, that look. "What for?"

"Well, you know I was talking to her about that investment property for Shane. For his retirement money. No sense letting it just sit there. She said if I was interested, I needed to do it today...." He sighed as he took off his hat and scrubbed a hand over his prickly head. "Look, I can just borrow your phone...."

"No, you can't. You have a signing in three minutes. Call Diane, tell her yes. I can do that."

"Cool. Oh, and could you call Shane and tell him to expect her call? He might wonder if she just calls him out of the blue, and he'll need to sign the papers and shit." Shane was good about signing stuff, but that might be stretching it, to have a sheaf of deed paperwork show up out of the blue.

"I surely can." Frank smiled, a weird little twist of his lips. "You just leave it all to me."

It wasn't like Frank to be so fucking accommodating, but for once Galen didn't question his motives. He'd call Shane later, have a nice long talk about what all he wanted to do. Explain everything.

"Thanks, Frank. I got to go." He clapped the man on the back.

"No problem," Frank said, voice trailing after him. "No problem at all."

Shane wandered around the house, the dogs following him as he picked up the piles of mail on Galen's desk, then put them back down unread in front of Galen's dusty monitor, the poor old thing replaced by a shiny new on-the-road laptop. This was fucked. Deeply fucked.

This whole thing.

He.

Fuck.

It didn't take long to look at the whole house—the bedroom, the bath, the room they'd turned into a game room with a pool table and an old juke box, the kitchen with its red chairs. God, he'd been so fucking impressed that Galen'd had real chairs. Matching chairs.

It was still kind of cool.

Shane stood in front of the answering machine and hit the Play button for the thirtieth time. "Hey, Shane. Frank. Galen asked me to call, have you talk to that Diane Wilson lady about listing the property. He's considering getting a place up here. Can you get that done, bud? Thanks."

Thanks.

Jesus.

Maybe Wade was right. Maybe it was over and he was just too fucking stupid to pay attention. Maybe he ought to take Wade up on his offer, just get on that big old boat and take being loved good and steady over being the guy at home. Waiting.

Getting old.

Fuck.

Shane picked up the phone and dialed, needing to talk to Galen, needing Galen to tell him it was all going to be....

"Dude, Shane, you okay, buddy?" He blinked at the receiver. Jesus. Jesus, what was wrong with him?

"Shit. Uh, no. I misdialed. How's it going, man?"

"Same old, same old. Who you calling?"

"I.... Galen. He's... we're thinking of selling the land. He's not running the bait shop anymore and stuff."

"Yeah? Damn. You moving up north?" It felt good, real good, to have someone sound like that about him. Like his leaving might be the end of the world.

"Me? No. No, man. I have a job." Hell, he could have any bartending job in this town that he wanted. He knew that now. It was a fucking good thing to know.

"Oh. Oh shit. You... you're cool? You want me to come get you? I will, in a fucking second." He knew. He knew all he'd have to do was open his arms and Wade would be there, showing him that he wasn't alone.

"I know. I'm good." Except he wasn't, was he? And Wade was a fucking temptation he didn't need right now.

"Well, you know I'd let you stay with me, huh? We could stay on the boat, be real beach bums. Save you on rent and stuff."

Rent. Right. Shit. His fucking head was killing him. Why would Galen have Frank call him? "I've done the beach-bum thing. It's overrated."

"Come on, meet me for supper. I know you're not on the

schedule at the club, and I know you're needing, honey. Come on, Shane."

And when was the last time Galen knew that? When was the last time he even knew the name of the hotel Galen was in? When was the last time they'd...? Weeks. It had been weeks. Longer.

He needed to talk to Galen. They needed to fix this.

"No. I got plans tonight, man. Maybe tomorrow." Tonight he was going to deal with this shit, tell Galen it was time to come home. To sit down. Talk.

He hung up without another word and dialed straight through this time. *Come on, Len. Please. Answer the fucking phone.*

"'Lo?"

Oh, thank God. He smiled, fingers tracing the lines of the weird little painting Galen'd hung by the back door, this watercolor, fingerpainty thing.

"Hey. Hey, Galen. It's me. Shane." *I miss you. Bad.*

"Hey, darlin'. Look, I don't really have a lot of time. Did you get Frank's call? I keep hitting dead spots. My phone is crapping out."

His belly went icy. "I did. Yeah. I wanted to...."

"Cool. Take care of that paperwork for me, darlin'. I'll call you tomorrow and tell you all about it. I gotta run. The guys are waiting. There's a press conference, and I'm damn near at the door. I'll call. Tomorrow. We'll chat."

He heard a shitload of applause before the phone went dead, hand falling to his side.

Tomorrow.

Tomorrow, if things didn't come up and if the phone worked and the meetings didn't run long and....

Tomorrow, if Galen didn't have anything better than a bar manager who was just sitting and waiting and praying for things to get better.

Shane could almost see himself in the glass of the back door. Almost. Jesus, this wasn't a fucking dream, and he....

Yeah.

Time to wake up, stupid. Before he found himself in deeper shit than he was in right now. Before he ended up taking the second-best offer because he didn't have what it took to keep the first one on the hook.

He hung up the portable and grabbed Goob's and Kahn's food bowls, making sure they were clean. Two sets of hopeful eyes stared up at him, two tails wagging. "No, we're just going to get our shit together. It's time to go. We've been here long enough. Come on. I got some calls to make before the morning."

Tomorrow Galen could forget to call all he wanted.

Tomorrow he'd be gone.

Chapter Thirteen

"FRANK, I can't get through to Shane. Did you get him when you called yesterday?"

Damn it, he should have taken the time to talk when Shane had called him. Galen hated that he'd let Shane down again, and now Shane wasn't answering the goddamned phone so Galen could say he was sorry and he was coming home in a few days and he missed Shane so bad it hurt. Two months was two months too long.

They were at the breakfast buffet, Frank looking spiffy in his suit and tie. He gave Galen's jeans and boots a glare, nodding to Galen's head. "That cowboy hat is a ridiculous indulgence."

Galen's teeth ground together in the back. "Shane, Frank. Did you get him?"

"No. I left a message. I did get Diane, though." Trying to stare him down, Frank curled his lip. "Shane is an indulgence you really can't afford either, Lenny. When you move up here, you'll have to give him up."

Galen felt his mouth literally drop open. "When I move where? What the fuck are you talking about?"

Frank shrugged, picking at a piece of grapefruit. "It's like I told Shane. You're going to have to make a commitment here. You're going to have to sell your place."

"Sell my...." Eyes widening, he went back a few sentences. "You told Shane I was selling my place?"

"Jesus, keep your voice down!" Leaning across the table, Frank snarled at him. "You didn't have the balls to do it, so I did. I need your head and your dick here, Lenny."

Hands clenching into fists, Galen leaned right in too, into Frank's space. "You fucking told my lover that I was selling my house."

"Do you really want me to go into how damaging it is that you're openly gay, Galen?"

"Who are you?" He'd never liked Frank all that much, but the man had a head for business, and the initial plan for Galen's involvement had been so good Galen had gone ahead, despite his doubts. Showed him what a fine judge of character he was. He should have listened to Shane.

Shane had said Frank was bad for him. Someone knew what was what.

That flat, emotionless stare was all lizard brain, like Frank was incapable of understanding any kind of strong emotion. "Your business partner."

"No. We had a contract where I helped with your marketing. Luckily, I had a good lawyer when we drew it up, and I can get out of it."

Planting his hands, Galen surged to his feet, the urge to fly across the table almost overtaking him. The only thing that kept him from throttling Frank right then and there was Shane. If he got arrested for assault or something, he'd never get home to make it right.

"I'm out of here," Galen said, turning on the heel of one self-indulgent cowboy boot. *Fuck this shit.*

It was time to go home.

He drove until he couldn't see, then pulled into a rest stop and walked the dogs, the Mississippi wind blowing hot against his damp cheeks.

What the fuck was he doing?

What the fuck was wrong with him?

He couldn't just drive forever—he had to stop somewhere. Think. Breathe.

What did people do when they left home? Where did they go? He had money; that wasn't it this time.

This time he didn't have a plan.

He opened his phone and dialed the house, just needing to hear Galen's voice on the machine, telling him they weren't home, leave a message after the tone, blah, blah, blah.

Shane listened all the way to the end, then stopped and reached for the map. Where to go?

North? He could go to some big city and tend bar for rich bitches. *Nah.*

California had movie stars, and he was already feeling old, and plastic boobies didn't interest him.

New Orleans probably needed....

Baton Rouge.

Momma.

Oh, she was only another few hours. She'd know what to do. She might even let him in to sleep for a little bit.

Maybe.

Okay. Plan. He liked a plan.

Momma's. Then New Orleans.

Go him.

Beeeeeeep.

"Darlin', would you pick up the phone? I need to talk to you. Come on, honey. It's not true, okay? Shane?"

Galen waited. And waited. Shane never picked up. *Goddamn it.*

An hour later he tried again.

Beeeep.

"Shane, come on. Frank is.... Well. He's a solid gold ass, and I should never have trusted him. I called and picked up messages. I know what he said, and it ain't happening, okay? Please, darlin'. Call me back. I got a new cell. It's guaranteed to get through."

Galen rattled off the number, hoping against hope that Shane was just out having a beer. Or something. Not running. Then he hung up and waited some more.

Beeeep.

"Okay, Shane, I got a flight. I'm coming home. You just wait there, please? Fuck, darlin'. I want to make this up to you, okay? I'm so sorry we got all crossed up. I love you."

Galen knew when he said it that it might be too little, too late. He just hoped to hell he got there before Shane decided to take off or something. *Jesus, please just let him get there.*

Chapter Fourteen

J ESUS, HE was tired.

Like bone-deep tired.

Like driving for twenty hours with the dogs tired.

He pulled up to the little frame house with the great big rose bushes and the little iron fence and....

Oh shit.

What if she didn't let him in?

What if she screamed at him?

What if she hated him now?

Shane just sat there, the Jeep slowly cooling down, the dogs starting to whine, Goober scratching at the window, wanting out. *Shit.*

The front door finally opened. Galen's momma popped her head out the door, pink curlers still in her hair. When she saw him, she bounced down the stairs and came right over to the Jeep. "Shane! What are you doing sitting out here? Come on in. I was just making breakfast."

"I.... Hey, Momma. I.... Uh. I'm not sure you want me to. This is Khan; she's Galen's." He wanted to hop out and give Momma a hug so bad it hurt.

"Hi, Khan." Momma scratched ears and took the licking and wagging, but soon enough she was opening the door for him, pulling him out, and hugging him just as hard as he needed. "It's so good to see you, honey."

"Oh, Momma." He held on tight, heart fucking broke. "I'm so sorry."

"Huh?" She pulled back a little to look at him, a tiny frown creasing the lines around her mouth and eyes. She had Galen's eyes. Or, you know, Galen had hers. "You look so tired. Come on. I'll let you sit, and I'll cook, and you'll tell me all about it. The dogs can go in the backyard, and we'll let mine out, and they can all get acquainted."

"Momma. Momma, I left Galen." He wouldn't go in and eat her food and shit without her knowing. It wasn't fair.

Her eyes went wide, and her mouth dropped open. "Oh shit, honey. We're gonna need waffles. Come on." She grabbed his arm and hauled him into the house.

"Oh, thank God." He slumped a little, the dogs barking and scrambling at his feet. He hadn't been sure what he'd do if Momma turned him away.

"Hush, you mutts." Her voice was like thick syrup, so Louisiana it hurt, but soothing too. Momma just got the dogs fed and tucked away, playing with her own pack of mutts. Before Shane knew it, he had a glass of milk and a piece of left-over cake and a seat at her table.

"I... I don't know what to do, Momma. I didn't know where else to go. I... I stopped in Chattanooga. Looked. They wouldn't open the door to me there, though."

He'd known it.

He hadn't even gone up to the door.

"Oh, honey. What happened?" Tightening the sash on her robe, Momma bustled around, stirring batter, tossing bacon on the griddle.

He sighed, put his head on his hands. "I.... He doesn't

want me anymore, Momma. He's gonna sell the house, and he had someone else call, leave me a message. He's moving up North without me. He's never home, and.... I don't know, Momma. Maybe he's finding better options with all them rich Yankees."

He sorta thought better of Galen than that, but people changed.

"Moving up North? My Galen? No. No, honey. That has to be a mistake." She turned, spatula waving wildly. "Did you ask him?"

"I did. Sorta." Shane shrugged. "He just told me we'd talk later. He was having a press thing." He picked up the napkin holder—it had strawberries on it. Little painted strawberries. "He's a big deal now. He's got important shit to do."

Hell, they hadn't seen each other in eight weeks.

"Oh...." Something in her voice made him look up, and man, she was mad. Her eyes just flashed. Shane got ready to slide under the table, but it was Galen she started cussing. "I'm gonna murder him. Can't even talk to you? Sends someone else to do it? That boy...."

"He just...." His chest hurt, deep down. "You can't make someone stay in love, Momma. At least I can't. I didn't come here to make you mad at him. I just...." He just didn't know what else to do.

"Shane." She pressed her fingers under his chin, making him look at her. "I think something is just mixed up. I know he loves you."

"I want to believe that. I do. There's this guy at home— he's pretty, he's rich, he's got a boat, and he loves me. He's asked me a dozen times to just sail away with him, and I can't. I can't do it, and I feel so fucking stupid because Galen's gone, and I'm... I'm getting older, Momma." Jesus, he sounded like an idiot.

She just hugged him, arms squeezing tight. "We'll figure

this out. I'll call Galen and kick his ass. You'll see. You don't need to be running off with someone."

"I don't." He leaned in, squeezed her tight. "I love you, Momma. I'm so sorry. I just needed a place to stop."

"Well, you're gonna stay here as long as you need to. You're family." She patted his back, loving on him, humming just like Galen did. Only girly.

"I won't stay long. That ain't fair to Len. He's your boy. He needs you." He let his eyes close a second. Shit, what was wrong with him? He wasn't even good enough for his own momma to love and he was here, borrowing Galen's.

"Baby. Stop. You know what? You need to sleep. I can tell you haven't been sleeping." Pulling him up, Momma pointed him to the bathroom, then handed him fluffy towels and soap as he stumbled down the hall. "Now, you take a shower, and I'll get the guest bed made up."

"Can you give the pups some food? They'll be hungry." He headed in, nodding, letting her take care.

"All taken care of, baby. Go lie down. You take that load off a little." Her kind voice just followed him, making him feel at home for the first time in so long.

"Thanks, Momma. Love you, huh?" He kissed her cheek, then headed to get clean and sleep.

Maybe for like a zillion years.

Figured that when he wanted to go home, the weather would turn off horrible. The plane had been an hour and a half late taking off. His connecting flight in Chicago had been cancelled completely, and he'd had to scream at some poor guy at the desk to get another flight.

'Course, that had relieved his spleen some.

"You look tired, man," the guy next to him said. He was

cute, sounded like home in that Cajun sort of way, and looked worn to the bone himself.

"I am. Been gone too long. Ready to go home."

"Ah. Having honey troubles, eh?"

Lord, how long had it been since someone said stuff like that to him? Maybe since last Thanksgiving when they went to Baton Rouge. Was it last year? Maybe three years ago....

"Yeah. You could say that. But it's my fault, not his...." *Shit.* Galen trailed off, figuring it probably wasn't a good idea to tell a good-looking Cajun he was gay. The man might just get up and kick his ass.

"You cheat on him?" He got a sideways look, kinda speculative, and Galen had to work not to laugh. What were the odds of him getting a queer seatmate, especially one so damned pretty?

"No. I don't intend to start either."

That got him a big old grin, the man's brown eyes sparkling. "Ain't no harm in looking, though, right?"

"Not a bit."

The guy leaned in close, lowering his voice. "It's a long enough flight. Wanna talk about it?"

Surprising the hell out of himself, Galen nodded, feeling the need to just say shit out loud, get it out. Sometimes a stranger made that easier. "Actually, yeah. I do."

"Shane, honey. Are you going to call Galen?"

He shook his head, face buried in the newspaper, trying to wake up. He'd been dreaming about zombies in New Orleans chasing him through the Café du Monde and trying to eat his balls. "I don't know what to say."

Was he supposed to apologize?

Was he supposed to scream?

Was he supposed to just ask? *Hey, Galen. It's been weeks. Weeks since we saw each other. Talked. Laughed.*

Months since he felt like they were something special.

Since he felt like he was enough.

"How about 'I miss you'?"

"I've said that enough, Momma. I ain't telling him that, ever again."

She sighed, patted his shoulder. "Oh, honey. I bet you do. I really bet you do."

Chapter Fifteen

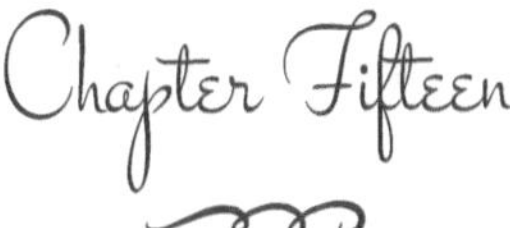

SHANE GRABBED his duffel, shoving dirty laundry and shit all in together with the clean.

Him and Momma'd been watching the news and....

Hurricane.

Not here. Not even up north with Galen.

But home.

With Galen's house. Galen's life. Right there fixing to get whomped.

Goddamn it.

A smarter man would just sit tight.

Hell, a smarter man would laugh and tell himself Galen deserved this.

A smarter man would *definitely* not be driving into a big-assed storm to save his possibly ex-lover's house.

Good thing he wasn't very smart, huh?

GOD ALMIGHTY. GALEN GOT TO THE HOUSE AROUND 6:00 a.m., and it had never felt so damned empty. He was so fucking tired he could hardly see, and the damned rain was coming down in sheets. The wind howled around the house.

Howled. The dogs. They weren't there. They hadn't met him in the yard or at the door. *Goddamn it.* Shane's Jeep was gone, the dogs were gone.... So was the dog food and bowls and everything. *Fuck.*

He needed some sleep. Hell, he needed to know where Shane was.

Galen grabbed his cell and tried calling Shane again, sighing as it went straight to voicemail. Growling, he reared back to throw the phone before thinking better of it. He might need it if the landline went out.

Christ, the storm was just getting worse.

There was no way he could call around to see if Shane was with Wade or one of the other guys. None of them would even be alive at this time of the morning, and God knew he wasn't sure if his pride could take another blow like that. Asking if they'd seen the man he let down over and over. Galen grabbed a bottle of water and headed to the bedroom, his head feeling like it was going to explode.

He'd catch a few hours of sleep, then get up and start hunting.

He'd bring Shane's ass home to him no matter what it took. Damn the storm and Frank and everyone and everything else in the world. There was no way he was gonna let Shane go.

No way.

MOMMA.

Storm's coming for Galen's house. I can't just leave it empty. I got to go take care of things. I got the dogs. I took some Cokes and made a couple of sammiches. I left you twenty dollars under the cookie jar.

I'll call. You tell Galen to stay put, yeah? Stay safe.

I love you so.

Shane

GALEN WAITED FOR THE PHONE TO RING. SEEMED like all he'd been doing lately was wait for it to ring, then waiting for someone to pick up. Then leaving messages when no one did. He'd been up since ten, listening to the storm rage outside, listening to the phone not ring back.

Goddamn that fucking Frank. If Galen ever intended to see the man again, he'd rip that thick head off the guy's bull neck and piss down the hole. He didn't intend to, though, so it was a moot point.

Come on, Momma. Pick up.

"'Lo?"

Oh, thank God. He'd started thinking she'd never fucking answer her goddamn phone again.

"Momma. Where the hell is Shane? I came home, and he wasn't here, and he's not with that Wade guy...." He'd finally broken down and called Wade at about nine, waking the man out of a solid hangover and getting a frantic "He's gone?" response.

"Well, you know, son, you'd think you know where your man is...."

"Not now, Momma." He rubbed his forehead, hurting something fierce. The damned storm was making his sinuses ache. "I know what happened, and it's all a mistake. I just need to talk to him."

Galen needed to make it right, if he could.

"You're damned right you do, son. If you'd just seen how he looked at me, like he'd lost his whole world."

Oh for fuck's....

Wait.

What?

"He's with you? Oh Jesus, tell me he's with you." A day of driving and he could be right there.

"No, honey. He was, but he heard there was a bad storm coming y'all's way, and he was worried about the house. He just left with a note. I found it this morning, honey. He must've left in the night. He took the dogs."

"Shit." Shit. Shane wasn't answering his cell. Hadn't been for days. "When did you go to bed?"

That way he at least had a time range for Shane leaving.

"I don't know...." He heard her sigh, the sound familiar and worried. "We stayed up and watched the news, so ten thirty? He was talking about heading to New Orleans, but the second he saw that storm barreling down on y'all's place, I could see him start to worry."

"Yeah?" Hell, he knew it was something big, but he hadn't even watched the news. He'd been out of his mind with other kinds of worry. "Can you call his cell? Maybe he'll answer for you."

"I been trying, baby. I hate to think of him driving tired, in bad weather."

"You're not helping, Momma. If I knew where he was, I'd go get him." He'd hunt that fine little ass down and never let it go again.

"Don't you growl at me, Galen Michael Frost. You need to pull your head out of your ass and decide what's important for you, figure out what makes you happy, and go with it."

"I have, Momma. I promise. I.... You got no idea how I felt when I heard Frank's message, knew what had sent Shane running...."

A fucking vacation timeshare. An investment. That was what Frank was supposed to set up. Something he could help Shane invest his retirement fund in. The fucking lying bastard. And Galen had trusted him when he fucking knew better.

"I told him. I told him you'd never do that, son. I know you." The faith in Momma's voice helped. It helped a lot, knowing she believed in him. She might give him all kinds of hell for at least a year, but she knew him.

Now the question was why the hell Shane hadn't.

"I'll call you when he gets here, Momma. Don't worry. I'll make it right."

Somehow.

Chapter Sixteen

T HE WIND was howling, the rain barely starting to hit the Jeep. *Come on. Come on.* Shane was so fucking tired it hurt—bone-deep. He'd been on the road since 2:00 a.m., and the weather had held at windy and drizzly, up to about dark on the other side.

Then all hell had started to break loose. *Fucking weather.*
Fucking storm.
Fucking Florida.
Fucking Galen.

Goob and Khan were howling to beat the band, the Jeep was getting blown all over the goddamn road, and he needed to get home—get the lanterns set up and the windows covered and....

It was still home, damn it, and he needed to get her stormworthy.

Shane pulled down the gravel road toward the bait shop, howling along with Goob and Khan, which was way fucking better than screaming at them to shut the fuck up.

Home.

They knew, though. Knew they were almost home. How

the hell dogs knew this shit.... Fuck, that twisted cypress almost took him out, crashing right off to the side of the Jeep.

"Jesus." He wanted to stop, but he knew if he did, he'd just be fucked, so he floored it. The Jeep vibrated, tires jittering on the wet gravel. *Goddamn it. Come on. Come on. Just a few minutes more.*

The sound of his tires squealing in mud almost made him cry out in rage. He was so....

Whoa. The outside floodlights were on.

Goddamn it. Nobody better be squatting in the house. He'd kick their asses.

He managed to get the Jeep to the bait shop, and then he gave up. Hell, he needed plywood anyway.

Yeah.

Plywood.

"Y'all get your hairy asses into the house. Right now. If there's a stranger, Khan, bite their balls off."

Khan and Goob took off, their howling turning to high-pitched barks of joy. Oh. Maybe it was someone they knew, coming out to check on the house. Maybe Wade decided to dock the boat. Shane headed to the bait shop and grabbed one of the boxes of camping gear and....

Dude.

Where was the toolbox?

"Shane? Shane! Is that you, darlin'?" The light from one of the lanterns cut a swathe through the storm, and damned if that didn't sound like... Galen.

"Len?" *Oh. Oh shit.* He didn't. He wasn't. He wasn't ready to.

Shit.

"Shane. Come help me board up the last two windows. And get the damned dogs inside before the gators get them."

Okay. Okay, he could handle all-business Galen.

He didn't answer, just slid the gear across the porch and

went to help, getting one board up before getting the dogs in and heading back for the Jeep to get his shit and the pups' dishes.

Wait.

Maybe he should just go.

Maybe he....

The rain started coming harder, hitting fast enough that it stung his skin, drenching him, just like that.

Fuck.

Galen appeared out of the rain and dragged him toward the house, all wet and bare skin and... Len.

"I...." Jesus, the man looked *good*. So fucking good.

They ran hard, the tree branches slapping the living shit out of them, the wind swirling around them, trying to knock them off their feet. *Christ.*

Christ.

"Shane! The back door! It's not boarded yet. Help me get it shut." It was banging back and forth, the dogs in the kitchen, barking at it like crazy.

"Okay. Okay." Together they managed to get the door shut, the glass shattering, sprinkling them and the kitchen. Shane braced himself against the door, face turned away from the shit blowing in, sticking in his skin. The fucking wind sounded like a freight train, just headed straight for them. "Get me a board!"

"Got it!" They worked like a real team, just like they always had. Just like Galen didn't mean to leave him all washed up.

It didn't matter. They had to save the house. And the dogs.

He was keeping both of the fucking dogs, no matter what.

Damn it.

They fought the storm, both of them grunting and groaning, cussing up a storm of their own. Then the board finally fit into place, the last nail going in, and the fury suddenly became muted, the wind not so close, so immediate.

Galen stared at him, those dark eyes so serious, so careful. He just stared back a second, not knowing what the fuck to say.

Hey, Galen. Came back to save the house you're selling?

Hey, Len. Left you, but I worry, so I drove all night.

How's the football business, stranger?

None of that worked even a little.

"I better get the glass up. The pups'll get into it." Good. That was good. Business. Broom.

"Yeah. Yeah, I'll corral them in the master bath. No windows." Galen dragged both dogs off, howling and whining. The dogs. Not Galen. Galen was eerily silent.

He swept and filled up both sinks with water, trying his damnedest not to look at the fucking answering machine. Christ, he was tired.

And there was glass all in his shirt.

The sound of the fridge opening and closing made him jump. Galen handed him a beer, smiling a little. "Hey, darlin'. Perfect timing."

"Yeah. Yeah, that old cypress went as I came in." He popped the top, sucked the beer down, the cold hitting his empty stomach with a splash.

"I heard it." The man stared hard at him, looking tired and worn. Unshaven, bags under his eyes, all pasty; Galen looked beautiful. "Been trying to call you."

"Yeah. I didn't have my phone on." He just stood there, trying to get his brain to do something. "I don't like them much, those phones."

"I know. I just needed to tell you what happened, Shane. I was starting to figure you'd never want to hear it 'til I talked to Momma." One long step forward brought Galen right to him, hands landing on his shoulders.

"I...." He took a deep breath, just breathed in the scent of rain and Galen and home, let it fill him up for a second. "This is a bad idea, Galen. I'm real tired. I don't know if I can deal with shit right now."

Not when he was feeling like the world's biggest idiot.

"Shane? Honey, look at me. I want you to know one thing before I feed you and put you to bed, okay?" Look at that man. So much like his momma. Those eyes were just the same. "Frank was lying."

"Why?" That didn't make any sense. Of course, none of this made any sense. "Are y'all? I mean, does he want...?" Shane sighed, shook his head, just sick with it. "Fuck this. I'm going to bed. I'll sleep in Momma's room, if you want, but I'm going to bed."

"No, I don't want you to sleep in Momma's bed!" Galen shook him a little. "This is all my fucking fault. But I want you, darlin'. So bad." Len pulled him into a bone-crushing hug, just holding on like the man was never gonna let go.

"You're gonna get glass on you." He leaned hard, nuzzling Galen's shoulder, telling himself to just stop, to just step away. He couldn't, though. He loved the stupid son of a bitch. Always had.

"I don't care." Kissing his cheek, Galen led him back toward the bedroom. Which was all candlelit and boarded up like Fort Knox and... somehow safe. "Get changed and cleaned up, darlin'. I'll get some soup."

Shane nodded, heading in to wash his face, strip down, and put on something dry. Goob and Khan watched him the whole time, tails still, ears held low. "It's okay, guys. It'll be okay."

One way or the other. That's what Momma'd say.

He got his shorts on and plopped down into the bed.

"You feel better? Get the glass off?" Len came in with

biscuits for the pups and canned chicken soup and iced tea for them. It all seemed so normal that he wanted to scream.

"Yeah." He sat there, stared at his hands. He'd never left anyone before, much less come back. Well, he'd left Galen once, but that hadn't worked out all that well, had it?

Christ, his head hurt.

"Shane? The storm isn't gonna blow out anytime soon. I'll keep watch. You get some sleep." Those broad shoulders slumped, and Galen patted him on the arm before putting the tray of soup and all on the nightstand. "You need anything, you holler. Okay?"

"Okay." God, he wanted to apologize; he wanted to push into Galen's arms and just take a kiss. "You... for once you picked a bad time to come home, huh? Weather's for shit."

"No, I got home just in time." Galen shrugged. "At least I hope I did. But you need to rest. You're in no place to hear what I want to say. I just.... Please just say you'll listen when you're feeling better?"

"Have I ever not?" A little flare of anger caught him, just a little one. "I'm the idiot who's been waiting around for you."

"I know. I know that." That wasn't shouting. Not really, but he could tell Len was on the very edge of it. Fine tremors shook Galen's hands. "I'm sorry, Shane. I know I'm an asshole, and you got no reason to stay around. But I love you."

"Stop it." He stood up, head pounding, beer hitting him like a ton of bricks. "I don't. I mean, you just go and you got all these people and all this stuff that's important, and I'm a fucking suds-puller, and I got nothing to give you, and then there's Wade, and... I don't want to just stay here and get old and shit and wait for you to decide you don't want me."

Christ, he'd got diarrhea of the mouth.

"Shane." That agonized look tore at him. "I quit. I've got my lawyer ending the contract now. I'm not going back to work with Frank. I came home for you. And. Jesus. You weren't here. I don't ever want to do that again." Len was on him again, right in front of him, hands hovering over his shoulders, like the man was afraid to touch him.

"I couldn't. Wade keeps asking what's wrong with me and —what?" *Quit?*

"Wade can't have you." This time Len did touch him, gripping his upper arms. "You hear? And Frank can't tell you I'm selling the house. Shit, darlin'. I asked him to do me one favor. He was supposed to just get us an agent to do some investments.... Lying sack of shit. No wonder you hated his ass."

"He's nasty. I told you that." *Investments. Investments.* Shane's knees buckled. Oh fuck. He was a fucking idiot.

Len caught him, easing down to the bed and pulling him down so he sat on Galen's lap. "I'm sorry. I know.... When you called me. I should have talked—" The boards on the window bowed in, two of the candles blowing out.

"Jesus." He looked around, shook his head. "You think we need more boards?"

This fucking storm was kicking ass. This wasn't no small tropical storm. This was a real hurricane.

"I think we might." Shaking his head, Galen stood him up and moved around the room, checking their defenses.

"Okay." He grabbed his flip-flops. "I'll grab what I can. You watch the dogs so they don't get out."

"You be careful," Galen said, giving him a hard look. "I want your ass in one piece, darlin'. I mean it."

"Yeah. Yeah, I hear you. You stay in here with the dogs." He headed out the side door to the covered porch, the debris just slamming everywhere. Jesus. Jesus, he'd never make the fucking shop. Shane figured he'd give it a try, though, dropping as low as he could and heading around the side of the house.

Galen's big hand fell on his shoulder, yanking him back.

"The dogs are in the bathroom! The tools are up front. I'll get the boards." The wind took Galen's voice and shredded it like paper, the sound bouncing crazily.

"You ain't going without me!" *No way. No. Fucking. Way.*

Galen stared at him for maybe two seconds, but it seemed like an hour. Then he got a sharp nod, a hard, stunning kiss, and a wild grin. "Come on, darlin'! It'll be a hell of a ride!"

His own grin answered Galen's, without him even wanting it to, and his fingers slid into the dark hand offered over to him. Goddamn, he had lost his mind.

They made a run for it, the storm tearing at them, even Galen's strength no match for it. They staggered to the shed, the fury of it all actually driving them to their knees once.

Soaked, sore—they just stood there, panting, dripping. "We can't stay here. It's getting worse."

"I know. Don't know how we're gonna get the boards up. Maybe the cart? That way they're flat down. We'll get less resistance." Galen was looking around, a big old bruise coming up by his eye where something had hit him.

"Drag 'em on the ground, yeah? That wind gets under the edge, we're fucked." He winced as glass broke, deeper in the shop. "We can't stay here, Galen."

"We got to go. Grab the edge of that stack and we'll haul. Hell, if you have to, you sit on them and I'll pull." Nodding, Galen grabbed his side of the wood, waiting on him.

"Keep your head down." He grabbed hold, saying a little prayer for stupid assholes and goofball dogs.

"You too." That was it. They charged out, determined as all fuck. Jesus, she was blowing like a two-dollar whore in a back seat.

It felt like the fucking wind was biting him, taking chunks out of his arms and legs. They pulled and tugged, losing the top two boards. They had a near miss right at the back door, one of the windows bowing in against the board, then shattering out, shrapnel flying every which way. Christ.

Galen gave one last mighty heave, and the boards slid right up on the back porch. "Get the door, Shane!"

"Got it!" They got the door open and slammed shut again. "This is fucked."

That wind wasn't *natural*, damn it.

"No shit. Okay, you take the one in the kitchen that just busted out. I'll get the bedroom." All business suddenly. Of course, Galen hated getting all bruised. Like that was Shane's job or something.

He headed for the kitchen, arms heavy as fuck. Jesus. He was moving to fucking Idaho.

Or Iowa.

Or some weirdassed vowel-starting state without hurricanes.

The hammer fought him, the nails flying like buzzing bees. But he finally got it, and man, two layers of boards made it easier.

When it was up, he just sat.

Hard.

There wasn't a piece of him that didn't fucking hurt. In fact, this piece of floor worked just fine for him, napping-wise.

"Hey, darlin'. Come on. The bedroom's pretty safe now." Galen lifted him gently, pulling him along.

"Huh?" He blinked, legs moving without his brain following.

"Bed. We just need to bunker down." They moved through the hall, listening to the house groan.

"'Kay." He nodded, a scared sickness, deep in his belly. "I wish you'd've stayed up north. You'd've been safe with that son of a bitch there."

"No. I had to come home and find you." Those dark eyes looked almost wild, Galen hopped up on adrenaline.

"Yeah. Yeah, I kinda get that." Because the thought of Galen here in this alone? Sucked rocks.

Galen kissed him again, tasting like saltwater and swamp, which was kinda gross. But not, because it was Galen. "Let's get some rest, darlin'. Like you wanted. Then we can talk."

"Yeah." He pulled Galen down onto the bed—gross or not—because God *damn* it, he needed to hold the bastard.

Needed to.

Len settled right in, holding him so tight it made him sweat. Looked like he wasn't the only one who wanted to feel that they were right there. Together.

It wasn't all right, but it wasn't all wrong, and Shane took it and held tight.

Just like his heart wanted him to.

Chapter Seventeen

G ALEN WOKE up to utter stillness.

The quiet was shattering, making him sit bolt upright on the bed and stare around. At the sound of the bedsprings creaking, the dogs started raising a ruckus in the bathroom, and Galen remembered them with a jolt of guilt.

After climbing carefully out of bed, Galen avoided the debris and went to let the pups out, oofing when they leaped on him.

Goob went right to the bed, back legs churning as the silly hound tried to hop up to get to Shane.

"Oh now. He's sleeping, mutt. Let him rest."

"Huh?" Shane groaned, patted the mattress without even waking up. "'Mon, y'all. Sleepin'."

Oh. Bless his heart. Galen let Goob settle in, then crawled back in on his side, Khan hopping up on him. He didn't even want to look. The storm wasn't over; they were just in the eye.

"Mmm." Shane cuddled into him with a happy sigh. That fucking sound gave him hope, because it meant something, that he could still make Shane feel that.

Of course, who knew? Maybe Shane thought he was Wade. Sighing, Galen tamped down on the jealous thought. Shane had come home for him and their house. Not Wade. No one could kiss him like Shane had and not care.

Doing a little snuggling of his own, Galen pondered checking the windows. Just in case.

Shane's hand moved, slow and easy, tracing his belly, one muscle after another. Loving on him. Humming, Galen curled into the touch, letting Khan have his back. His own hand settled on Shane's hip, fingers tracing the too-sharp hip bone.

"Mmm. Len." Shane stretched and smiled, eyelids moving some as he tried to wake up.

"Shhh. I got you. The storm is at the halfway point. It's okay." He crooned it a little, jonesing on having Shane in his arms.

"We're all here?" Shane gave each pup a scritch without opening his eyes. "Jesus, I had the worst dreams."

"Yeah? What did you dream about? Tell me and I'll make it go away." God, if only it would be that easy. Maybe he hadn't damaged them beyond repair.

"Dreamed you...." Shane frowned, eyes popping open. "I dreamed I came here and you'd gone. Are you moving up north, Len?"

"No." That was the God's honest truth, and Galen put it all in his voice. "No. I quit. For real. Walked right out on Frank and called my lawyer. I want to come home."

"Why?"

"I love you, darlin'. I.... When I couldn't get ahold of you, and then I found out what Frank did...." Galen smiled a little, shaking his head. "Well, it was a good thing we were in public, or I'd've wrung his neck like a turkey."

"You love the work, Len. I know you do, else you wouldn't... I mean, I know I'm not...." Shane sighed, shook his head. "I know I'm not all that, and I can see I'm losing it some. That's not gonna get better. I'm not gonna get any better."

Galen drew back, staring Shane right in the eye, his gut churning. "I did that, huh? Made you feel like you weren't enough. I'm sorry, darlin'. I don't love that work. I don't. I was just...." He sighed, shaking his head again, harder. "I just agreed to do it, and then I had to do the best I could."

"I get that." Shane nodded, slid down out of the bed, and headed for the bathroom. The man was covered in little scratches and bruises, just like he was.

Waiting, Galen stared at the ceiling, trying to figure out how to make Shane understand. He got it now. He did. He was ready to focus all his damned need to do everything he did well on Shane.

It didn't take long for Shane to come out, dressed in a pair of soft shorts, looking miserable. "You hungry, Len? There's bread and peanut butter."

"Darlin'...." He reached out with one hand, trying to get Shane to come sit with him. "You need some food? We could do that."

"I hate this." Shane looked straight at him. "I fucking hate not knowing what to do, not knowing whether I should go or stay. It makes me fucking insane."

Galen climbed off the bed and went to Shane, hands landing on those pretty shoulders. "I love you. I want you to stay." The hardest thing he'd ever had to say was coming up. "But I want you to do what you want, darlin'. I want you happy."

There. He was a big old girl.

"You sound like Wade."

Jealousy flashed again, hot as lightning, loud as thunder in his ears. "Yeah, well. I guess Wade has it just as bad for you as I do. But I ain't willing to give you up to him, goddamn it." He could only do selfless for so long. Galen needed Shane too damned much.

"Don't fucking snap at me. Wade's fucking been here, waiting on me to decide that I don't love you, and I *do*." Shane's chest slapped against his, the sound surprising the fuck out of him. "I love you, you bastard, and I just kept *waiting*!"

"Shane." Groaning, he pulled Shane even closer, trying to give the man a kiss that would explain how much that fucking meant to him.

Shane held back, staring at him, shaking a little. "I'm not waiting for you to decide I'm not who you want, Galen. I can't."

"Goddamn it, would you listen to me! I came back for you. I know I'm a fucking idiot, okay? I know I hurt you. I'm fucking sorry!" He was shouting, right into the void left by the eye of the storm, but he couldn't stop. Desperation made him crazy.

"Good!" Shane could fucking beller, coming right up to him, shaking him but good. "You're *my* fucking idiot, you asshole! And I got dick without you. Nothing but that fucking bar and those guys and those fucking parties. It ain't *real*, Galen!"

"No. No, this is real. Just you and me and this, okay?" Oh, please. Please let Shane mean it. Not that he wanted Shane to think the rest of his life was shit, but Galen knew the football and the press and all the fucking investments were bullshit too.

Shane nodded, staring at him. "Yeah. You and me. This. This fucking house and the pups. I'm not what I used to be. I need this now."

"Stop it." Now he did grab Shane again, shaking him a little. "Neither of us is as young as we used to be. But you're all that to me. Every fucking thing in the world."

"I don't have to be everything. I just need to be something."

"Then stick around and be mine." The lines around Shane's mouth broke his heart. Those blue eyes just looked so lost. Galen stared into them, willing Shane to understand what he knew. He was home to stay.

Shane's head tilted, just like Goob's when he heard something scratching outside. "I drove into a fucking hurricane to save your fucking *house*, Galen. I am yours."

Something touched off a little spark there, making him shake Shane again. "It's our house, darlin'. Yours too. You know that, right?"

"I...." Shane looked like he'd just been whacked with a flying tree branch. Shit. Just....

The low rumble of the wind started again, Goob and Khan starting to howl.

"Jesus. Great timing." Galen sighed, then grinned a little. "You can yell at me more in a minute. We need to check the kitchen and front room before it gets any worse."

That got him a grin right back, Shane reaching for him, fingers squeezing his arm. "Yeah, yeah."

They got to work, moving like the team they always had been.

There would be a hell of a lot more storm before it blew itself out. But at least now Galen figured they were ready to weather it.

Chapter Eighteen

THE THING about having a big fight and not fucking right after was the weirdness.

Shane sat and listened to the wind. Galen sat and listened to the emergency radio. The dogs tore around the house like idiots.

It was deeply fucked-up.

Really.

"You ever been in a big hurricane before?" He was a fucking bartender. He could make small talk.

"Huh?" Len glanced over, those dark eyes all but black, taking in every detail. "Once. When I was a kid."

"With Momma?" He sorta stared, caught in that look. It didn't matter, not even a little. He loved the man.

"Uh-huh. We had this little house on the edge of the bayou, and man, it all but blew apart. We were waiting on some feller to come get us.... Last time we waited on anyone to save us, I guess." Galen got up and came on over to sit by him, grabbed his hand and just held on.

"No shit? I bet your momma was pissed." He held right back, shoulder against Galen's. "She's looking real good. I... I want you to know that I didn't go to her to fuck with you. I just didn't know where else to go."

One big thumb stroked over the back his hand. "I'm glad you felt like you could. She thinks of you as family, darlin'. Flat out."

"Yeah." He nodded, leaned a little harder, watching the walls breathe. "I quit being manager at the club before I left. They'll let me back to work the bar." He hated managing. He liked the office with the locking door, but the hours? Sucked.

"No shit?" Turning, Galen bumped noses with him, staring at him. "For real? That mean we can take a vacation?"

"I want to. I miss that." He nodded, staring back. "I know you said I only needed a few more years, but I don't want to do it. I'll tend bar and work parties and shit."

"That's fine, honey." He got a slow, light kiss. "I got some ideas on how to get your retirement fund going." Galen held up a hand, stalling him when he opened his mouth. "It's all stuff that someone else can handle for me. No phones. No traveling."

"I don't want to take your life away. I just...." He just needed Galen. "I need more of you than I was getting." See him. See him trying to talk and shit.

Snorting, Galen leaned in, chin on his shoulder. "I was eating a bottle of Tums a day, babe."

"That's bad for you." He turned his face and took a kiss. "Those people, they're bad for you."

He meant it too. Those rich, too-smart people, they wanted shit that wasn't theirs to have. That never made anybody happy.

"Mmm." Galen's lips moved on his, slow and easy. "Yup. You were so right about Frank, darlin'. No more."

He had to admit, it was good to hear. Len was all about extremes. If he said he'd never talk to Frank again, he never would.

"Good. He... he really pissed me off." They were gonna have to talk about Wade too, and the partying. Sometime.

"I know." One hand cupped his cheek, Len nodding and meeting his eyes. "I'm sorry."

"Yeah, well. I'll just have to take it up with him." The idea actually felt really fucking good. Really.

Something crashed outside, another tree coming down.

Assuming they lived.

"Shit." Khan tried to jump over the couch, sending shit crashing down inside too, and Galen got up to grab her collar, settling her right down. He got a glinting grin. "I'd like to see you take on Frank, darlin'. You'd kick his ass."

"I would. He's been trying to fuck with my family."

"Yeah." The wind just screamed, the whole house groaning, and Shane figured that was about his opinion on Frank too.

"Where would you want to go?" They'd have to clean up and shit, but he could vacation. He so could.

"Well, I don't want to go north...."

Shane blinked, looked over at Galen. Then the laughter started, hard and sharp and coming from somewhere deep inside him, just ringing out. Len laughed right along with him, slapping one long thigh, just hooting. Oh. Oh, they were gonna hurt something.

He rolled, arms crossed over his chest. "Jesus, I love you. I swear I do."

Before he could even get himself upright Len was right there, kissing the rest of his breath out of him. That was no gentle, sweet thing, that kiss. It was hard and needy and full of fire.

This time, Shane jumped at it, pushing so close that it almost hurt. His. His family. His fucking lover. His Galen.

One arm wrapped around his back like Len was trying to pull him right inside, that big hand flattening between his shoulder blades. Len's tongue pushed into his mouth, tasting, taking his lips. The only thing to do was push right back, let Galen feel him. Let Galen know he was right fucking there.

Maybe let Galen fight for it a little.

They tumbled right off the couch, hitting the floor with a thud, Galen pressing down against him. That big body felt so damned *good*, all long legs and heavy muscles. He got one hand tangled in Galen's short hair, holding their lips together. The other hand was on that ass, happy as a pig in shit.

Galen humped against him, pressing down, kissing him until he could *feel* the bruises pop up. "Love.... Oh, Shane. Jesus. So good."

"Yeah. Yeah, Len. More." Wilder than that fucking storm, Galen just took hold of him and ran with it.

His shorts slid right down under Len's hand, and the sweats Galen had changed into went away as well. Then it was just skin and sweat and heat. He got one leg hooked around Galen, tugging them to where Galen's cock nudged his balls, his prick rubbed on that fine belly.

"Oh fuck." That long body heaved on top of his, Galen just moving faster and faster. "Missed you. So bad."

Shane didn't have anything to say to that, so he just nodded, offering all he fucking was. "Come on."

"Uh-huh. Oh. Oh damn." That cock slid against him one more time, Galen shuddering, sending wet come sliding all along his thighs. The smell hit him—all male and strong and reminding him of so much, so many reasons it had been good—that he shot, shoulders rolling with it.

Galen held him, kissed him, moaning happily for him. And laughing when the dogs peered down curiously at them from the couch.

"Think we made as much noise as the storm."

"You think?" Chuckling, Galen eased down beside him,

leaning all along his side. "Kinda like one of those hoodoo rituals to scare off the weather, huh?"

"Damn superstitious bayou baby." He settled in, blinking a little slow.

"You know it." Galen kissed his cheek, the sound of the wind seeming less threatening. "It'll blow out soon."

"We got a lot of work to do."

"We do. But we'll do it, darlin'. Together."

Chapter Nineteen

THE SECOND time Galen woke up to quiet, he knew the storm had blown over.

He had Shane in his arms, the dogs curled up against them, and the roof still hovered over their head. Hell, he figured that was a good sign. Galen grunted, moving his arm out from under Shane's head, shaking it awake.

The dogs needed out, and he needed to get an idea of the damage.

Shane popped awake, head coming up, eyes wide and blue as a cloudless sky. "It's over? Is it done? We got lights back yet?"

"No lights yet," Galen said, checking the switches. "But the wind's not howling. Want to help me take the dogs out?"

"Yeah. Yeah, let me get my jeans." Shane stumbled across the floor, still in pure automatic mode.

"We got time." Hell, neither of them had to go to work or anything.

"Huh?" He got one of those confused blinks, and then Shane shook himself awake a little more. "Sorry. Right. What was I doing?"

"Coming over to tell me good morning?" Galen spread his arms, giving Shane a good look.

"Oh. Cool." Shane headed right over, arms wrapping around his waist and squeezing tight. "Mornin', Len."

"Mmm." He draped his arms around Shane, so easy and right and good. "Hey. You look less pooped."

"Yeah. I musta slept hard." Shane lifted his face for a kiss, natural as anything.

Closing his eyes and saying a little thank-you to the god who watched out for fools and ex-football players, Galen bent and took that kiss, tasting Shane nice and deep. Shane leaned, letting him in, hand on his hip, thumb drawing lazy circles.

One hand flat on the small of Shane's back, Galen let the other hand travel, tracing lines of muscle and bone, learning Shane all over again. "You need to eat more, darlin'."

"You need to cook more. I been going out a lot."

"Yeah. I hear you. They kept making me eat flaming cheese." He laid his cheek right on the top of Shane's head and held on a little.

"Oh, weird. You smell good." Shane had something dark and swirly on his shoulder, like a bruise but not. He brushed his finger over it, but it was still there. He leaned, took a good, hard look. Ink. Shane had ink. "It's a *G* and an *S*. I got it a while ago."

"I... damn, Shane. That's pretty." His heart set up a slow, steady pounding. "You're... I.... Damn." Pulling back, he hauled Shane up to kiss the man silly.

He did love the way Shane went still and then cuddled in, lips soft in contrast with the raspy stubble on the pointed chin. Galen tasted and loved on his man a little, lips pushing Shane's mouth open so his tongue could slide inside. Oh fuck, that was good.

Those long-fingered hands slid up his arms, holding tight as Shane's tongue slid against his, pushing a little. The tiny show of aggression had him groaning, had him pushing Shane back against the wall, turning until they smacked against the door frame. He put his hands under that tight little ass and lifted, holding Shane right where he needed the pressure the most.

One of Shane's legs wrapped around him, heel digging hard into him, keeping him tight and right. They rocked, hips punching back and forth, their cocks sliding along one another. Galen figured he was in heaven. Sure enough. Shane started sucking on his tongue, pulling hard in time with the slip-slide of their cocks.

Oh. Oh, that was fine. His skin felt hot, tight, his lips swollen and tender. His prick slid against Shane's, wet at the tip, so hard he ached. "More, darlin'."

Shane's lips found his jaw, the suction sharp and stinging, bound to leave a bruise. Shit! That had him jerking, his hands sliding a little. Growling, he bent to suck his own mark up on that tanned skin, right where Shane's shoulder met his neck. Shane's muscles clenched, that rough cry just what he needed to hear.

"Yeah. Oh, darlin'." His voice sounded like it had been torn up by the storm, rough and needy. Galen bit down on the bruise, worrying it.

"Yours." Shane twisted, muscles rubbing against him hard enough that it burned. Then sharp teeth caught his bicep, hard enough to ache.

"Mine! Oh, honey. Mine." That was all he needed to know. Shane might not need to be everything, but Galen didn't do anything halfway. Heat sprayed up over his belly, onto his cock, Shane's moan filling the air along with the scent of come.

His head fell back, giving Shane all of the skin of his throat and chest, his hips pumping as his balls drew up. Just a little more....

"Mine." Shane's lips wrapped around one of his nipples, sucking good and hard.

"Uhn!" Yeah. He shot so hard he saw stars, his eyes rolling like dice. Shane was right there, holding him, urging him on. It was better than any dream he'd had on the road.

"Fine bastard." The words were soft, just whispered against him, but damn, they felt good.

"Me? You're the one with the tattoo." That was making him all tingly. Still.

"Bunch of us went together. I wanted something... good."

"Works for me, darlin'. I love it." He winked, letting Shane slide to the floor. "I might get me one."

"Yeah? Gonna let me watch?"

"Hell, yes." The thought of how he'd felt, watching Shane get pierced when they'd gone on vacation in New Orleans. Yeah. It was inspiring.

He got a grin. "Cool. It's kinda hot. Made me buzzed."

"Long as no one else got to see the hot part." He knew Shane hadn't cheated on him, but he just... he didn't want anyone to see Shane all het up.

"Nah. Shit, I had Tim Richards bring me home and pour me onto the couch after we all went back out for a few." Shane looked a little embarrassed, a little ashamed.

"Well, that's okay, then." Better than Wade. He stroked Shane's hot cheek. "You okay?"

"Yep. I just... I did a lot of partying, you know? It wasn't working for me like it used to."

Oh. Oh yeah, Galen remembered how that felt. Really. "Well.... We'll make sure you don't have to."

"Yeah. Got better things to do than miss you, huh?"

"You know it." Something creaked, crashed. "Like clean up the yard."

Shane snorted, chuckling and reaching up for his hand.

"No shit. God knows, Vic's prob'ly on the deck wanting chicken."

"Oh. I wonder if he's back. Bad storms bring them in." They got jeans and mudders on, and Galen hauled Shane to the kitchen door, the dogs starting to bounce and dance.

"Come on, beasts. Outside to do your business." Shane pulled the boards away from the door, face going a little gray as they got to see outside. Lord. They didn't have to worry about being bored.

"Shit and shinola." The place looked like a car bomb had come on up in the yard and gone boom.

"Yeah. Yeah. I better get up on the roof, huh? Check the shingles?"

"Be careful." His first instinct was to say no, but if Shane wanted to do the work, Galen needed to let him.

"Yeah. I'll look first, make sure we're sound." Shane headed out, hollering at the dogs.

"Good man." Galen set to clearing what he could of the porches, stacking wood and pieces of window, avoiding the small glass. Man, he ought to put on more clothes.

"Roof looks good. The bait shop's in big trouble."

"Yeah?" Well, shit. That would take some time and effort. "The back porch is okay. The front needs a new post."

They spent the next two hours cataloging everything, mourning the loss of a couple old cypress trees.

Filthy and tired, they both jumped when a pickup truck headed their way, Red Cross sign on one side. A guy who looked about as tired as Galen felt waved. "Y'all okay?"

"Hey. Yeah. We're without power, though. Any idea when that might get back?" They needed it for hot water, for everything.

"Couple days, at least. Maybe more. I got bottled water, propane. Some food."

"You're a lifesaver." Galen smiled at the guy, picking his

way over to shake hands. "We did okay, really. It's mostly the outbuildings."

"Dave." He got a firm shake. "Most folks did about the same. It wasn't as bad as they thought."

"Galen. Lord, I'd hate to see it worse. Shane! Want some water?"

"Hey, yeah. We oughta."

Shane waved from the roof, the Red Cross dude waving back. "I'll leave you a case. You might need it."

"Thanks. If the garage survived intact, we've got propane, so we ought to be fine." It was nice to know folks weren't as bad off as Galen had feared.

"Do you have a way out if you need it? That little Jeep down the drive is totaled."

"Shit." Galen glanced up at Shane, hoping he hadn't heard. "Yeah. I got a truck. It'll need to be cleared, but it's good."

"Good deal. I've got other folks to see. You two be safe."

"We will. Thanks again." With a case of water they could get on until things got back to rights. Hell, if they had to, they could go get a little generator.

The guy toodled off, swinging wide around the fallen trees, just bouncing on the seat.

Picking his way back to the house, Galen shouted up. "Come help me drag this water to the house, darlin'."

"Sure, Len. Gimme a couple." Shane swung down, monkey-walking down the ladder.

Stopping to stare a bit, Galen stood, hands on his hips. Yeah, that was his. *All* his. The rest was just garnish on the plate.

Shane headed his direction, then stopped, head tilting. "You okay?"

"Huh? Hell, yes, darlin'. I am surprisingly okay, considering what all we have to do." Except the whole Jeep thing. "We need to get you a new car."

"Oh dude. No. The Jeep?" Shane sighed, shook his head. "I was afraid it wasn't safe where I left it, but I couldn't get closer."

"I'm sorry, babe." Meeting Shane halfway, Galen gave the man a rib-creaking hug. "She was getting rusted out anyway."

"Yeah. Yeah. Still." Shane leaned in hard, hands wrapped around his waist.

"You okay?" It would be hard for Shane to give up the one thing he thought of as his. But Galen would work toward getting Shane to think of the house as his too. It had never occurred to him that Shane didn't think of it that way already.

"Yeah. Yeah. I got enough to put a down payment on something, and I can work the bar for the payment, huh?" Shane kissed his jaw, sighed softly.

"You have more than enough, darlin'. We need to talk about this whole real-estate thing. But that can wait until after vacation." No business. Not now. Galen squeezed, hugging hard.

"Mmm." Shane's back popped, and he got a gasp, a shiver. "Oh. Oh, that felt good."

"Yeah? You all stiff and sore? We can stop, have some food." They had cans....

"You...." Shane looked around, looked a little stunned. "Man, I don't know where to start."

"We started. Time for a break." Brooking no argument, he pulled Shane into the house and brushed weird stuff off the kitchen chairs.

"I.... You want me to make something?" When had Shane started fluttering?

"Nope. I want you to sit and talk with me while I create food." That was his job, right? And Shane's was to be easy in his skin and let Galen be the big man around the house.

"Okay. I don't... I'm not sure what's here."

"Well, I know you didn't use up all the canned peaches." Slinging an arm around Shane's back, Galen just stood a minute, soaking in the feel of that hot little body. "If we have to go eat Vic, we will."

"You are not barbecuing my gator, Len. I will beat you."

"Yeah? I'd like to see you try." He pinched Shane's butt, just a little. Man, he was feeling better all the time.

"You're full of piss and vinegar."

Yeah. Yeah, he was. He felt like he was finally coming home.

"Hey, we got through the storm. I figure this is a good sign." He took a kiss, right on Shane's open mouth, bruising in its intensity.

He could fucking feel Shane's heart pounding against him, Shane groaning, kissing him back good and hard before pulling away. Panting. Hard. "You wanted something to eat."

"It can wait." Suddenly he needed a lot more than food. Galen pushed Shane back, stumbling until they fetched up against a wall. Pressing his hips against Shane's, he grabbed both of Shane's wrists, pressing them up over the man's head.

"Galen." Those bright eyes looked shocked. Hungry. Fucking hot, and damned if they didn't get hotter when Shane tugged against his hands.

Sometimes a man forgot what was good in his life. Maybe it took a shock to remind him. Galen figured this was that time for him *and* Shane. Grinning a little, Galen tightened his grip and took another kiss, tongue pushing between Shane's lips.

Those long, lean muscles jerked, Shane pulling good and hard. When he didn't let go, he got himself a deep, hard kiss, Shane pushing back. Fucking A, it felt good. Right. Finally. Galen pushed one leg up between Shane's thighs, lifting his lover off the floor, holding them up with sheer stubbornness.

Shane pushed down, rubbing hard enough that it had to ache. Felt damn good too.

"Oh, darlin'." They broke the kiss, both of them panting. "What I'm going to do to you."

Shane chuckled, nipped his chin. "Promises, promises."

"Oh. Don't dare me, darlin'." It had been too fucking long. He picked Shane right up, slinging that lean body over his shoulder, and headed for the bedroom.

"Galen!" Fuck, those were the prettiest thighs, leading right into a tight, tight ass.

"Shane...." He grinned, waiting for the pinch. His free hand came up to pet a little, feeling Shane up.

Those fingers goosed his ass, right on cue. He grinned, bounced Shane a little. Some shit never changed.

He dumped Shane on the bed, thanking his stars they'd already cleaned it off to sleep, and came down right on top of that sweet body, his hand pulling Shane's arms up over his head again.

"Hey." Shane arched, rubbing on him like a cat, those little rings catching in the hairs on his chest.

"Hey, you." He stared down, sort of learning all the new lines on Shane's face, reacquainting himself with that smile. "God, you feel good."

Oh, look at that smile. That was enough to get his motor running, even if he hadn't already been in gear.

Galen rubbed, bending down to bite and lick, sucking up tiny bruises all along Shane's inner arm. His damned motor was screaming in high gear.

"Oh. Oh fuck." Shane's muscles jerked and shifted, his lover's hips bucking in time.

"Mmm-hmm. Gonna tear you up." Everything else could wait. *This* was reconnecting. Fuck all that talking. Galen bit down, right at Shane's chest, right next to one pierced nipple.

It was like touching Shane with a live wire. He got a cry, hands jerking violently in his grip. "Yes. Fuck. Len."

"Yeah." *Shit, yes.* His cock could pound nails, and he rubbed through their sweats. That little ring called to him, and Galen grabbed it with his teeth, pulling hard.

Mmm-hmm. Look at that body bow, stretching up for him.

Tanned, lean, body compact but perfect, Shane was still the most beautiful thing he'd ever seen. His hands got slippery with sweat, and he wished to hell he knew where the damned cuffs were. But they could do that later. For now he'd keep Shane too distracted to break his grip. Biting tended to do that.

Shane started babbling, begging for him, for more, harder. Shane was damn near crazed, hips bucking and rolling under him, pushing up and slamming into him.

He pressed down as hard as he could, letting himself feel Shane all along his body. But soon enough he had to let go with one hand to get the clothes gone. Now.

"Want you." Shane got those hungry lips on his upper arm, sucking good and hard, making his hips jerk.

"How do you want me, darlin'?" Galen asked, bucking hard. "Want me to fuck you?"

Those bright eyes caught hold of him, staring him down. "Good and hard, Len. So that I can feel it deep."

"You'll feel me for days." Pushing up, he pulled Shane's ass up to the cradle of his hips, stroking Shane's cock a couple times before leaning to search for the lube.

Shane's wrists were twisting in his hand, tugging. "I can't touch you like this. So fucking *fine*, Galen."

Hell, he'd forgotten he still had Shane's hands in one of his. Go him, finding the slick all one-handed. He grinned down before bending to take a breathless kiss. "You'll have all the time in the world to touch, babe."

"All the time?" Shane nipped his bottom lip. Hard.

"You know it." There. Jesus, that lube was hard to open. He squeezed it one-handed, getting his fingers wet so he could slip them between Shane's legs.

"Talent, talent." Oh man, if Shane could tease, he wasn't doing his job.

Pushing against Shane's hole, Galen slipped one finger in, going right for the tiny gland. He really needed to work on driving Shane crazy.

One leg went up, slid right up along his thigh, Shane bearing down against him.

"Oh fuck, darlin'." His muscles went all tight and shivery. Galen concentrated on Shane, though, pushing in and pulling out, getting the man ready for him.

"Galen." Shane jerked when he pegged that little gland, eyes rolling back in his head. "There. Right there."

"Here?" He hit that spot again and again, watching the flush creep up to cover Shane's chest and neck, making the bruises stand out more.

"Uh. Uh-huh." Shane twisted, belly clenched so fucking tight.

The sweet cock that slapped Shane's belly wasn't shabby either. Made his fucking mouth water. But he concentrated on pushing two more fingers into Shane, getting him all open.

"Oh. Oh fuck. Galen." That was it, just like that. Shane was right there, lost in it, not thinking of a fucking thing but him.

"Love you like this. Love how hot you are inside. Gonna. Soon." Pulling free, Galen settled between Shane's legs, pushing the head of his cock where he needed it the most.

"Love. Now, Galen. Right. Fucking. Now." Shane pushed, trying to bear down, trying to take him in.

"Shhh. Hush now. Breathe." He waited for Shane to open

back up again, to take a deep, long breath. Then he pushed right in, sliding home like he belonged there.

Those tight muscles rippled around him, working his prick, just driving him out of his fucking mind. Galen groaned, finally letting go of Shane's hands so he could use one of his own to prop up on, the other to pull at Shane's cock. He needed to feel it.

"Yes." Shane's hands landed on his shoulders, squeezing tight. Shane damn near fucked himself, riding his cock good and hard.

"More." His hips slapped against Shane's body, the sound as erotic as anything he'd ever heard. He could smell Shane, all sweat and saltwater and work, and when he kissed that sweet mouth, he figured he'd tasted heaven.

Oh hell yes. Shane just gave and gave to him, bucking on him and kissing him like he was all that.

Galen's balls drew up, telling him it was all over but the shouting. His thumb pressed against Shane's slit for a long moment before he gave one more good stroke. He needed Shane with him. He got it too, Shane squeezing his prick so tight his eyes rolled, heat spraying out over his hand. Jesus Christ.

That was it. He lost it, hips sawing back and forth as he pumped into Shane's body. The storm may not have killed him, but Shane just might.

"Jesus. Len. I. Wow." Shane chuckled a little, holding him tight. "Damn."

"Yeah, darlin'. Yeah." He dropped his head to give Shane a kiss, holding on right back, happy where he was.

He couldn't wait to do that again. Because that? That was working far better than all the "I love you."

Galen figured it would do.

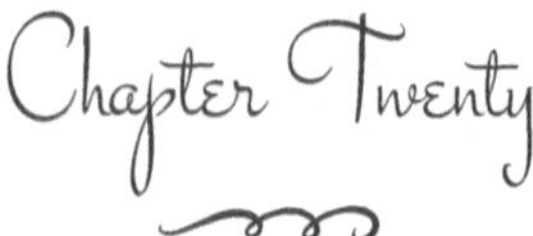

Chapter Twenty

F UCK, IT smelled foul.

Shane was in the shop, mucking shit out, trying his damnedest not to hurl at the mold and funk and stink.

Shit, you'd think there was a lizard rotting under the sink.

Still, the house was solid, Galen was working on the deck, and they'd spent two days clearing the road. That county municipal dude said they'd have lights late tomorrow and the water was safe to bathe in. All in all, it wasn't bad.

Well, except for the Jeep.

Dude.

She looked like a beer can at the end of a jock's frat party.

He shook his head and pushed another pile of sludge out the door, whistling under his breath.

"Shane? Shane, honey? Are you here? I finally got them to let me fucking dock. I was so goddamn worried!" Wade's voice rang out, seeming to bounce off everything and fill up the air. Shit. Shit, he hadn't even worried about where Wade was, what Wade was doing in the storm. Shit. What kind of a friend was he?

"I'm in the bait shop, man. How'd you weather it? The boat okay?"

"The boat's a little dinged, but it's all right. Man, you never called me back, even before the storms came in." Wade barreled in, blond curls bouncing. "Man, this place stinks."

"I didn't. I went for a drive. I needed some air." He needed to think. He needed.... He needed to see Momma.

"Oh. You could've come out on the boat." Wade's green eyes studied him, sort of guarded.

"No, Wade. No, I couldn't. I went to see family." Man, this was weird. "You didn't get hurt any, did you?"

"Nope." Wade winked, gave him a grin. "You could check, though."

Uh. No. No, he didn't think he could.

Another shadow fell over the door, Len's big body filling all the available space. "Hey, darlin', I heard someone pull up. You okay?"

"Yep. Wade came to check on us."

Thank goodness.

"Oh hey, Wade. Good to see you're okay." Man, Len was looming. Wade probably didn't know it, but Shane had seen it before.

Wade looked back at Galen, nodded. "Same to you, man. I was worried Shane was out here by himself."

"Yeah. I figured you knew better." Galen smiled slightly, staring Wade down a little. Not nasty. Just not all sweetness and light. "We managed."

"Good. Good. I would hate for something bad to have happened to him. Do y'all need anything? There's lights on the boat...."

Oh, Wade was a sweetheart. Really.

"No. No, we're supposed to have lights soon, and we've got a shitload of work to do."

Even Len unbent, coming over to clap Wade on the back.

"Thanks, Wade. We're good. Unless you got something fresh on the boat you want to share for supper."

"The McDonald's is open, man. That's supper." Wade wasn't a cook. In fact, Shane wasn't sure he'd ever seen Wade eat something not wrapped in paper....

"Well, we could do that, then." Look at Len. He looked kinda like Vic the gator when he yawned.

"Nah. Y'all go ahead. I need to go to the condo, see if it's all cool." Wade shrugged, gave him a look. "If it's all good, Shane?"

"Yeah, Wade. Yeah. I... I quit at the club. Me and Galen, we're looking into other things."

"You what?"

"I quit working the club for a while." He held Wade's eyes. "It was time to do something else." He hoped.

"Uh-huh. Well...." A hard flush crawled up Wade's tanned throat, into his cheeks. "Well, good luck, man. You'll do great. I know it."

God, he wanted to apologize. Wanted to just hide. "Thanks, buddy. Call us, man. We'll hang out."

"Sure. Sure. I'll give you a call when you get cleared out a bit."

"We'll have a beer on me, okay?" Galen chimed in, those big, tight muscles relaxing some.

"Yeah. Yeah." Wade looked... broken.

"See you, buddy. Don't be a stranger."

He watched Wade walk off, and he chewed his bottom lip, just guilty as all hell. *Fuck. Fuck.*

"You okay, darlin'?" Shit. Len always knew when he wasn't. Always.

"That was weird. I...." He met Galen's eyes. "He wanted me to go with him; he wanted lots of stuff. He's a good guy, you know? But...." But Wade wasn't Galen.

"I'm glad you didn't." Those dark eyes burned for him. "I

know he's your friend, Shane, but I'm glad you came back to me."

"I had to. I love you." It was stupid and girly, but there it was.

"I love you right back, honey." That rough voice went low, growly, and Galen stepped right up to grab him, kissing him until his vision went all fuzzy.

Oh.

"Hey." He kinda blinked, swayed a little.

"Hey." Smiling, Galen twirled him around. "What do you say we play hooky and get out of the nasty for an hour or two? See what's washed up on the beach?"

"Yeah. Hell, yeah." Just a walk. He could so do that.

"Cool. I need to stretch my legs." Holding his hand, Len wandered out into the yard, which was taking shape again.

"It's looking better, yeah? Starting to look like it used to." He laughed as the pups barreled out, hunting them.

"Yeah. Come on, you mutts. We're going to have a walk." Listen to that howl. The dogs were tired of being cooped up too.

Khan bounded over, heading straight for her person. "You'd better brace yourself...."

"Oof." Len caught the silly girl midair, turning to kind of fling her so she landed a few feet away. Khan tilted her head, wagged, and then ran right at Len again. Someone had a new game.

He hooted, reaching down to scritch Goob's ears. "Look at them, boy. Look at those two."

Goob wagged and leaned, just panting away.

Khan romped all over Galen for five minutes before she was ready to walk. The silly girl seemed to love flying around like a demented bird. Then they got moving, heading the truck so they could go to the beach.

"It's so quiet out here, with the electricity off, huh?"

"It is. Not bad, though, aside from the smell." That sideways grin had him hooting, remembering that he and Galen had *fun* together.

"You know how many lizards gotta be in that shop?" He cackled as Goob started hunting, looking for lizards.

"I don't want to think on it. Or snakes." There was a cooler in the truck, and Len shrugged when he pointed at it. "I thought we'd get some ice, get some drinks. Have supper on the beach too."

"Yeah? I can do that. I can so do that." It was sorta weird, sorta like a dream, having this back.

"Good." They got the dogs in the back of the king cab and headed out, Galen reaching over to hold his hand.

They drove in the quiet for a while, about until Shane got twitchy. "Whatcha thinkin' about, Galen?"

"Huh?" Len glanced over, smiling a little. "I was just thinking about how I wanted some fried bread."

The answer just tickled him, relaxed him, made him nod and chuckle. "I could demolish a funnel cake with strawberry."

"I could too. Maybe one with bavarian cream." That shit was nasty, but Galen loved it. Could power it down.

"Mmm-hmm. Funnel cakes, corn dogs—have we ever gone to a fair together?" He'd gone this spring with the guys, goofing off and getting drunk.

"I don't think so. I mean, we've done the boardwalk." Galen squeezed his hand before letting go to shift gears again. "You okay, darlin'?"

"Yeah. Sort of. It's different. I'd worked myself all up, been living another whole life, kinda." He didn't know how to explain.

"What's that mean?" Now Len was frowning, kinda glancing at him every few seconds. "I mean, I guess I can figure it."

"I don't know. I think it means that I thought I'd lost you, and I didn't, and I'd got used to... fucking up." Was that just making it worse?

Galen pulled off at a small public beach, not the one with the pier like he'd thought. Of course, Len kinda parked and sat, turning to face him, searching him with those eyes. "Fucking up? How?"

"Partying, mostly. I...." He shook his head, chewed his lip. This was a bad idea. "I was just not living right."

"Shane." That voice went all wonky, wobbling a little. "You weren't.... No. I know you wouldn't do that."

"I wouldn't cheat on you. Hell, Galen, if I was gonna do that, I wouldn't love on you like I did." It was bad enough he'd thought on it, thought serious about Wade.

"Then we're good." Those big hands landed on him, unbuckling his seat belt so Galen could pull him across for a kiss. "I knew you wouldn't do that, but Christ, you've been talking scary."

"It was scary." He didn't know how else to explain it.

"Okay. Okay, tell me what happened. Just one night of it." Len eased him in, held on tight. Okay. Okay, Len had done this shit once, right?

He leaned, stared out the window. "Things just get out of hand so fast, you know? You have a couple beers and somebody hands you something, and suddenly I was flying and with folks I didn't know, you know?"

"Oh, babe. I'm sorry." That big body had tensed some, but he could tell Galen wasn't gonna unload on him or anything.

"It's my fault. I just got...." *Weak? Bored? Stupid?* "You know I'm not all that bright. I never have been good at that whole peer pressure thing."

"Shit, darlin'. You're not an idiot. Would you quit thinking you are?" Galen tilted his face up and stared right into his eyes. "I left you alone too much. Got too wrapped up in work. We *both* fucked up."

"I'm a grown-up. I'm supposed to be able to do this." He just didn't.

"Do what?" Shaking his head, Len sighed. "It's all trial and error. If my momma's taught me anything, it's that."

"Yeah. Well, I've tried a lot and erred some."

"So have I." Heavy brows drew down. "Do we need to get you tested for anything, babe?"

"Tested?" He blinked, utterly confused and maybe a little hurt. "I said I hadn't cheated on you, Galen."

"No. No, I know, but there's other things that can.... Oh, for fuck's sake." Galen kissed him. Hard. "Never mind, honey."

Wait.

Wait.

Other things?

Shit.

Shane frowned, moving away a little. *Okay. Damn it.* "We'd best let the puppers run, huh? Before they eat their way out of the truck?"

"Yeah. I.... Yeah. I'm sorry, Shane. That was out of line." Shit. Galen looked completely flustered and guilty as hell.

"It's okay." God, what if he'd...? What if...? Jesus. "Come on, pups. Let's go." He opened the door and headed down toward the water, the dogs running for the ocean.

Len caught up with him, pulled him around, stared down at him. "Shane. Please, darlin'. Don't. I was just... well. I should know better. You've never done most of the shit I have."

"I'll go see a doctor. Make sure." He didn't think he could make Galen sick from taking pills and stuff, but maybe.... Hell, he didn't know. He wouldn't risk it, though. Jesus.

"You never used a needle, honey. I know you didn't.

That's the only thing I would worry about." Len was shaking his head, frowning. "I should never have asked."

"Needles? No. No, Len. I don't... shit, there isn't anything feels good enough to do that, 'cept get these pierced...." His heart stopped racing quite so hard.

Shit.

"There you go." Now he got a smile, a little wobbly, but right there. "I'm just stupid."

"No. No, I didn't." Shane stopped, took a deep breath. *No. More. Talking.* "Just don't stress on it, 'kay?"

"Okay." Looping one arm around him, Galen steered him off toward the water, whistling up the dogs.

The sun was just starting to go down, the light trying to fade. It was kinda sad.

Kinda.

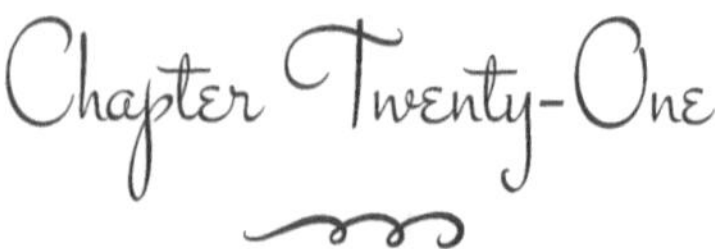

Chapter Twenty-One

GALEN WATCHED Shane sleep.

It was the first time since their trip to the beach that there had been no weirdness. No awkwardness.

If he could just learn to keep his goddamned mouth shut, maybe things would go better. Fucking accusing Shane of shooting up. That had never been Shane's thing, and he knew it. No, all that shit came from his own issues. Galen sighed, glancing at the clock. Maybe he should get up. Go clean the kitchen or something. Stop thinking. He sure wasn't gonna sleep.

Shane's eyes popped open, baby blues just staring him down. "Galen?"

"Hey, darlin'." He let himself smile, for real, loving the way Shane woke up all rumpled and blinky. "I didn't mean to wake you."

"'S okay. You good?" Shane reached for him, just petting away, loving on him.

"Yeah. Yeah, I was just having trouble sleeping." He put

his hand over Shane's, holding it against his belly. "I was fixing to go clean the kitchen."

"I can help." Shane blinked slow, leaning into him, cuddling a little. "You unhappy, Galen?"

"No. I'm glad to be home and tickled as fuck to have you here. I'm just worried I'm fucking it up." Three in the morning seemed a lot easier than sundown on the beach to say shit like that.

"I'm sorry." Shane sighed some, cheek on his shoulder.

"Why? What I did back in the bad old days isn't your problem. That's mine. You're not me, darlin'. I just need to remember that." That and the fact that no matter what Shane might have done, Galen loved him.

"No, I'm not. I was just goofing with the guys. Playing."

"Yeah." Sliding on the sheets, Galen slipped back down into bed, snuggling up to Shane's side. "Sometimes I just get diarrhea of the mouth."

"Shh." Shane patted his hand, easing him some. Easing him down.

Snuggling in, Galen nuzzled against Shane's throat, trying to ignore the big old voice of guilt eating at him. "Sorry, darlin'."

"Let it go, Galen. We're okay. Get some sleep."

"Yeah? Okay." He wanted to be better than that, but they'd been apart a good bit. Hell, Shane had said himself that he'd had a whole other life. Which kinda pissed Galen off, because he hadn't. Not really. He'd worked, and he'd worked out, and he'd dreamed of Shane.

Shane'd been partying and making friends and getting ink and shit and not even letting him know.

His fingers automatically found that ink, tracing the twined letters of their names. At least it meant Shane had been thinking of him. But damn, he wished he'd been there.

"I wanted something that I could feel, you know? Something that wouldn't fade."

"I'm not sure I do know. But I like it." Galen just…. He hated it. Not the tat. The fact that Shane had been so unsure.

"Cool." Shane nuzzled, took a deep breath. "You smell good."

"Mmm. I probably smell like water rot." They were still mopping water out of the weirdest places. "You good?"

"Nah, you smell like home." Shane was blinking, nice and slow.

Home. Yeah. They could work with that. Galen relaxed, his tense muscles easing slow but sure. "Love you, darlin'."

"You do. I know." Shane hummed, nodded. "Love."

Well, at least Shane knew that much.

The rest of the cleanup could wait until tomorrow. At least.

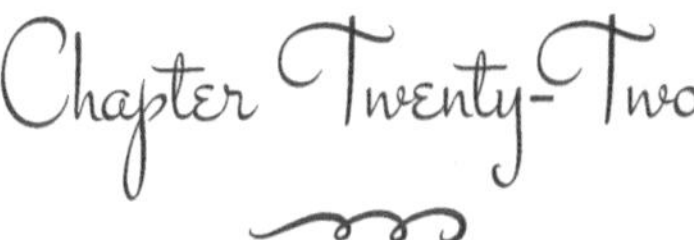

Chapter Twenty-Two

TWO WEEKS they'd worked on the house and the shop. Two weeks and the lights were on, the phones were on, the roads were cleared.

Two weeks and Frank'd started calling.

Writing.

Emailing.

Threatening.

Galen was going to blow a vein, Shane could tell.

Finally Galen answered and things got loud as hell, and Shane just headed down to the bait shop to potter.

He'd been down there about an hour, working over some inventory boxes, when he heard someone clear his throat. "Shane?"

Oh man. Wade. "Hey, man. How's it hanging?"

The man looked like hammered shit, dark circles under the big blue eyes, tan a little faded.

"I've been sick, honey. I'm better."

"Oh shit. That sucks. Come on, have a seat." He cleaned off a chair, helped Wade over. "You want a Coke?"

"No. No, honey. Shane. That ain't what I want."

"Well, what? I'll fix you up."

Wade shifted on the little chair, pulling off his gimme cap to tug at those pale curls. "I been thinking, Shane."

"Yeah?" He grabbed a chair, sat. Shit, he hated to see the man look so tore up. He did.

"Uh-huh. I mean, it's gonna sound crazy, I guess." He got a ghost of a grin, Wade's cheekbones looking sharper, the hollows beneath deeper.

"Well, tell me, then. You know I ain't scared of crazy." He chuckled, reached out and patted Wade's knee. "Shit, buddy, you and me have had a couple adventures, haven't we?"

"We have." Grabbing his hand, Wade held on tight, fingers gripping his. "You could…. It's not too late, Shane. I got the boat tricked out for a long tour; you quit your job. Come with me."

"What? Oh, oh, honey. I thought. I thought you knew that…." No. No, this wouldn't work. Not at all. Much as him and Galen felt broke sometimes, Galen was his one true thing. "You're good to me, Wade, you are, but…."

"But what?" Leaning in, Wade stared right into his eyes. "He doesn't love you like I do, Shane. How could he, and be gone so long?"

No. No, Galen loved him like no one ever would. God knew, he'd tried to love Wade, he had, a little, but his heart just couldn't. It wasn't his anymore. "This ain't about Galen, Wade. This is about me. I love him, and I'm gonna stay 'til he don't want me anymore, and it'll be worth it for me, yeah?"

"How? I mean, I just don't see how." Wade's face twisted all up, those eyes going cloudy. "You told me yourself you were worried he'd never come home."

Yeah, but Wade hadn't seen Galen when Shane had showed up during the storm, hadn't seen how Galen held him at night like he was the most precious fucking thing in the world.

"I did. I do, but…. Shit, Wade. I can't explain it. He's it for me. He's home." Galen was…. Galen. Nothing else had held his attention in his whole life.

"Shane, honey?" *Oh. Len. Thank God.* "Hey, I finally got that asshole off the phone." Galen popped his head in the shop, staring from him to Wade. "Well, hey, Wade."

"Hey, Galen. I just came to tell Shane goodbye. I'm heading out for a while. Take the boat through her paces."

Oh. Oh damn it. Shane felt like the world's biggest asshole, hurting a decent guy. He felt like a bigger prick for knowing he'd do it again, if he had to.

Len nodded, coming to put an arm around him. "Well, you be careful, huh? But that sounds like you'll have fun."

Wade gave Shane another long, slow look. "You're sure, huh? About what we talked about?"

"Yeah. Yeah, I'm real sure. Come see us when you get back in port, huh? We'll have supper. Len makes a good steak."

God, he needed a shot.

A double.

"Shane does a great margarita too." There wasn't a bit of nasty in Len's voice. Shit, if anything there was sympathy, which was weird. Len usually growled.

"Yeah. Yeah, see y'all." Wade stood, squeezed his hand once real quick, and then just walked off without looking back.

Goddamn it.

"You… you get shit dealt with with Frank?"

"Hell, no. He's gonna keep trying to hound me. I called my lawyer. We're not answering the phone." Turning, Galen grabbed him and squeezed, hugging him hard. "You all right?"

"Yeah. Yeah, I will be. I could sure use a drink, though." He leaned in. "I don't think he's gonna come back, Galen."

"I'm sorry because he's your friend, darlin'. But I'm glad you chose me." Tilting his chin up, Galen took a kiss that surprised him, pushing him, taking it deep.

Wade just slipped away, along with all the other shit, leaving him just as clear as glass and solid as stone.

Like he could've chosen anything else.

They broke for breath, Galen staring down at him. "Come back to the house with me, Shane."

He nodded, reaching up to cup Galen's cheek, touch a little. They went arm in arm, Galen bumping hips with him, hand moving on his arm. Hot. It was muggy, almost steamy, but Galen was the hottest part.

"Mmm." Those fingers on him just did it for him, bone-deep.

The kitchen was starting to look bright and light again, all the boards gone, and Galen shut the door behind them, pushing him up against the counter to kiss him. The counter bit into his ass a little, Galen's heat solid against his front. He opened his mouth to say something, but that just got him another kiss and another. God. Galen was gonna eat him up. The kisses bruised his lips, made him short of breath. And that counter might just dent his spine. Damn. Damn, he wrapped his arms around Galen's neck, head just swimming.

One hand cupped his butt, sliding between him and the hard edge of tile, lifting him right up. So damned strong, his Len.

"Galen." He got his legs around Galen's hips, meeting those eyes as he did. Jesus, that look damn near burned him.

"Mine. You got that, darlin'? Mine." Galen sucked up a mark on his neck, right where the one Len had put there was fading away. Made his whole body feel like a live wire.

"I know. I want to be yours." Maybe he needed it. Either way, it was what he was.

"Oh God." That grin was razor-sharp but fucking happy, Galen's dark eyes just sparkling. "Need you."

He nodded, one hand tracing that mouth. "So take me. I'm right here."

"Yeah." Someone liked that idea. Hoisting him up, Galen sat him on the counter and started working on his clothes.

"You're hungry." He lifted his arms, old T-shirt going flying, and he reached for Galen's wifebeater.

"I am." Shrugging out of the tank, Galen worked their buttons and zippers, pulling and pushing and growling when things went too slow.

Shane chuckled, trying to help, fingers stinging when Galen swatted them away to tear his fly open. That big hand closed around him, pulled at his cock a couple of times. Just to get him revved up. His ass left the counter, whole body jumping, the air electric as shit, like the storms were gonna come back.

"That's it, darlin'. Look at you. So fucking amazing." That thumb rubbed right under the head, Galen's blunt nail scraping the tiniest bit.

"Oh. Oh, there. There, Len." His eyes went wide as his thighs went taut.

"Yeah? Like that?" All the way up and down, Galen touched him just the way he needed, sliding along his length. His belly quivered, his toes curling.

"Uh. Uh-huh." Jesus. Jesus, that felt. Galen was gonna kill him.

Reaching up, Galen put two fingers against his lips. "Get me all wet, darlin'. Need to be in you soon."

"Uh-huh...." He moaned and took those fingers in. Oh. Oh, Galen tasted... so good.

"Fuckin' hot, darlin'." Galen kept up a string of sweet words, telling him how pretty he was, how good he felt. *Yeah. More.*

Hot as a box of firecrackers in a barbecue, Shane pushed closer, one leg propped on an open cabinet door so he could spread wide. Galen pulled those fingers free and slid them down to press between his legs. The stretch had him moaning, had him trying to open up even more.

"Galen." He slid off the counter a little, pushing himself down onto that touch.

"Sweet Jesus. Shane." In and out, Galen moved, stretching him, wetting him. Galen was flushed, panting, growling for him.

He wanted to say a lot of shit—yeah and love and want and yours—but he was awful busy, so Shane just moved faster, muscles starting to warm up. He didn't think Len was ever gonna get to the main event, but finally he got more than Galen's fingers, that fat cock pushing at him. Len dragged him down, pulling at him until he sorta fell right there, right where Len could be inside him.

"Yes...." His head fell back, arms braced on the counter so he could help move himself on that heavy prick.

"Uhn." Grunting, Galen moved back and forth, pushing up at the same time. Fucking A. He was just gonna explode.

"Jesus. Jesus, Len. I...." His cock was slapping between them, hard as Chinese algebra.

"Touch yourself, darlin'. I got you. I won't let you fall." No. No, Len wouldn't let him fall.

He nodded, finding his balance, one hand wrapping around his prick. *Oh. Oh hell yes.*

"That's it. Oh fuck." Moving faster, Galen hoisted him up a little, arching his back, putting just enough distance between their chests that Len could see what he was doing.

Shane showed off a little, working his cock hard, almost too hard, the ache giving him just what he needed. Len's eyes were just glued to the center of his body, almost black with need. That big cock pushed at him, opened him wide, and damn. Every muscle in Len's body strained, giving him a show of his own.

"Yours. Yours, love." He jerked hard, ball sac aching as he shot, spunk splashing on his belly.

Nodding, growling, Galen went crazy for him, hips pumping hard. He felt it deep inside when Len shot for him, filling him right up. His. Galen was his too.

Hell, yes. His muscles were trembling, tired and shaking.

Leaning for a minute, Len rested against him, holding him against the counter. Then big muscles shifted and Galen heaved, lifting him up. "Bedroom?"

"Uh-huh. So fucking strong." It still stunned him, after all this time.

Kissing him hard, Galen turned and headed for their room, managing not to trip over the dogs. They landed on the bed, both of them panting and laughing.

"Hey. Hey, Len." He wrapped tight around, taking one quick kiss after another.

"Mmm-hmm. Hey, darlin'." Those eyes stared right into his, serious, sure. "Thank you."

"What for?" He just stared back, heated through.

"For staying with me. For telling Wade no. I didn't hear much, but I heard that. I love you, darlin'. So much."

"I know." Shane nodded, sure he'd done the right thing, staying where his home was. "I couldn't go with him, no matter what. I need you."

"You got me, Shane. You'll see. I'm home for good." That was it. That was what he needed. Just Galen and home and some time to make it right.

"Good." He guessed a better man would hurt more about Wade, but he wasn't all that. He just loved.

That was all.

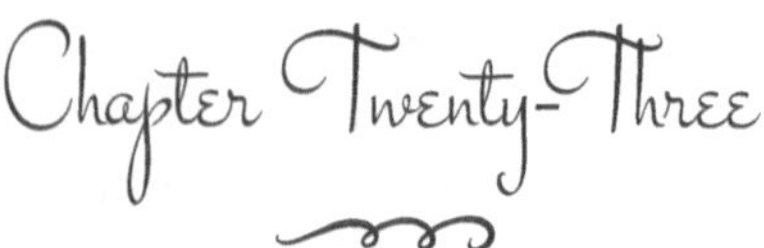

Chapter Twenty-Three

THE BAIT shop finally smelled like fresh two-by-fours instead of mildew and dead lizards. Oh, it was far from done, but Galen thought they were making progress. It felt good, to be out there working with his hands, listening to Shane whistle and scrub the new glass cases they'd just gotten in.

They had all the fans on, the place a little stuffy, but it worked. Hell, he got to see Shane's thin T-shirt clinging to every cut of muscle, outlining those little nipple rings.

"I think I need to get a tattoo to go with yours, darlin'," Galen said when Shane finished the bottom shelf and straightened up.

"Okay, Len. Nemo did mine. He's real cool. Sorta biker-looking, but cool."

"Yeah? Did it hurt bad?" Not that he was afraid of pain; he just kinda wanted to know about Shane's tat.

"No. It itched more than anything. Like a sunburn." Shane pulled up his shirt, showing him the ink again. "The weird part was someone shaving me there."

"Shaving...." *Oh fuck.* How long had it been since they'd

done that together? Last time he'd seen it, Shane had been texting him pictures on his cell phone. His now defunct cell phone.

"Mmm-hmm. There wasn't much hair, not like if I'd got it down here." That hand motioned to that sweet, taut lower belly.

"Uh-huh." Galen couldn't help it. He stared. Hard. "That would be pretty, though."

The muscles rippled, just like he'd touched them. "What would?"

"A tattoo. Right. There." Drawn like Shane was a lodestone, Galen moved close, touched that sweet skin.

"On you or me?"

"You. Though I would get one too. Might be better to put it on my back, though. Where I'm less hairy." Grinning, he stroked up and down, watching Shane's muscles twitch.

"Yeah. You'd look funny, piebald." Uh-huh. Shane was all into him being fuzzy. His Shane, though, he could strip that fine body down to bare skin.

"We'll have to think on it." Flattening his hand on Shane's belly, Galen thought more on taking the man up to the house and having at him in the bathtub. He could feel each muscle, rippling, shifting, could smell the way Shane's cock was lifting.

"You're getting a little fuzzy, darlin'." Tugging at the tiny hairs, Galen grinned. "We could go have a bath."

"Mmm. We could. We've worked it hard." Look at those cheeks go pink. Hell, yes.

"We have." The floors were squeaky clean, new laminate hardwood put in the day before. The cases were in place, the new cash register ready to go. Time for a break.

"Come on, Shane," Galen said, holding out a hand.

"Oh, for fuck's sake. You're telling me that you left everything behind for this piece-of-shit place? Jesus, Galen. Are you *stupid*?"

He recognized the voice about five seconds before Shane did, Shane's pretty eyes going furious, just like that. Galen turned, his voice calm and even when he spoke. "You're not welcome here, Frank. Take it up with my lawyer."

"Fuck you. I came to find out what was wrong with you." Smarmy little blocky fuckhead.

"There's nothing fucking wrong with him." Shane grabbed a two-by-four, hefted it. "Not a thing."

Staring at Shane, Galen tried to come up with something to say, but he was flabbergasted. He'd seen Shane defend the bar, but damn.

"Look here, you little shit—"

"No. No, I don't fucking *think* so." Shane stepped forward, wood slapping on one palm. "You ain't coming to our place and speaking to Galen like that, you hear me?"

Frank sputtered, and Galen wanted to laugh, but that would just make things worse. He put a hand on Shane's arm, just to let the man know he was still there, and looked Frank right in the eye. "We're not in business anymore. Not after what you tried to do. Now get your ass out of here."

"You're giving up all we've done for a cheap piece of ass?"

Shane's arm tensed, a low warning noise sounding. "I ain't cheap, and you're a fucking liar, man. Len can do better."

Galen's own muscles went tight and hard, and he growled, hands clenching. "He's not a piece of anything. He's it, Frank. He's my other half. I know that now. Now get."

Frank opened his mouth, and that piece of wood swung out, smashing into the side of the shop. "That's your warning."

Goddamn. Look at that.

Frank gave him a look that burned with rage, but the man turned tail, cussing all the way. When he was out of range, he shouted, "You haven't heard the last of it, Frost. I told you he was an indulgence you couldn't afford!"

Shane stepped forward, glaring. "Don't make me fucking hunt your ass, you lying sack of shit!"

"You keep him away from me!" Frank hotfooted it to his car and tore out, spitting mud from under his tires.

Galen watched, grinning a little at the way Shane was still vibrating.

Shane watched Frank leave, then carefully put the two-by-four back in place. "You still want that shower?"

"I do. In fact, I think I need it more now than ever." Frank made him feel grungy.

"'Kay, Len." Shane headed toward the house, all het up.

It was fucking hot.

Following that swinging ass, Galen stuck his hands in his pockets, a little shell-shocked. Shane had scared off Frank. Shane had fucking threatened to beat the bastard. Shane, who had always yelled at him for fighting and starting shit in the bar and all. That finally got his ass in gear, and Galen put on a burst of speed, catching up with Shane outside the bathroom. He grabbed one shoulder and swung Shane around, hugging that lean body close.

Shane looked up at him, eyes still flashing. "Hey."

"Hey." Damn. Look at that man. Galen was so hard he could pound nails. "You're something else, darlin'."

"I ain't letting anyone come here and threaten us."

"No. No, you're not." Jesus, that was weirdly hot. "Mine."

He bent and took a kiss, letting Shane know how much he appreciated it. Shane's body slapped against his, Shane meeting him halfway, the return kiss melting him, bone-deep. Wrapping his arms around Shane's body, Galen let the kiss go on and on, his whole body on fire with it.

Shane's fingers were in his hair, holding him close, keeping their mouths together. They rocked a little, both of them unwilling to give up control of the kiss, passing it back and forth. He tasted Shane deep, tongue pushing in and out in a slow, heavy rhythm. Shit, he was caught in it, caught in Shane and the kisses.

Staggering, they made it to the bathroom without losing contact, hands and mouths moving, searching. Galen gave up all thought, letting it take him where it would.

Shane's hands were fucking everywhere, teasing him and touching him, both of them starting to strip down like they hadn't touched in days.

So sweet. His hands shook as he touched Shane's shoulders, his chest, fingers sliding down unerringly to pull at Shane's nipple rings. God, he loved the way that made Shane shiver. Those little nipples went rock-hard, Shane groaning and nipping his bottom lip hard. Growling, he bit right back, pushing Shane harder and faster. His thumb rubbed one tiny ring back and forth, feeling Shane's groan more than hearing it.

That little bit of flesh got hot under his fingers, Shane's ass moving in time with his touches. Every movement had him grunting, trying to get closer, trying to get Shane more naked.

"Honey, I need…. We need more skin."

"Uh-huh." Shane tugged his shirt all the way off, rumbling. "I can't believe that bastard came here."

"Neither can I." Hell, it had never occurred to him that Frank would dare brave him in his own den. The man was essentially a coward. Galen tugged at Shane's shorts. "He's gone. Now it's about us."

"It was about us then." Shane wiggled out of them, ass shaking.

"It was. Jesus. You. I can't believe you sometimes, darlin'." His hands moved as fast as his mouth, tracing Shane's ribs, Shane's hip bones. Hard and wet-tipped, Shane's cock got to bobbing, trying to get his attention.

It worked. Oh, Lord it worked. And suddenly Galen had to taste, something he hadn't done in too damned long. He slid right to his knees, nuzzling, rubbing his bristly cheek against Shane's prick.

"Galen!" Oh, if he was getting that sort of response, that desperate need, he'd not done this nearly enough. Licking, tasting, Galen worked his way up to the tip before sucking Shane in. No teasing, just pushing all the way down to the root. Shane's hands landed on his shoulders, slapping down as those lean hips started moving, cock fucking his lips.

Yeah. Oh God, yeah. Galen glanced up, meeting Shane's eyes, watching them burn for him as he sucked. He tightened his lips and let Shane take what he needed.

"Galen. Galen, fuck. I need." Yeah. Yeah, he could see that. He so could. Shane was eating it up, belly jumping with each thrust.

He flattened one hand on that sweet stomach, fingers stroking. He could just see a tattoo there. One he got to watch Shane get. He sucked harder, his eyes finally closing as he pulled on Shane's prick with heavy suction.

"Love...." Shane's cock throbbed, swelled in his lips, seed just spilling, filling his mouth.

That had him moaning, his own hips humping the air. *Oh fuck. Yes.* Shane tasted like everything good in his life, making the memory of Frank completely disappear.

Shane didn't even go soft, just kept shifting, moaning his name. Needing him. Christ.

It took effort to let go and climb to his feet, but Galen ached, needing to feel Shane against him, needing something. Anything.

Shane muscled him back toward the bed, groaning, pushing him. The backs of his knees hit the bed, and Galen tumbled down, pulling Shane on top of him. "Oh. Good."

"Uh-huh." Shane rubbed a little, crawling up his body, ass rubbing Galen's cock a minute before the tip pressed right against Shane's hole.

"Oh Christ. Shane. Darlin'...." He pushed up, knowing he should take more time, more care, but he needed in.

"Yeah." Shane lifted up, bore down and just fucking took him in with a groan. Galen grabbed Shane's hips, pulling down, pushing up. Shane was tight, hot, perfect, squeezing him on every stroke.

"Love." Sweat beaded on Shane's chest, rolling down the muscles.

Nodding, he sat up to lick at the corner of Shane's mouth, tasting, before he pressed his lips to Shane's, taking a hard kiss. Yeah. Yeah.

Shane grabbed his head, tongue pushing hard against his, fucking his lips like he was fucking that tight ass. They moved faster and faster, sweat running off their skin, both of them gasping for breath. God, yeah. He pushed harder, hips pumping up. Close. They were both fucking close—he could feel Shane around his cock, hear it in those deep, growled groans that pushed into his lips.

Balls drawing up tight, Galen yanked Shane down on him, sinking so deep he might never recover. He shot hard, his head falling back, his mouth open on a harsh cry.

He barely caught the hint of damp on his belly before he had the weight of Shane on him.

"I got you, darlin'. Right here." He murmured it into Shane's neck, stroking that sweaty back.

"Mmm-hmm. Love." Shane sighed, then sank down on him, cuddling in.

"You know it. Love you." God, Shane had been all tooth and nail. For him. For them.

Galen didn't think he'd ever seen anything that made him more proud.

Chapter Twenty-Four

MM. THE bed smelled good.

Like sex.

Like them.

Shane chuckled, rubbing his cheeks on the pillows, jonesing on the fact that Galen was all over them.

Fuck, he was easier than advertised.

He heard another soft chuckle, low and growly, and he knew that was Len, watching him, jonesing on *him*.

"Mmm. Mornin', Len." He went to turn over, sit up.

Wait.

What?

"I thought we'd have a little fun, darlin'." One big hand slid down his back, cupping his ass. "Guess what I found when I was cleaning yesterday?"

The cuffs. Obviously.

"Man, you're either getting better at that or I'm sleeping harder...."

"I think you were half dead. All that hard work. Hard lovin'." Oh, listen to that. He might not be able to see Galen, but he could hear the smile.

"Hard lovin'." He shifted, knees sliding under him so he could stretch. "I might remember that."

"Yeah? Still feeling it?" Those big hands moved him, turning him over on his back. His hands uncrossed, his arms stretching out and up.

"Mmm-hmm." He sort of jonesed on it, that ache and stretch and burn.

"Love how you look like this." Now he could see Len, all big and fuzzy and naked. It was a good look on the man.

"Mutual admiration, huh? Look at you." He reached for Len, forgetting about the cuffs a second.

Oops.

"Uh-huh. You look. I'll lick." Len kissed his mouth, licking at his bottom lip.

"Mmm." Licking. He was a fan. Hell, Len could do amazing things with that mouth.

Laughing, making a soft burst of breath fan his mouth, Len bent and kissed his chin, then his throat before sucking hard. Making a mark. He arched, chin lifting as he let Galen have his way. Damn, that was fine, but when Galen's teeth started scraping his skin? It was way better.

The sharp sting when Len bit down over his Adam's apple had him gasping, wiggling, trying to get closer.

"Jesus. You. I. Galen."

"You, Shane. It's all you." That smile slid over his skin, finding the ball of his shoulder so Galen could bite down there too.

It was electricity, sliding right down his spine, and his fucking balls drew up with it.

Like he was sending a signal, Galen reached down, cupping his balls and rolling them. "Hot for me, darlin'?"

"When have I not been?" He spread wider, thighs shaking some.

"Never. I know it." Len went to sucking up a mark on his

chest after that, right beside his nipple. The fire inside him flared even higher, making him grunt.

"Gonna make me lose my mind." His nipples went tight, aching around the rings.

"No. Just lose yourself for a bit...." That grin was pure evil. He got to see it for like, five seconds before Galen bent again, working his nipple rings.

"I...." *Fucking shit.* He arched as Galen pulled, chest following those lips, the pressure just the hottest thing ever.

"We need to get your chain...." Len was nipping, licking, working him like there was no tomorrow.

"Uh. Uh-huh." Jesus, that was hot. It started a ball of flame, right in the pit of his belly.

"In fact...." That big body levered off of his, Galen bending to rummage in the drawer of the bedside table. "Woo! Here it is."

His abs went tight, drawing up his knees, his balls. Fuck, but he wanted. Then Len was back, his hands holding that glinting chain, moving to clip the ends to his nipple rings. The pull came immediately as the chain settled.

"Galen!" He stretched up, almost sitting, eyes rolling like thrown dice. The pull at his arms made him wince a little, but it wasn't such a bad thing, remembering he was at Len's mercy. Nope. Not such a bad thing at all, with one hand tugging at the chain, the other cupping around his cock.

"Oh. Oh sweet fuck. Galen." If the man stopped, he was going to commit murder.

"You are." Winking up at him a moment, Galen rubbed one thumb up the underside of his cock, pulling hard at the chain at the same time. "Very."

His thighs spread, knees drawn damn near up to his armpits, balls tight as they could be.

"Uhn. Oh God. Look at you." Len went a little wild,

kissing him all over from his chest to his belly to the insides of his legs, where Galen bit hard at his thigh.

"Please. Please. I fucking need so bad." He couldn't even fucking focus. All he could do was jerk and beg and want.

"What do you want, darlin'? Want me in you?" Oh, like Len didn't.... Jesus fuck. That mouth slid down between his legs, tongue licking behind his balls, right down to his hole. He might have screamed, he might have not—what he did know is that if he didn't come soon, he'd lose what was left of his motherfucking mind.

Galen didn't waste too much time, though, licking at him, opening him up with both thumbs. The man drove him to the very edge, making him pant and beg and threaten, but Len finally moved up to settle that heavy cock right where that mouth had been.

"Now. Now, Galen. I swear to God, I need it right now." He was on fucking fire like he hadn't been in months, maybe longer.

"Right here, Shane." Surging forward, Galen pushed into him, right where he needed it, inside him. The pressure pushed his hips back, pulling at his arms, making him moan.

One thrust, two, and then that amazing prick slid against his gland, lighting him on fire. His eyes went wide, spunk pouring from him. Len cried out, dark eyes meeting his, and those muscled hips pumped once, maybe twice, before Len came for him. Hard.

Shane was pretty sure his lips were moving, but there wasn't anything sensible coming out.

He thought he might be broken.

Galen was shaking, sort of hovering over him, arm muscles quivering. "Need to untie you, babe."

"Uh-huh." He just stared a little, watching Galen. "Love."

"Love you." Smiling, Galen pressed a kiss to his lips, loving on him a moment before levering up to loosen the cuffs.

He groaned as he brought his hands down. Ached. So good.

Big hands closed over his wrists, massaging the soreness out so slow and sweet that it made him moan. Oh. God, Len knew how to make him feel right.

"Jesus. You. This is. So good...." Fuck. Perfect.

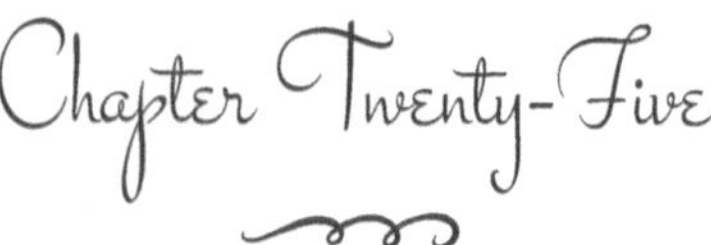

Chapter Twenty-Five

THE HOUSE was as secure as it was gonna get. The dogs were set with a buddy of theirs. They were packed. Galen grinned to himself, loading the last case into Shane's new truck. Man, it seemed weird to be packing up and leaving again, but this time he was doing it right.

"You all ready, darlin'?"

"I. Yeah. Yeah, I am." Shane still looked a little lost sometimes, like he couldn't figure out why he wasn't at the club.

He knew Shane would probably go back and tend bar. Something. The man needed to work, and it was a social job, one that got Shane the kind of personal interaction and shit that he needed.

But for now, they would wander.

"Cool. Come on, honey. We'll go play." They'd decided on the mountains. Not Vermont, like they'd done on their one Christmas vacation. The big mountains. Colorado. They were gonna road trip it.

He got a grin, a dark hickey right at the curve of Shane's

jaw. "Man, this is the longest vacation ever. We're going to have a ball."

"Shit, yes. We're going to eat and fuck our way across country." Man, he could see that. Just him and Shane, naked at every opportunity.

Shane hooted, hopping up into the cab. They had snacks, a cooler, music, and a kickass camera. They were ready.

Galen eased out of the yard and hit the road, cranking the truck up and burning off, knowing Shane loved speed. He wanted to laugh. Wanted to hear more of Shane's amazing chuckle.

"You excited, Len? I'm ready. I dreamed about that cabin we rented. Looks like heaven. Just you and me."

"Yeah? Dreaming, huh? Yeah, I'm excited, darlin'. It has a hot tub." They'd pored over all sorts of brochures, making sure they'd be a little isolated but have all the comforts.

"And a grill. And a big old bed." One hand landed on his thigh, Shane petting a little.

"Uh-huh." Oh, that had his foot dancing on the gas pedal, but Galen held it together, knowing it was early days on this road trip to be so distracted. "A great big one."

"Remember our last road trip? Thanksgiving with Momma?"

"Oh good Lord. Yeah." Man, they'd had some times. This one might prove to be the best. He patted Shane's hand. "Remember how rubbery that Yankee cranberry thing was?"

"That was foul. Your aunt makes the best biscuits, though." They headed north, easing onto the highway. They hadn't just talked in forever. It was weird. Cool, but weird.

"Yeah, but did I ever tell you about the time she put in cream of tartar instead of baking powder?" They laughed and chatted, and before Galen really blinked, they were two hours down the road and needing to stop.

Shane looked fucking amazing—T-shirt and jeans, skin tanned nut-brown, little bite marks visible every little bit.

All he could do was jones on that, watch Shane boogie on into the convenience store while he got gas. God, that man made him happy.

He headed in to do his business, and Shane was at the counter, talking to a couple girls, a cook, and a big burly truck driver. Jesus, Shane'd never met a stranger.

Galen grinned and headed for the bathroom, then came out to grab a Goo Goo Cluster and put it on the counter. "You all set?"

"Yep." Oh good Lord. Peach rings. Red Bull. A bobble-head alligator and a ball cap that said "Hell, Yeah."

Someone was having a grand time. Galen added a shot glass to the mix, knowing he could get Shane to do some private bartending soon. He got this grin that just made his belly tight—happy and sexy and pure fucking fun.

How the hell had he let himself miss that?

They got back to the truck, and Galen had to take a kiss. Just a little one, where no one would see.

"Mmm. Hey." Shane grinned against his lips, nose brushing his. "Northward-ho, huh?"

"You know it." He cupped the back of Shane's head, holding him there for another kiss. Yeah. That was what he needed.

"Thank you." The words were damn near moaned.

"You're welcome, darlin'. We should hit the road. Get to the hotel so we can...." *Well. Yeah. Hoo, yeah.*

"I'm all about that." Shane blushed, eyes flicking to the back of the truck.

"Shane.... Oh, darlin'. There's too much crap back there." Man, they should have stayed in the bathroom. Except that was kinda nasty.

"I know. I...." Shane cupped his cock, just a second. "I brought a bag of our.... Uh. Stuff. It's back there for us."

"No shit?" Jesus, he was gonna batter his way out of his jeans with his cock. Just like that. He pushed into Shane, missing the pressure of that hand already. "Need you."

"Uh-huh. The straps. A plug. Stuff." Shane was hot as a two-dollar pistol.

Galen almost killed them both taking another kiss, his elbow hitting the horn about the time Shane's tailbone hit the gearshift. They both jerked back, then started hooting, the cab of the truck filling up with the sounds.

Clapping his hat back on his head, Galen patted Shane's thigh, right up near his cock. "Save that for me, darlin'."

"For the rest of time, man."

That was enough for him. Just to know that.

It was getting better every fucking day.

THEY HAULED THE SUITCASES INTO THE HOTEL room, both of them bumping shoulders and chuckling.

Shit, that kid who had checked them in looked about three-quarters stoned and smelled.

Well.

Damn.

"Shit, Len, we should've asked about where to order pizza." Shane got the fan blowing, looked out the window. *Dude. Brick.*

"We got the phone book. And the hotel doolie usually has a few suggestions." Hell, their room key had a Pizza Hut on it.

"I was making a stoner joke, dork."

"Oh." Len kinda looked at him, head tilted just like Goob's did.

He rolled his eyes, grinned. "Man, you missed all the fun part of being high."

"Probably." Shrugging, Len opened one of the suitcases and pulled out their bathing suits. "I never did things halfway, you know?"

He nodded, chewed his bottom lip a little. "That's okay. I never do things better than half-assed. It has to have a good side. You want me to grab some towels?"

"Huh?" Those sloe eyes met his, and Galen grinned, relaxing. "No. I want you to come here and kiss me."

"Oh. Okay." Better. He could so do that. He headed over, pushed into Galen's arms with a soft sigh.

"Oh, good." Galen bent, lips finding his, hot tongue slipping out to run along his mouth.

Oh man. He'd been wanting this all fucking day. He got one arm around Galen's neck, hanging on, his free hand sliding up that hard belly.

"Been thinking of this ever since that first truck stop," Galen said, lips sliding down his throat.

"Yeah. I had a serious hard-on for you." Still did. Prob'ly always would.

"Same here. If we'd had the room...." Len kissed him again, teeth stinging his lower lip.

"This.... Damn. This is better. This is private." He reached down, rubbing Len's prick through the old, soft jeans.

"Uhn. Yeah. Just us...." Len smiled that pirate smile, rubbing against his hand. Those long legs spread, bracing Len's big body.

"You smell good." He leaned a little, cheek rubbing on Galen's chest. "I could eat you up."

"Hey, I wouldn't say no to that." One hand covered his, Galen leading him right to the tab of the zipper on those jeans.

Hell, yes. He eased the zipper down, tongue sliding in to

taste the hollow of Galen's throat as he protected that heavy cock from those teeth.

"Better...." Len's cock pushed out, slapping into his hand, making the best noise. Oh, Len was hard for him.

"Mmm-hmm." He unbuttoned one button after another, heading down slow and easy.

"Shane...." Galen touched his shoulders, cupping the back of his neck. "More, darlin'."

"Be patient." He bit one hard little nipple, knowing full well he was asking for it later. Knowing? Shit, hoping he was asking for it.

"I can be patient. Can you?" That growl had him grinning. It didn't sound patient at all.

"You know it." He bit again, smoothing Galen's jeans down off those amazing, lean hips. His thumbs stroked Len's hip bones, and those muscles shifted, Galen starting to push toward him.

"See, not so patient." He went down on his knees, lips wrapped around the very tip of Galen's cock.

"No.... Not when you—fuck! Not when you do that." Steady as a clock, Galen started thrusting, moving in a heavy, natural rhythm into his mouth. He didn't tease, he just gave Galen what the man needed, what they both needed. He got his fingers around Galen's balls, tugging a little. Going up on tiptoe, Len moved for him, almost like a dance. Like the sexiest hip-shaking dance ever.

He moaned, eyes wide open, watching every fucking movement.

"Darlin'. I... damn. Hot. Such a fucking hot mouth." Yeah. Oh, he loved Galen's voice when they were like this.

Shane nodded, head moving, throat working, trying to pull more and more pleasure out of that prick. He could feel Galen's balls draw up, feel the fine tension in that big body.

Yeah. One finger slid back, nail scraping that line of skin behind Galen's sac.

"Fuck! Shane...." A low, raw groan was his only warning before Len was coming for him, filling him right up with heat.

His. Fuck, yeah. He took it all, his own hips fucking the air, humping a little as he jonesed on it.

Yanking him up when he'd taken the last lick, Galen shoved him down on the bed, tearing at his pants. He stretched out, fingers on his nipples, cock thrumming in his jeans. Fuck, yeah. Yeah. He did love him a road trip.

Galen got his jeans open, got them down his legs, dropped them on the floor. Then the man was on him, lips tight around his cock, sucking madly.

"Galen! Galen. Hot!" He wasn't going to last, so he didn't try. He just bucked and shot, eyes rolling in his head like dice.

Moaning, Galen licked him clean, stroking his belly and thighs, soothing him right down. Oh, that was the way to ease the stiffness from a day in the truck.

"Mmm. Yeah." He reached down, hands missing Galen the first couple times.

Laughing, Galen crawled up to snuggle with him. "We could nap. Go sit in the hot tub."

"'Kay." He was easy.

Happy.

At one with the universe.

On fucking vacation.

Chapter Twenty-Six

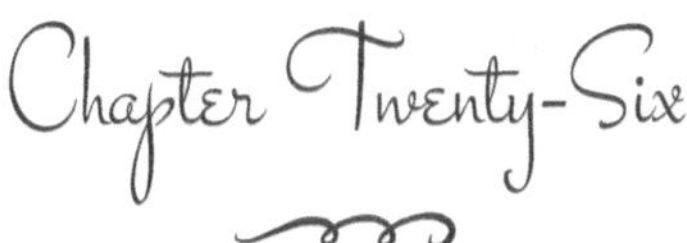

GALEN FLOPPED on the bed not covered in suitcases, patting his belly and groaning a little. He and Shane had pigged out at this little diner, chowing down on fried chicken and greens, biscuits and butter, and the best cobbler ever.

Sometimes Galen loved Georgia. He really did. Shane sprawled out next to him, one brown arm rubbing against his.

"I been looking at the map, darlin'. It wouldn't take much for us to swing on up through Chattanooga and see your folks."

Shane shrugged a little, eyes on the bedspread. "I could show you the house, if you want. It's in a decent part of town."

"Yeah?" Galen knew Shane and his people didn't talk, but he still wanted to see where the man had grown up. "Cool."

Shane finished looking at the little hotel services book and rolled away, stood, popping his back and stretching. Reaching out with one hand, Galen poked Shane's ass. "You okay?"

"Yep." Shane snorted, glute going tight. "You want to go swim?"

"I do." They hadn't made it to the pool in the last hotel, both of them a little too hot for each other. Today Galen figured it would ease the aches.

"Cool." Shane leaned down, kissed him nice and slow, eyes holding his and just staring.

"Mmm." He reached up and put one hand behind Shane's head, cupping the back of that warm neck, holding Shane there for more. The corners of Shane's eyes crinkled up, the bright blue warming up for him.

"Pretty, darlin'." Grinning against Shane's mouth, he licked at that bottom lip, still a little swollen from the night before.

"Mmm. Just yours, huh? You taste good. Sweet."

"Mine." He probably tasted like peach cobbler. Tugging, Galen got Shane back down on the bed with him, wiggling until they were comfy. "We could make out until we can't see. Then we could swim."

"Hell, yeah. You know how long it's been since we could do that together?" Shane grinned, legs twining with his. "So good, both of us having time."

"I do know, babe." He stroked and moved, searching for skin under the clothes.

God, that smile just came, more and more often, soothing shit in his heart that had gone all cracked and crusty. They rolled a little, both of them on their sides, loving on each other. Their eyelashes actually brushed together when they blinked, they were so close.

His Shane. They just breathed together, slow and easy. The heat of it surprised the hell out of him, the way he could see the gray streaks in Shane's eyes, the way he could feel the beating of Shane's heart against his chest. Every move of every muscle that shivered when Shane breathed translated into a kind of caress. Galen hummed happily, needing it so bad.

"You're so fucking fine, Galen Frost." Shane whispered the words into his lips, breath hitching a little.

"Yeah? Love you. That much I know." His hand slipped down to cup Shane's ass, nothing urgent, just a nice handful.

"Good." They laughed together, and fuck, it felt good. Solid.

Squeezing that hard little body, Galen finally took another kiss, letting his tongue trace the line of Shane's mouth, tasting sweet there too. Shane followed his tongue, chasing it for a second before easing away, pressing in to touch his teeth. All they could do was touch and rub, a slow slide of bodies and lips and hands that made him want to scream. But he was too fucking happy to make the effort.

Shane's lips found his ear, teeth on his lobe, digging in, tugging a little.

"Oh, darlin'. That's good." God, he loved how Shane made him feel. Like a ten-foot-tall god.

Shane groaned, started whispering to him—soft, low filthy words that crawled down his spine, settled in his balls. His eyes tried to roll back in his head, his hips shifting forward and back, his moans almost constant now. Shane wasn't so much taking control as he was taking Galen's breath away, and damn, it worked.

"Forever, Galen. Going to do this forever." Shane's fingers slid down his belly under his T-shirt, tangling in his short hairs.

"Yes." Galen arched a little, putting more room between them so Shane could touch him even more. He worked Shane's chest with his hands, sliding that shirt off and going right for that buff chest. Hard, ripped, the muscles built from hours and hours of work, they fascinated his hands.

Those nipples did it for him too. Those were his rings, done for him on their first vacation, and the symmetry wasn't lost on him. "We need to stop somewhere and get me a tattoo."

"Mmm. Yeah. My mark on your skin." Shane moaned low, tanned skin going a deep, rich rosy color.

"You know it." That flush felt so good under his fingers, that much hotter than the rest of Shane's skin.

"I want you." Bright blue eyes stared at him, burning. "I don't want this to stop, either, though. You turn me inside out."

"Whatever you want, darlin'." They could stay like this until they fell asleep, have a nap, love some more when they got up. Or they could go fast and hard, go swim, and come back and bask. Galen didn't care.

"I want...." The next kiss burned him down to the ground, lit him on fire. "I want everything."

Galen rolled, putting Shane under him so he could press down, get his hips moving. "You can have it, darlin'. I promise."

"Galen." That settled it, both of them starting to shift and move, rubbing good and hard.

"Yeah, darlin'." Leaning down, he took a kiss that curled his toes. Hell, it brought everything into sharp focus—the feel of Shane's lips, the way their chests rubbed together, the ache in his cock.

Those rings slid and flipped, up and down, moving against his skin with every rub. He could fucking *feel* it in each throb of Shane's cock. Goddamn. Yeah. Spreading Shane's legs, he rubbed harder, getting them good and lined up.

"Fuck, that's...." Their mouths slammed together, someone's lip splitting, the copper tang of blood sudden and sharp. His eyes went wide, his hands clenched on Shane's skin, and Galen started moving faster. More. Now. His hips were out of control, slamming down. He could fucking feel the bruises blooming under his fingers, Shane gone hot as a brand beneath him.

Shaking, grunting, he willed Shane to be right there with him, willed the man to just give it up. He needed to come so bad that he was losing his rhythm. Heat splashed on his cock, his belly, pouring between them. Hell, yes. Just like that. Grunting, Galen came hard, his whole body working and pushing and moving like crazy. "Fucking A, darlin'."

"Uh-huh." Shane nodded, blinking slow, staring at him in that dazed, sated, melty way.

That was Shane's best look. Ever. "Still want to swim?"

"Uh-huh. Could soak." Shane's eyes closed, hand wrapping around his hip.

His own hands were braced next to Shane's head, clenched in the sheets. Damn. Moving. Right. His bicep was kissed, his elbow, his wrist. Shane was melting into the mattress.

"Moving is overrated." Grinning, he kissed Shane's chin. "Love."

"Mmm-hmm. You know it." Shane pulled him down, settled him. "Nap. Then hot tub."

"Sounds good, darlin'." He took one more kiss before settling down against Shane, chin on that sweet shoulder.

Shane's sigh was pure happy. Pure-D happy.

And all his.

Chapter Twenty-Seven

T HEY PULLED into a long tree-lined road, the houses familiar but still different. The Johnson's place was blue now, where it had been white. The neat old brick mailbox in front of Chrissy Lynde's place was gone.

His folks' house, though, it looked the same.

Big and white, the front yard all groomed and shit. The roses beside the door were red, dark red, and they smelled like heaven in the late summer when the wind blew and....

Shane swallowed, pointed to the little park right across from the house. "You can park there, and I'll point out landmarks."

"Sure." Len gave him kind of a weird glance, but pulled into the park and looked around, smiling. "It's nice."

"Yeah. I used to come here every day after school. There used to be a couple picnic tables and a swing." Now there were benches and shit.

"No swings now, huh?" Reaching over, Len patted his knee, stroked a little.

"No. No, they're gone." He found a smile. "You want to take a walk?"

"Sure, darlin'. You can tell stories on your childhood self." They hopped out of the truck, and Galen came around to put a hand on his back.

"My best friend, Chrissy, lived in that house. She had a twin brother who died when we were twelve. It was weird. She's an actress now, on one of those soap operas. The kids that lived in the green house were bullies, but their mom made cookies every Tuesday." It had been worth it, for those cookies.

"Oh. Cookies. Momma made the best Snickerdoodles. Did you ever get those?" Len had the best momma, and expected everyone to have that too.

"She made peanut butter and then sugar. She was funny— this little lady with all this hair and tie-dyed T-shirts."

"So which house was yours?"

"That one right across the street—609. That window upstairs on the left was mine." His brother's on the other side.

"Yeah? It's got nice roses. We gonna go say hi?" Tilting his head, Galen laughed a little. "Or I can stay here if they'd disapprove."

"Oh, I don't—" His breath caught as the front door opened, his mom heading down the steps, mail in her hand. She looked good, older than he remembered, but real good— perfect and coiffed and still skinny and not smiling and....

"Mom." He stopped and stared, one hand lifted to wave at her, when her eyes met his. She looked at him, one eyebrow lifting, and then she turned tail and headed back toward the door.

Right.

Okay.

"So, you ready to go, Galen?"

Galen stared, not at him, but at the door that had just closed with a snap. "What the fuck? Shane?"

"What? That was Linda. My mom. She looks good. Let's

go, huh? Get some food on the way out of town?" What was there to say? There wasn't room in that house for a loser; there never had been.

"Shane, honey. Most people's moms don't just stare them down when they come to visit." Poor Len. He looked all pissy.

"Most people's moms don't have me for a son." Christ, he could use a drink. "There still beer in the cooler?"

"Sure. We'll get on the road, and you can have one." That look said they weren't done talking on it, though. Bless him, Len could be stubborn.

"Cool." He slid into the passenger seat, pulled his cap brim down. Looked straight ahead. Straight ahead.

Twelve years.

Twelve years and she still....

Shit.

Len got them out of the neighborhood, back down the way, heading toward the highway. "You want some Krystal's?"

"Ooh. Little burgers. I'm there." The farther they drove, the easier it got.

"Good. You've made an addict out of me." They'd stopped in Georgia for Krystal's, and Galen had approved of those little burgers wholeheartedly. It was cute.

"Yep. Where else can you eat a dozen burgers and not have guilt?"

"There you go." They forgot all about the beer, pulling into the little white-and-red fast-food place and settling in for a binge. Little burgers, pickles, fries, and a Coke the size of a small country—Shane fucking approved.

They got all through, nothing left but the napkins and the groaning, before Galen brought it up again. "Shane, what's with your mom?"

"When I went to the Keys, I called her and told her I wanted to stay. She didn't like it." He shrugged. "I told you my brother's a doctor, huh? Pretty wife. Kids. Money. They've got a son that's everything they want. They don't need the loser son."

"Loser...." Those dark eyes stared right into his, the brim of Galen's gimme cap making them look shadowy and serious. "Honey, you're not a loser."

"Sure I am. I'm a queer bartender that's heading toward midthirties. It's okay, Galen. I am what I am." He couldn't be more. He was just lucky he'd fallen for someone who was more, was amazing. Christ, that was a depressing line of thought. "So where do you want to find a hotel?"

"Somewhere not here. I can drive a couple more hours." Galen nudged his foot under the table. "You may not be a doctor, Shane, but you're you. That should be enough for anyone."

"It should, but it's not. Every so often I call or write, just to see if they've changed their minds, but they haven't. After twelve years, I guess they won't. It's not a big deal anymore."

"No, huh?" That look was too damned shrewd. "Well, it shouldn't be if it is. You're a big boy, darlin'. You've got a life."

"Yep." He'd done okay. He wasn't starving. He wasn't dead. He had a dog and a lover and a gator. Hell, he even had a new truck to replace the Jeep.

"So don't let her get to you. You need a momma, you got mine. She loves you fierce."

Galen's momma was a hoot, for sure. A pretty good judge of character too, when he thought on it.

He nodded, sort of unsure what Galen wanted. He didn't think about home often. Just every now and then.

"So, where do you want to stay tonight, darlin'?" Len gave him a grin, all eye line crinkles and laugh lines around the night.

"We'll find something. I can drive a bit." He finished his Coke, stood. "Come on, you. Let's blow this popsicle stand."

"You got it." They got in the truck before Len touched

him again, hand sliding up his arm to grasp his shoulder. "Okay?"

"Yeah. Yeah, I mean, it'd be nice, to think I meant something, but I know it can't happen, so…. Yeah."

"I'm sorry, honey." Squeezing, Len took a quick look around before leaning to kiss the corner of his mouth. "We need to find a place with a pool and actually swim."

"We can do that." He chuckled, nodded. "We can so do that."

That sounded way cooler than stressing over his old neighborhood.

GALEN WATCHED SHANE SLEEP, LEANING AGAINST the door of the truck and snoring a little. Bless his heart. They'd just kept driving a bit, heading west out of Tennessee, getting away from Shane's bad memories.

It sucked, but in a way, Galen understood better now. Much better. Shane's whole "I'm not worthy" thing made a lot more sense.

They hit the outskirts of Memphis, the lights of the city making it look almost pretty, which was a feat as far as Galen was concerned. He wasn't fond. But there might be something he could do in Memphis that he couldn't do farther out west.

"Shane," he said, poking the nearest arm. "Wake up and call information."

"Huh?" Those blue eyes stared over at him.

"I need you to call information on your cell, darlin'. We need a tattoo parlor."

"A tattoo parlor. 'Kay." Shane blinked, nice and slow. "Uh. Where are we?"

"Memphis? I think." A sign. Yeah. Memphis. Go him for being right.

"'Kay." It took a second for Shane's body and brain to get together, but he managed. Sort of. "There's some on Second Street."

"Okay." He could find Second Street, surely. They had a map on Shane's cell too, if they needed it. In fact, Shane gave him directions, and soon enough, they had two choices. "Which one looks better, babe?"

"That one there—the little one that looks like an apartment."

"Works for me." Parking was a bitch, but they found a ten-dollar lot across the way that looked secure enough, and Galen grinned over at Shane. "Let's go see what they'll do for me."

"Yeah? You ready?" Shane stretched, back popped. "You know what you want, or are we just looking?"

"I know. Someone else already did it, but I don't think he'll mind if I copy it." Holding his breath, Galen waited for Shane to meet his eyes again.

"Yeah?" Shane's eyes searched his, the smile growing, sweet and slow.

"Yeah. I like it so much I want one of my own." *Oh, thank God.* Shane liked the idea. So did he. It would mean something.

"That would be something, huh? Our ink." Yeah. Yeah, Shane was into it.

"It would." He leaned over, put his hand on Shane's thigh. "Where should I get it? My hip? My back?"

Shane reached out, touched his arm. "Right here. Where people can see it."

"You got it, darlin'. Let's go." He wasn't afraid of needles, at least, and given his past, that was a blessing.

"'Kay, Len." Shane was damn near bouncy, hand reaching out to almost touch him, over and over.

The studio was bright, full of flash art on the walls, and

clean. Shane had a good eye. Galen approved. He kind of let Shane go ahead, though. Shane was better at this shit.

Shane did his smiling, nodding, charming thing, showing this big old dude with scales inked all over him the fancy little *G* and *S* that was on Shane's shoulder.

"That's what I want," Galen said finally. "On my arm. Here."

Shane nodded. "Right there where the muscles curve. It'll fit just right."

The guy hummed and nodded and peered and finally said, "Sure. I can do that."

Galen watched Shane talk prices and shit and grinned, waiting to fill out the paperwork and all. Shane had just never met a stranger. Of course, when Shane stripped off his shirt and leaned over the counter for the guy to trace that ink, Galen was wondering if that was exactly a *good* quality.

Still, if he wanted that tat to be his too, he kinda had to let it go. Goddamn, he hated anyone else touching Shane. Those heated blue eyes never left him, though. Shane stared, watching him. Loving him. That alone kept him from growling, and before he knew it, the big guy was leading him to the back to sit and get prepped.

Shane stayed close, doing his own growling when the big guy suggested he could wait in the lobby. "No. This one I get to be here for."

Galen chuckled, winking. "You sure? I didn't get to see yours." But he nodded to the little steel-framed stool that the artist wasn't using. He wanted Shane there.

"I'm sure. You didn't get to see mine, so I have to be here for this."

"That's fair...." *Somehow.*

They got moving after that, and there wasn't much chatting. Just cleaning and setting up and stinging pain.

Shane leaned forward, eyes on his. "When I got mine, I

was all stressed out, and I needed something that made me believe you were coming home."

"Now you know, huh?" Staring right back into Shane's eyes made him feel like a fucking god, blocking out everything else—the buzz of the needle, the building adrenaline rush, everything.

"Now I know." One finger touched his chin, just once, just real quick.

That touch electrified him like nothing else, making his skin tingle. God, all of a sudden the feel of the needle was almost too much, too hot.

"Breathe." Shane smiled at him, and he could smell it, smell how much Shane wanted him. Damn.

"I am. Kinda." Galen grinned a little, trying not to breathe hard enough to shake his arm.

"I kept thinking about New Orleans, when I got my rings. About how it was, right after. About how you looked."

"How I looked?" Lord, Shane had been shaking, hard as nails when he'd gotten those little nipple rings. Galen had never seen anything so hot before or since.

"Uh-huh. Like I was something."

"Darlin', you are something. Something fine." He figured the tattoo guy wasn't gonna kick their asses, since he hadn't by now. He could jones a little.

Shane pinked but didn't look away, stared right into him.

The sting went on and on until he thought he'd explode, but every time the guy asked if he wanted a break he said no. Galen could handle it. All he had to do was stare at Shane and it was all good.

Finally it was over, Shane's fingers tracing just the edges of his ink, the skin throbbing—hot and tender and sensitive as hell. They went to the mirror so he could look at it. Damn. Look at that. Just look. His and Shane's letters, right there.

"My Galen." The words were whispered. Soft and low.

"Yours." His whole body felt like it might explode. "We need to find a hotel."

"Yeah. Now. Put your shirt on." Shane was vibrating against him, just shaking.

"Uh-huh. Thanks, man," he said to the artist, smiling a little but too damned tense to be overly friendly.

"Anytime. You not getting more ink tonight, man?" Those eyes were looking, too damn close.

Shane shook his head, laughed. "No. I have plans. Maybe on the way home. Come on, Len."

"You got it." They'd paid up front, so he grabbed Shane's hand and dragged him right out, the truck seeming miles away.

"That was the hottest thing...." Shane took the keys out, tossed him the phone. "Find a hotel."

"We shoulda asked the guy...." But this was Memphis. There'd be somewhere. Close.

"Yeah." Shane got the truck started. "I'll head for the highway. There's bound to be something."

"Soon." He reached down with the arm that wasn't throbbing and rubbed himself a little. Yeah.

"Don't you come. That's mine." Oh fuck. Hot. That little possessive growl did it for him.

"I'll hold on, darlin'. I can do that." Maybe. He hoped. Jesus fuck, Shane smelled good.

It didn't take Shane long to find a Holiday Inn and bully the little boy at the front desk into a room key. They got to the room before Galen grabbed Shane and ripped that T-shirt off so he could see the ink that inspired his. Just barely.

Shane flexed, fingers reaching for his belt. Each little muscle went tight, Shane's tanned skin flushing dark. Galen let Shane get his jeans open, get them off his hips. Then he bent and licked at Shane's tattoo, biting down just beside it.

"Fuck!" Shane jerked, hands gripping his hips good and hard.

"Yeah, darlin'. Good." His hips jerked, pushing into Shane's touch, his ass wiggling. God, he needed. Shane slid down, mouth dropping on his cock like a lead balloon, taking him down to the root.

"Fuck! Shane!" Jesus, he was gonna. Yeah. Possibly. Oh God. His hips snapped, and Galen tried to control it, but he couldn't. He had to go with it.

Shane's hands were fucking everywhere—his wrist, his balls, his ass, his hip.

"Shane. You're making me crazy. I need." His hands worked restlessly, touching Shane's shoulder, fingers rubbing that tat over and over.

That pretty mouth popped off. "What? What do you need, Len? I'll give it to you."

"You. I need you." That probably didn't make sense. Shane was giving him that hot mouth for all he was worth.

"I'm yours." Shane spun him around, tripping him on his jeans a little as that hot tongue slid along his crease. He fell forward onto the bed, bouncing on his hands when Shane's tongue pierced his hole.

"Yeah. Oh, Shane." Man, how long had it been? Shane rarely took the lead, and Galen rarely took Shane in. He would now. In a heartbeat. Shane hummed, the sound vibrating around his hole. Jesus. That made his thighs go rock-hard. His balls drew up, his whole body shuddering at how fast he was about to go off. "In, darlin'. In now, before I lose it."

Shane groaned, lips sliding up his spine as the noise of belt and zipper sounded. "You ready enough?"

"Ready. Now. Please." Pushing back, Galen braced on his elbows, feeling the new tattoo pull at the skin of his arm.

"I got you." Shane lined up and pushed in, cock spreading him, stretching him and filling him up.

"Uhn." Back arching, he pushed and rocked, needing more of the burn, more of Shane. "Love."

"Uh-huh. Love. Mine." They started moving hard enough their skin slapped together.

Galen was all but singing, his cries coming so close together that they sounded like a weird kind of music. Shane felt so good. So hot, so thick inside him. Callused fingers wrapped around his cock, tugging good and hard—just like he needed it. Fuck him. Shane was hot as a two-dollar pistol.

"That's it, darlin'. Oh, that. Right there." Shane's thumb hit that spot just under the head of his cock, and his whole body clamped down.

"Fuck. Fuck, Galen, *good*." Shane's hips jerked, cock sliding over his gland.

Good.... That didn't even begin to describe it. He managed maybe one more thrust into Shane's hand before he shot, hollering his damned fool head off.

Shane moaned, moving restlessly, all that rhythm lost as heat filled him. "Galen. Galen. Damn."

"Yeah. Feel you deep, darlin'." That just.... Galen wanted to bust with what he was feeling.

"Mmm-hmm. Deep. Love you, Len. I do."

"I know, darlin'. I know. Not leaving you. Want you." They shifted, kind of flopping so they could tangle.

"Yeah. Yeah, I know." Shane snuggled in, nose against his cheek.

"Good." What more could he say? He'd put Shane into his skin. The man had been in his blood for a long time. Hell, he'd braved a hurricane for them.

"Yeah." Shane patted his ass, resting against him.

"Where are we going next, darlin'? Did you look at the map?" They still had a few days before they needed to be at their cabin in the mountains.

"There's a couple of silly roadside things, but I think we need to go to Kansas City tomorrow, just goof around a day."

"Cool. Sounds like fun." He liked music, liked the idea of fucking around and touristing with Shane. Besides, barbecue.

"It does. We'll go play." He got another of those grins, pure happy.

He'd spend a lifetime playing with Shane if he could. Galen couldn't imagine it any other way.

Chapter Twenty-Eight

OH SHIT.

Shit.

He hadn't laughed so hard in weeks.

Months.

Maybe longer.

Galen was in rare form, joking and goofing off, climbing on street signs, dragging him through every cheesy gift shop in Kansas City and showing off his ink.

Shane was having a ball.

"Oh! We need to have barbecue, lover!" Galen stopped and sniffed, then pointed at a little hole in the wall. "There."

"Sure." He laughed, nodded. "You mean you're hungry? After the fudge? The popcorn? The hamburger the size of your head?"

"What? I'm a big boy!" Len had been working out every morning at the hotels they stayed at, and he was looking ripped, man.

Shane stopped, let himself take a brazen, slow look. "Hell, yeah."

Those tanned cheeks darkened above Galen's beard, just flushing dark. "You like it, darlin'?"

"Uh-huh." He fucking adored it.

"I like it you liking it. If you're not hungry, though, we can come back." Grinning huge, Len came over and popped his ass.

"Hey! I can eat." He headed for the restaurant door, copping a feel of Galen's balls on the way.

"Hoo yeah." Following him close, Len hummed happily, almost a blues tune, like the one they'd heard at lunch.

Fuck, he loved Galen like this. The man fascinated him.

Oh dude.

Smell that spice.

"Makes your mouth water. Hey, honey. Two please." After a wink from Len, the little hostess chick wiggled and giggled and gave them the best table available.

"Lord, Lord. She's gonna come over to get in your lap and ride." Shane winked, settled down. Man, look at that gal shake it.

"You'd tear her hair out." Flirty Len was all his, just like all the other variations. It made him happy, deep down.

"Yep. I'm the only one allowed to ride, man." Besides, his hair was too short to pull.

"There you go. I'm all about the ride. Oh man. Ribs and sauce and coleslaw." Galen bouncing was the cutest thing ever.

"And bread. Lots of bread. You want beer or tea?"

"Tea, I think. I better hold off on the beer. We need to hit the night life for some music later." One booted foot hit his under the table.

"There's all sorts of friendly clubs here. Dancing, drag shows—I bet I can find a bar that lets me pour." Although he wanted to dance, there was nothing like Galen rubbing against him.

"I bet we can. I could use some Jack. We could boogie." Oh, someone else was willing to dance. Woo.

"Works for me. I brought my leather pants."

"No shit?" Those black eyes settled on him, hot as lasers. "I want to see that."

"No shit. My pants, my silky white shirt. My chain." He could flirt too.

"Oh God." Yeah, he could see how that was making Len's nipples hard, could smell how hot Len was getting for him.

Shane preened a little, muscles tightening up, cock trying to perk up.

"So, ribs and what else?" The waitress was back.

"Coleslaw. Bread. Do you have sausage?" He winked at Galen, then looked at the girl, eyes wide.

"We like sausage," Len added, laughing with him. The little girl surprised them by cackling and nodding.

"Sure, guys. Sausage. You got it."

They both grinned, settling in with their tea. Blues music poured out of the jukebox, the smells of the food did wonders for his appetite, and hell, the ink on Galen's arm just kept catching his eyes. Every so often Len would look at it too, kinda wondering like. It rocked. It so did. He thought Len thought so too.

"Mine." It made him happy to say it. Hot and tingling, balls-deep.

"Yours," Len agreed, munching on the bread that had magically appeared. "Oh, good cornbread."

"Mmm. Butter." God, they were eating their way across America. It was a wonderful thing.

"Uh-huh." Foot sliding against his again, Galen licked butter off that amazing lower lip. "I can think of some great things to do with slick stuff."

"Perv." Hell, yeah.

"You know it. I have plans for your ass, darlin'." That grin spoke volumes. Kama sutra like.

"Mmm." He was *so* going to be on the receiving end of those plans. "You look like the cat that got the canary."

"Oh, I am. I have this wonderful, terrible idea." Lord, Len was wicked-wicked. It was a fine thing. It was like going on vacation together had renewed the man.

"You gonna share, Len, or you going to make me wait?" Jesus, he was just vibrating.

"You have to wait, darlin'. That's part of the fun." They got their food then, and it smelled so good, looked fine too. Len moaned happily, and it was like sex.

Meat and sauce that was spicy enough to singe your nose hairs, creamy coleslaw, ice cold tea—it was amazing. Hell, it was almost as good as home. They finally sat back, patting their bellies and grinning. "I think we'll have to wait on dessert, honey."

"God, yes. No more. I'll bust."

"Nope. We can walk some off. Dance the rest off with a beer, yeah?" Even the foot against his ankle felt heavy.

"Hell, yes. You know I love to dance." And with Galen? It was perfect.

"I do. It's been too damned long." They paid the bill and headed out to wander the streets, soak stuff in.

They found one of the dance clubs that wasn't too loud, wasn't too crowded, wasn't too young, and wandered in. Man, it was dark, but the place seemed clean, the clientele local. He approved.

They could dance the night away here without getting their asses kicked. Galen chuckled. "See if you can get me a whiskey?"

"If I can't pour it, I'll watch him do it. I promise." He headed over to the bar, nodding and smiling, ending up chatting up a huge bartender with a white smile in a round damn near blue-black face. The guy's name was Tag, and he was from fucking Samoa, which was cool, and he let Shane pour the Jack, which was cooler.

"You're a stud," Len told him when he came back with shots and beer. "Thank God you're mine."

Oh.

Oh dude.

He caught himself beaming a little, like the world's biggest dork. "Barkeep's a cool guy."

"Yeah? I bet you have his whole life story." That shot slammed down, Galen's throat working. Then one big hand closed around his, hauling him to the dance floor. "Shake it for me, darlin'."

He snagged his shot, took it, and then got to dancing. Oh man. Yeah. Hell, yeah. The music had just enough of an old school rhythm for Galen to really get into it, and man, that man had good hips. A fine ass. Long, long legs. They bumped together, slid apart, managed to tease just enough to make things hot, make things ache a little.

One hand landed on his ass, Len's thumb rubbing across the small of his back. Together, back and forth, they got a real bump and grind going. His nerves up and down his spine went fucking crazy, tingling and shit, making him all loose, riding this like the best storm. The best wave.

Those dark-dark eyes never left his, never looked away for a second.

Len was mouthing the words to the song they danced to now, hips meeting his in the best kind of sexual parody. Yeah. God, Len was hard for him. He started moving faster, heart pounding in his chest, beginning to sweat.

"Come on, darlin'. I know you got more than that in you." Someone was teasing him. Body and words.

"Don't make me beat you." Still, he moved close enough that Galen's hands landed on his hips. He leaned back, letting himself feel it.

"Nah, beatings are my job." Wild. Len was wild for him tonight, down and dirty.

His fingers just barely brushed the new ink, the skin raised. Hot. His.

Len's eyes went wide, that mouth he loved dropping open a little. "Shane.... Oh fuck." He could see Galen's nipples harden under the stretched tight shirt, could see the way that wide chest heaved for him.

"Yeah. Mine." He did it again, straddling one of Galen's thighs and rubbing away.

"I. Lord." Baring his teeth, Len pulled him away from the lights, right to the darkest corner of the dance floor.

"Jesus, you're fine, Galen. Fucking hot." He was going to lose it, right here.

"You're making me crazy. Love to watch you dance." Long fingers slid over his shoulder, right where his own tattoo sat on his skin.

"It's amazing." He grinned and stretched up. "Kiss me, Len. Good and hard."

Nodding, Len dragged him close and kissed him until his head got swimmy, the lack of air making stars appear before his eyes. Goddamn.

"Galen." He actually swayed a little, blood pounding.

"I know. I swear, we're gonna have wet jeans...." Those eyes were black with need, Galen's hands opening and closing on his skin.

"Jesus, I want, huh? Let's go back to the hotel." If this was his place, he'd've taken Len upstairs.

"Okay. Now." Grabbing his hand, Galen towed him like a man pulling a balky mule. Except he wasn't balky.

They weren't laughing as they headed back to the room, but it wasn't a bad feeling, just needing and wanting. They climbed up the stairs and got the card lock worked, and Galen barely got them inside before the man was on him. Hard hands, heavy chest, long legs; they all pushed up against him.

"Galen." He knocked Galen's cap off, tugging their lips together in a wild, toothy kiss.

He tasted blood at some point, but it didn't matter. Not one bit. Galen pushed back, tearing at his clothes. They managed to get shirts off, jeans open, his tennis shoes off and one of Galen's boots off before they hit the bed.

Len landed on top of him, pressing him down into the mattress, humping at him like crazy. There was no slow here. No easy.

He got his hand around their cocks, grabbing them together and squeezing.

"Shane! Oh, darlin'. More." That big body shook, Galen going wild for him, bucking and grunting and calling his name.

"More. Yeah. Love." He squeezed harder, eyes just rolling. "Gonna...."

"Me too...." Len shot for him, wet, hard bursts that rushed over his hand, spilling through his fingers.

"Galen!" He bucked once or twice more, then shot so hard his teeth rattled.

"Mmm. Dancing as foreplay." One big hand stroked down his back, patting his hip. "I love it."

Shane chuckled and nodded, floating down. "I hear you, Len."

"Happy, darlin'?"

"I am." He grinned. He was. "You?"

"Definitely." Len kissed him, stroking his shoulder, playing with his ink idly. "Can't wait to get to our cabin, though."

"Mmm. You. Me. Mountains. It'll be good."

"Oh yeah. Lord knows, I still haven't gotten my evil plan set in motion, huh?" Damn, Len was a tease.

He reached down, goosed Len a little. "Come on. Shower and then we can flip channels 'til we fall asleep."

Life was all about the little things.

<h1 style="text-align:center">Chapter Twenty-Nine</h1>

T HE CABIN was everything Galen had hoped it
would be. Rustic, yet filled with all of the modern
amenities, and with this huge bed that beckoned all
sorts of naughtiness.

They'd been there three days, trying out the bed in a whole
host of ways, so much that they'd had to head down to town
to buy more lube. Now Shane was napping, naked as a jaybird,
a shaft of sunlight from the open window slanting across one
hip bone. Made Galen's mouth water, it surely did.

The vacation had been the best idea ever. They'd recon-
nected, learned each other again, and loosened up enough to
play. Which meant, of course, that it was time to enact his evil
plan.

Galen pulled out the little backpack he'd found that Shane
packed specially for them, laid out everything carefully. There
were cuffs, which he might skip for now, and Shane's nipple
chain, along with a cock ring and a plug. His cock stirred just
thinking about it.

He'd start with the chain. Yeah. He grabbed it and knelt
on the bed, one knee between Shane's legs, and attached one

end of the chain. Shane's nipples both went hard, like they were calling for him. Ready for him to play.

God, he loved it when Shane was so attuned to him, so ready to rev up. He clipped the other end of the chain on, letting it drag a little, pull down.

"Mmm. Galen...." Shane's forehead wrinkled, the briefest smile crossing his face.

"Mmm-hmm. Time to wake up, darlin'. I'm ready for that plan." He pulled the chain a little, making it tight, watching the flush rise on Shane's throat.

"Oh...." Shane stretched a little, one leg sliding up along his side. "Mmm. Feels fucking good, Len."

"You know it." Reaching down, he pressed Shane's leg on the bed. "Now, darlin', hold still for me."

"Hmm?" Shane's eyes opened, his lover smiling up at him. "Hey, Len."

"Hey, babe." Bending, he dropped a kiss on that sweet mouth, fingers lingering on one of Shane's nipples. "I want to play."

"Yeah. Yeah, I can play." Hell, yes. The way that little nipple drew up let him know that.

"Good. You need to get up and do anything personal-like, now is the time...." He wasn't gonna be done with Shane for a long time.

"I'm good." Shane reached for him, hands sliding up his arms, thumbs digging in.

"Okay." Grabbing Shane's wrists, he pressed them back to the bed beside Shane's head. "Now, let's talk about the rules."

"Rules?" Shane's skin went a sweet pink, tongue flicking out to wet those pretty lips.

"Yup." He stared right down into Shane's blue eyes. "You're gonna do exactly what I say, when I say."

"I am?" Shane arched a little, rubbed against him, heating right up.

Palm flattening against Shane's belly, Galen nodded. "Yes, yes you are. You wanna know why?"

"Yeah. Yeah, Len. Why?"

He leaned down until his breath fanned Shane's lips, until their bodies almost touched all the way up and down. "Because I like it that way."

He got a rough, needy sound, Shane rippling against him, cock hard against his belly.

"Think you can do that, darlin'?" he asked, easing back up, letting his cock slide against Shane's balls.

"I can." That stubborn look was back, set chin and needy eyes. Fuck, that was hot, that little edge, that challenge.

"Good, darlin'. Real good. Now, you just stay there." He got the ring, the lube, and the plug and brought them back with him, showing them to Shane. "I think the plug first."

He could spend hours watching that flush crawl up along Shane's belly. Galen licked it, tracing the heat under Shane's skin with his tongue before pushing up to lube the plug. "You like that, huh? Want me to see you all full, ready for me."

"'M always ready." Shane spread a little, cock bobbing over that six-pack.

"You're something else, Shane. Mine." His fingers spread lube around Shane's hole, and he knew how cold that stuff was, how it would make Shane jump.

"Y... yours. Fuck. Cold." Shane bowed up, ass leaving the mattress.

"Shhh. You have to be still, darlin'." Galen put an extra growl in his voice, pushing the end of the plug against Shane's body, working against the natural resistance.

He got a low moan, Shane's hole stretching, spreading for him, sweet as anything.

"So pretty...." The plug slid all the way in, the base settling against Shane's skin, and it was too fucking hot. Galen stared for a long moment, proud as hell of the way Shane stayed still for him.

He could see Shane's body working the plug, muscles tensing and relaxing, over and over.

Stroking Shane's thighs, Galen murmured and growled, loving on Shane, telling him how fucking perfect he was. "So hot for me, darlin'. Doing so good. I think you get a reward."

"Rewards are good, huh? Fuck, that's hot."

"It gets better." The tip of Shane's cock was damp, shining in the low light, and Galen kissed it, licking the moisture off. *Ta-da. Reward.*

Shane shuddered, cock bobbing, bouncing hard. "Galen."

"I got you, darlin'. I never let you fall, do I?" He wasn't physically holding Shane this time, but he was always there. Right there. "Now hold still."

Every breath that fell on Shane's cock got him another shiver, but Shane went still when he snapped the cock ring in place, the sound almost shockingly loud.

"Oh. Oh sweet fuck." Those eyes were huge, focused as fuck. On him.

Galen let himself touch, from the nipples, so hard and red, to the belly, all the way down to the cock and balls, bound in leather. Finally he jostled the plug before rolling off the bed and going to pour himself a whiskey.

"You're fucking beautiful."

"Where are you going, Len?" Shane shifted, leaned up on one elbow.

"Did I tell you to move, honey?" There. The bottle of Jack sat on the little kitchen table, and he wandered back with it and a glass, pouring a shot.

"No...." Shane's nostrils flared at the scent of the whiskey. "That'll always make me think of you."

"Yeah? Make you think of the night we met? I wanted you so bad." Just like he did now. Galen sipped his drink, his free hand sliding down his own belly to wrap around the base of his cock.

"You looked like a wet dream, sprawled out in that chair watching me. I didn't have a chance."

"Didn't want you to." That was what they'd almost lost, with him gone so much. That heat. The flare of necessity they felt right now. Tossing back the last of his shot, Galen wandered to the bed to push Shane down and kiss him until neither of them could see. When their lips parted, Shane's hands were in his hair, one leg wrapped around his hip as they ground together, cocks sliding, side by side.

Laughing breathlessly, Galen pushed off, holding Shane down on the bed. "Darlin', you're not doing so good at the whole listening thing."

"Huh?" He got a confused look, a happy grin. "Galen, my cock was listening to your kisses just fine."

That had him swallowing hard, the urge to stop the game on him like white on rice. There was so much more to do, though. He jostled the plug a little, just because. "It listens way better than you do."

Shane's chuckle got lost in a moan, that focus back on the plug and what it was doing to Shane's ass.

"That's it, darlin'. Now grab the headboard." The cuffs would just get in the way later, so Galen left them off.

It was sexy as hell, the way Shane reached, stretched, and grabbed the headboard for him. "Like this?"

"Just like that." Instead of starting at Shane's arms, though, Galen scooted down and started at the ankles, licking his way up to the back of Shane's knee. Shane moaned, toes curling. He could see Shane's sac, tightening up, wrinkling.

Nuzzling there a moment, Galen contemplated. Inner thigh? Hip? Yeah. One sharp hip bone just called for him to suck hard, bring the blood to the surface.

"Oh. Oh fuck. Gonna leave a bruise." He sure as shit was.

"I remember that, standing in my apartment after... looking at your bruises.... Shit."

"I like the way you wear them." Look at that. Reddish pink, but in an hour it would be purple.

Shane panted, lips parted and swollen as Galen found another spot, right above Shane's pubes. Licking a little, he tasted salt, heat, and Shane. His favorite. Then he pressed his lips and tongue down and went to town. He could hear Shane babbling, just pouring love and pleasure and praise down on him. Grabbing those lean hips, Galen moved, leaving a trail of tiny bruises across Shane's belly.

No one bruised like his darlin'. No one. Shane arched, just a little, then settled. Waiting for him.

"Mmm. Taste so good. Have I ever told you how I love your skin? I must have...." Galen licked at the little glory trail, moving down before moving back up, fingers stroking Shane's balls while his teeth pulled at the nipple chain.

"Uhn. Once. Once or twice. Maybe. Fuck, that's good." Shane's whole body shuddered, shaking under his touch.

"So good." There. He found the base of the plug, Shane's body stretched so tight around it, so hot it all but burned. Pushing at it made Shane shake, so Galen did it again.

"Galen!" Shane's head just rolled, toes curling.

"Soon, darlin'. Soon. I want in you so bad, but I love how you look, right now." His hands shook, his whole body tight, hot, sweat running on his skin.

"Need you. Need this, yeah?" Yeah. Yeah, he knew. He knew now that Shane needed him looking, needed to have him paying attention.

God willing and the creek didn't rise, he'd never forget that again. Finally, Galen just couldn't wait. He reached down, slipped the plug free, and grabbed the lube to get himself wet. "Now."

"Yeah. Yeah. Now." Shane's eyes were on his cock, lips open, tongue slipping out.

Putting on a show, he pulled at his cock, slicking it up before he muscled between Shane's legs. Yeah. The head of his cock hit Shane's tender skin, and both of them groaned. Shane's eyes were burning, just on him like a touch. Those thighs spread farther, Shane's hole rubbing against the tip of his cock.

Moaning low, Galen pushed, his cock sliding right in, the feel of Shane's muscles closing on him so good. Hot. Amazing.

Shane's hands slid up his arms, fingers brushing his ink.

"Oh. Fuck, darlin'." That touch hit him like an electric shock, and Galen started moving, hard and fast, not able to hold back a bit.

"Uh-huh." Shane met each thrust, their bodies slamming together with sharp slaps.

"Sweet. Oh, darlin'. Sweet." It occurred to him to reach down and unsnap the cock ring, letting Shane free.

"Oh." Shane's eyes went wide, almost shocked. "Galen. Soon."

"Now." He kinda demanded it. Okay, he really demanded it, squeezing Shane's cock, needing to feel it. Heat sprayed over his fingers, Shane's ass jerking and squeezing around his cock. Galen lost it, his body shuddering and pumping, his own cock jerking as he shot deep inside Shane. Man, he loved it when a plan worked out just right.

Shane was there to hold him, arms wrapped around him as he settled down against that hard little body.

"I like the way we play, darlin'. I surely do."

"I like us, Galen."

"So do I, Shane. All the way." Galen kissed the side of Shane's throat, starting to think they could weather any storm.

Chapter Thirty

Look at that sky.

Shane stretched out on the lawn chair, staring up into the wide, bright sky. His tan was going to be perfect by the time he went home.

Just perfect.

The wind was blowing, and he was lazing, and....

"Galen, do you think I ought to go back to bartending when we get home?"

"Huh?" Len flipped over and propped up on his elbows. "What, honey?"

"Bartending. Maybe during the busy season, just for cash for us?"

Len tilted his head. "If you want, darlin'. You don't have to, but I know you. You'll have to be busy."

"Yeah, but I... I could work the bait shop." He'd like that. Hell, he'd really been working on the place, repairing, cleaning, setting up.

"Yeah?" That got him a happy grin, Galen nodding easily. "That would rock. Hell, you've put a lot of time in down there."

"I have. I had thoughts for it, depending on what you wanted to do." A couple cold cases for sodas and sandwiches. Maybe boat rentals.

"Like what?" Now Galen actually looked engaged, ready to listen to him. *Him*. Not like in that corporate raider way either.

"I think some snacks. Drinks. An ice machine. We could even rent out boats for the tourists...."

"Yeah?" The fact that Len didn't agree with him right off actually gave him hope that he was on the right track. That meant Len was actually thinking about it, not humoring him.

"Well, I just think we could make it somewhere both locals and tourists could come. I know lots of folks who aren't near as much into fishing as they are playing outside in the sun."

"God knows, you know the area better than I do. You got the connections." Len propped his chin on one fist. "It could work. You got enough saved for the minimal investment it would take, and you'd get to keep any profit."

"Well, what about you?" He didn't mind putting in for it, but the house, the shop—they belonged to Len.

"What about me? I think it's a great idea, darlin'. God knows I was letting it go to ruin." One dark eyebrow went up. "It's as much yours as it is mine."

"Is it? I mean, then we ought to talk about it as our profit, huh?" *Right?*

"Okay." He could see Galen turning that over. "I'll be pretty much a silent partner, though, huh? We'll work out a percentage if you want."

"Galen." He arched an eyebrow. "You give me a budget, I'll run the shop. I'm smart enough to do that."

"Works for me." Grinning, Galen blew him a kiss before flopping back down and flipping like a cheese omelet. "Oh, that sun is good."

"Uh-huh. Like magic. You didn't get enough rest while you were playing corporate raider."

"I didn't get enough of anything but hotels. Well, and gyms. I worked out. A lot."

Yeah, he could still see it in Len's muscles. Heavy, pretty muscles. "It's a good look for you." He turned over to get sun on his back. "What are you going to do when we get home?"

"Well...." Len's chair creaked, and soon enough warm hands were rubbing oil into his back. "I'm not good at being retired-retired. But I'm not gonna do something that requires me to travel. Or be on the phone all the time. My lawyer thinks I should try online stock trading. Something I can do two or three hours a day and then turn off."

That sounded boring as hell.

Galen would probably love it.

"Two or three hours a day is a good schedule. Leaves hours to play and cook and goof off with me."

"There you go." That one little move Len did with his thumbs made him melt. "My accountant, my lawyer... they all keep reminding me I'm retired. That I need to pace myself. I figure I'll get you to remind me more often."

"Mmm-hmm. I could cuff you to the bed when you get all busy." He'd be more convincing if he wasn't all moany.

Len pinched his ass. "No. That's my job."

Oh. Right. Len had that thing about being tied down. Still, the man could tease him about it now, instead of getting all funky. "Less pinching, more rubbing."

"Got it, darlin'." Happy laughter made him ease back into a puddle. That and the renewed rubbing, which felt fucking amazing.

"Mmm. You've got good hands, Len." If the puppers were here, they'd be bouncing and barking and shit.

"You have good skin." Fingers digging into his shoulders, Len bent and kissed his neck. "You okay?"

"I am. Missing the dogs some, but I'm happy. You?"

"God, yes." Licking a little, Len chuckled against his skin. "This has been a blast. So glad we took off. You think the dogs are okay with Momma?"

"Sure they are. Momma loves them." Loved all of them. Hell, she was so tickled that they were on vacation it was a little weird. She even drove all the way to get the dogs when their sitter flaked.

"You're right. She calls them the grandkids." Len sounded completely baffled by that.

"Well.... Khan's got your eyes...."

"Bitch." That got him a little slap, not even enough to sting, just enough to feel.

"Oooh. Baby, baby!" They both started laughing, the lawn chairs creaking.

Len finally stopped rubbing and just leaned on him, chin on his shoulder. "I could go for some pie. Maybe some tea."

"Sounds good, Len." He turned his head, kissed Galen's jaw, just happy as a pig in shit. "Sounds real good."

"Yeah. We still have some ice cream, huh?" They rocked a little, humming.

"We do. We'll have to get some groceries tomorrow, but we're good."

Galen felt so fine, hot and heavy above him.

"Cool. Of course, moving kinda sucks. I like it right here." A kiss landed on his neck, making him smile.

"Good thing we're on vacation, huh? We can just stay a bit." He got a hold of Len's hand, twined their fingers together and squeezed.

"We can." That rough hand curled around his, Len playing with his thumb. "We can just be."

"Thank God."

Another kiss, this one on his cheek, and Len was getting up, hauling him up too. "We have that Irish cream."

"You want coffee or on the rocks?" He leaned into Len's side as they wandered in.

"I think in coffee." The cabin was far enough up in the mountains that coffee wasn't out of the question; it would be nice.

"Good deal. You cut the pie; I'll get things started."

They got pie and ice cream and coffee with booze, and it was quiet and easy and right, like it used to be. Only better. They'd fought for this.

Hell, together, they'd earned it.

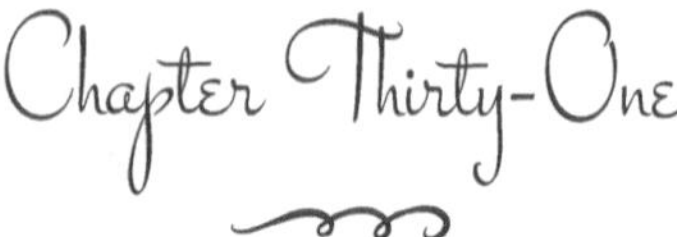Chapter Thirty-One

GALEN HATED to leave Colorado, but it was time to go home.

He and Shane had really had a blast, loving and playing, sitting in the hot tub and eating and.... Yeah. A fucking fine vacation.

They were almost to Momma's, though, where they'd pick up the dogs. They'd left the mutts with Jake, one of the guys from Shane's bar, but he'd had to leave town, and Momma had gone to grab them, taking them back to Louisiana.

"You ready for some home cooking, darlin'?" he asked Shane when he turned off the interstate.

"I am. She... she's not pissed at me, right? I mean, for everything?"

"Why would she be pissed at you?" Shit, he was the one who had fucked up, not Shane.

"Well, you're her son, man, and I left. I'd be pissed at me."

"Well, you know she already thinks I'm a fuckup." He winked over, barreling down the back roads he knew by heart.

"Right." Shane chuckled, slapped his thigh. "You're mine." Those fingers touched his ink. "Mine."

"Yeah. And if I am, she's your momma. It's all good." He hoped she'd made gumbo.

"Okay. You think she's made us a pecan pie?"

"I bet so." Shane loved Momma's pecan pie. She loved to make it and watch them eat it up.

"Man, I'm ready to see the pups. Poor Goob is the little one with all the monster dogs."

It did his heart good to see Shane still bouncing, still eager, even as they were on the way back home.

"He's strong as an ox. He'll be fine." Hell, Goob had taken on alligators.

"Well, sure." Shane bounced as they turned into Momma's driveway.

Grinning over, Galen pulled in and parked. As soon as the wheels stopped, the dogs spilled out into the yard, barking their fool heads off.

"Goob! Khan!" Shane opened the door and two beasts were in the truck, wagging and licking and howling.

Galen laughed, reaching to rub ears and tails. "Did we leave you with the evil Granny?"

Khan got right up in his face, eyebrows lowered, grumping and growling and muttering at him.

"I know, baby. I do. She's good to you, though, I know it. She has bones." Sweet baby girl. Khan panted, licked his chin, butt whacking the steering wheel over and over.

"Lord, boys. Y'all'd best come in. It's hot."

"Sure, Momma." Pushing the dogs away, Galen hauled his ass out of the truck, and man, his ass stuck to the seat.

Shane pushed out of the truck and into a hug from Momma. "Hey, lady! How're you?"

"Good. How are you, honey?" She hugged that man so hard that Shane grunted, and Galen couldn't help but laugh.

"Better. So much better, Momma." Shane kissed her cheek. "It's good to see you."

"It's good to see you too." She kissed Shane back before coming to see him, giving him a stern look. "You'd best have fixed everything."

"Doesn't it look like it?" Slinging an arm around Momma's waist, Galen herded them all inside.

"You both look happy. Real happy." She kissed his cheek and leaned. "The house looked better than I'd feared."

"Yeah. Shane and I, we worked on it." Together. That was the best part about it. "We got the shop pretty well fixed up too."

"Good. And you?" Momma turned, searching his eyes. "You're better? Happy?"

"I am. I can't even tell you. Goob! Stop chewing that." Goober had a mouthful of Shane's suitcase.

"Goober!" Shane laughed, started chasing the basset. Of course, as soon as the chase was on, there went Khan.

Momma started laughing, clapping. "Run, honey! Run!"

It was a wild romp that ended with panting dogs and sweaty Shane, and that was one of his favorite things. Well, not the panting.

Momma leaned in toward him, smiled. "He looks happy, honey, like himself. You did good."

"Thanks, Momma. Did you make pie?" Pie was important. He and Shane *needed* pie.

"I made chess and pecan. I wasn't sure which you'd want."

"Oh, you're the best Momma ever." Galen squeezed, loving on her a little. She just had so much love in her. "He was worried you'd be mad at him."

"Me? Hell, I just wanted to make it better. You boys need a lot of mothering."

"We're not too bright sometimes." Oh damn, the air-conditioning made him dizzy when he walked into Momma's house, his head getting all swimmy.

"You're mine, and I love you both. Shane, honey, quit messing with the dogs and come pour tea."

"Sure, Momma."

"Don't forget to wash your hands."

"Yes, Momma."

Some things never changed. Thank God for that. Galen washed up and helped Momma set the table, breathing deep. Fuck, it smelled good. Shane and Momma were teasing, laughing. Then Shane's eyes landed on him, and he got this smile that just.... Damn. Everything came into focus, everything they'd been working for the last month or so. He'd almost lost that, and it scared him. Fear was good, though. It would keep him from doing it again.

Shane settled down next to him, and Momma sat on the other side. There was gumbo, pie. Dogs.

Sometimes a man had to remember that the simple things were the best. Galen figured they worked for him these days. Mostly retired was the way to go.

"Eat your gumbo, son. I made it just for you."

"Yes, ma'am." The bright tomato and okra flavor made him smile, made him feel like a kid again. "You make bread?"

"Oh! Shane honey...." She pointed to the microwave, and Shane hopped up, fetched a pan of cornbread.

He gave Shane a grin. "Cool. That's mine, but where did you put the rest of y'all's, Momma?"

"Uh-huh. You only get half. Me and Momma get the rest." Shane winked, grinned. "Greedy."

"You know it. All that mountain air gave me an appetite." Butter on the bread, a little beer.... Life was fucking amazing.

"You look like you're healthy enough, mountain air or not." Momma winked, and Shane nodded.

"He looks great, Momma."

Galen gave Shane a slow grin, thinking about how Shane

had admired him just last night in the hotel. Made his cheeks heat up.

"Uh-huh. Y'all quit thinking nasty thoughts." Momma swatted his hand with the back of her spoon.

"Ow!" Hell, he couldn't help but think nasty thoughts. Shane was built for it, and God knew, Galen couldn't resist.

Shane chuckled, shook his head. "He's as pure as driven snow, Momma."

"I used to be, anyway. Somehow I drifted." Oh, that corn-bread was good. He crumbled it in his gumbo, even though Momma thought that was uncouth.

Shane and Momma both chuckled, Momma muttering, "Driven under a Mack truck, maybe."

"Now, Momma." Lord, it felt good to see everyone smiling, to feel like he'd stopped letting folks down. How many times did a man have to learn that lesson? Couldn't tell him nothing. He'd been that way all his life.

Shane's hand slid under the table, petting his knee, just looking all kinds of settled.

They ate and laughed and chatted and fed tidbits to the dogs, which had Momma protesting. He put his hand over Shane's at some point, holding on while they worked on dessert and coffee, smiling like a fool.

"You boys staying a couple days, or are you heading on?"

"I think we're heading on tomorrow," Galen said before Shane could finish drawing a breath. "I figure we'll have you down for Thanksgiving this year."

"Yeah? I'd like that. I could come stay a few days, and then you boys could come for Christmas, if Shane's not working."

"The bait shop'll be closed, Momma." Shane squeezed his fingers.

She stared from one of them to the other, her dark eyes so dear and familiar and sharp as a hawk's. "You're not going back to the bar, honey?"

"No, ma'am. I think I'm going to make some improvements to the shop, manage it. I'm too old to be clubbing six nights a week."

"Oh. Good for you!" Hopping up, Momma went around and kissed Shane's cheek. "I'm so proud."

Shane looked shocked.

Pure shocked.

"Yeah? Thanks, Momma."

"You're more than welcome, honey." Patting Shane's cheek, she bustled around, coming out with a cheap-assed bottle of champagne that had enough dust on it to choke a horse. "We should celebrate."

Shane looked at the bottle, lips just *barely* twisting. "We should. Let me open it and pour out. Do you have any orange juice?"

"I do!" Look at Momma, just bouncing. Galen winked at Shane when her back was turned, blowing the man a kiss.

Shane grinned, nodded. Shane'd make it right.

The champagne was passable in the orange juice with some ginger and God knew what else Shane put in it while he wiggled and hummed and danced. Mainly he drove Galen crazy.

Momma leaned against Galen's arm, just beamed. "You did good, son. Real good."

"Thanks, Momma. It was touch and go." He said it low, but it was the truth. He'd almost lost Shane.

"It would've been a shame, honey. That boy loves you like you're the center of the universe. A momma can't ask for better for her son."

"I couldn't ask for more either." He squeezed her waist, hugging on her, thankful for all of her help.

"Love you, Galen. I surely do. Y'all... y'all'll be okay moneywise, with Shane at the bait house, huh?"

"Oh hell, Momma. He's got more money saved than he

knows, and I've got a good settlement from Frank. Asshole showed up at my place, did I tell you?" *Shithead.*

"Oh good Lord. Did you knock him in the nose?"

"Shane puffed up like a rooster. Ran him off with a piece of wood." That still tickled him more than a whole chicken full of feathers.

"No shit?" Momma started chuckling, shaking her head. "What a good boy. He knows what's his, huh?"

"He does." Shane bebopped back over, grinning, and Galen reached out his other hand to poke one hip. "Right, darlin'?"

"Yep. What?" Shane sat down on the floor, Goober barreling over into his lap.

"You know what's yours. Like Goob. All yours. Silly mutt." Shane was gonna have to wash up before Galen would kiss him again, that was for sure.

"Yep. Just like Khan is yours." At the sound of her name, that huge beast came running.

Heading for him.

And Momma.

And Momma's sofa.

Galen caught her in midair, oophing when her back legs scrabbled against his crotch. "Oh Lord, girl. You're getting huge."

Shane and Goober were rolling on the floor, both looking like they were cackling.

Oh. They needed some ass-whooping. "Get 'em, Khan," Galen said, dumping her right down on Shane and Goob.

Khan went to town, growling and barking, tugging hard on Goob's ear while Shane tickled her belly. Finally Galen joined the fray, figuring it wasn't fair to let his girl get mauled. He grabbed Goob's tail and reached for Shane's ribs, doing some tickling of his own.

It was Momma who was laughing hardest of all, clapping

and snapping one picture after another, just going to town. Shane ended up in his lap, laughing hard, Khan and Goob flopped together.

Galen kissed Shane, not hard or long, just happy. He squeezed, happy as anything. "Love you, darlin'."

"Love you, Len. You too, Momma." Shane settled, easy as you please.

Momma beamed, taking one last picture. "I'm happy. I've got my boys. Y'all should stay at least one more day."

Shane chuckled, leaned harder. "You have things that need doing around here, Momma?"

"Oh, I just want to go shopping, maybe get you to clean out the gutters...." She looked so hopeful it was hard to say no.

"What do you think, honey?"

Shane grinned. "How could you tell that face no?"

"Yeah, that's what I thought." Grinning at Momma, Galen shrugged. "We'll stay. Just for you."

Hell, they'd been away this long. They could stand a few more days of vacation. Shane could stand a few more days of feeling what it was like to have family too.

All the way around, it worked for Galen.

And the way his lover and their dogs leaned and smiled, it worked for them too.

OME. HOME. Home home home." Shane grinned over at the beasts, who were running around furiously, smelling and pissing and exploring like mad.

Galen had steaks on the grill, the bug zapper was going, and Shane had a beer and his favorite chair.

Life was good.

"Uh-huh. I swear I saw gator tracks." Len flipped the steaks before bringing him some chip and dip, sitting on the end of his lounge chair.

"Yeah? Good. Means Vic made it." He reached out, started rubbing Galen's shoulders, the suntan oil making things nice and slick.

"Looks like. Oh, that feels good." Head falling forward, Galen let him touch, big body shifting under his hands.

He scooted forward a little and started really working. Digging in. Touching.

"Uhn." Those muscles went all relaxed for him, Len kinda slinking down on the lounge, really letting him have a go.

"You're fine." Shane closed his eyes, rubbing and rocking,

the smells of the water and the plants just right, just like they ought to be.

"If you think so, I'm damned happy." He did. Galen had dusted off his gym in the spare room, working out like an hour a day. It was amazing what some weights could do. Of course, he spent eight hours a day in the bait shop, chatting and lifting and hauling and shit. It was fun, hard work.

Like Len could read his mind, a chuckle floated up. "You enjoying the shop, darlin'? Happy to have a day off?"

"I am. It's good work. Hell, I got the best company whenever I want it." Galen, Goob, Khan—it was just like being home, but with coolers and bait.

"How's that boat holding up?" They'd gotten him a couple boats to rent out, the first one an old used clunker that he'd fixed up himself.

"Shit, some days I just want to hit it with a hammer. Hard. Still, I got the transom fixed and that fucking carburetor working. You need to turn the steaks?"

"Probably need to take them off and let them rest." Letting them rest these days meant putting them on a Tupperware cake thing with a lid. Khan was a remarkable steak thief. Galen turned and dropped a kiss on his mouth before going to futz with the grill.

Man, look at that ass.

Really.

He so approved.

Turning to look over one shoulder, Len grinned at him. Wiggled a little. "You're staring."

"I got something to stare at."

"I like it. Don't stop." Oh, someone was getting all growly in the good way. The steaks got set aside, safe from the dogs, and Len came back, the front of those cutoffs showing that someone was interested too.

"I won't. You're just... you're it for me, man."

"Ditto, darlin'." One of Len's hands slid behind his head, cradling it and holding him in place while that hot mouth closed over his.

He opened up, pushing up into the kiss. Hell, yeah. That was what he needed.

Galen kissed him like there was no tomorrow, and like they had all the time in the world. It made him moan, made him wiggle. His hands wrapped around Galen's arms, fingers tracing that ink. His.

A low moan sounded, Galen crowding him. "Shane.... Good."

"Uh-huh. Want." He did too. He wanted that cock, that mouth.

"Yeah. The steaks are resting...." Galen dropped beside the chair, leaning down and nuzzling at him.

He moaned, reaching to get himself a handful of ass. "Love your mouth, Len."

"Well, what do you want, darlin'? My mouth or my ass? I could suck you. Or you could do me." Those dark eyes twinkled for him, Galen making him choose between heaven and paradise.

"I'm supposed to *choose*?" Jesus.

"One now, one after supper." Laughing, Galen kissed him again, lips pressing against his, tongue teasing him. He moaned, tongue pushing back against Galen's.

They passed control back and forth, Galen's big hands closing on his shoulders, pulling him right up against that fuzzy bare chest. His cock throbbed against his zipper, aching to get out, to push free. Goddamn, his Galen was a hot bastard.

"Can smell you, honey." One hand slid down to close over his cock, pressing through the denim of his shorts. "Want you."

"Yours." He bucked up, rubbed against that touch. "Come on."

"Mmm-hmm." Len opened his zipper and pulled him out, got that hand wrapped around him, pulling gently.

"More." He might have to kill Galen or die when the fucking chair went.

"More what?" Fucking tease. Len finally got down to business, though, mouth dropping down over the head of his cock.

"Jesus!" His eyes rolled back like dice, hips pumping in short, tiny bursts. A low, rough noise was his reward, Len sucking at him, lips and tongue working hard along his length. Shane let himself babble—tell Galen all about how good it was, how fucking happy he was.

Len's hands were everywhere, stroking his thighs, reaching down to cup his balls. That mouth was relentless, moving up and down, up and down.

"Gonna. Gonna. Galen!" He arched as good as he could, pumping and jerking into Galen's mouth.

Swallowing him right down, Len took it all, moaning for him. Around him.

His ass landed hard on the chair, bouncing a little. "Damn. Good. Len."

Licking his lips, Len knelt up, arms braced on the chair. "Very good. Taste fine, darlin'."

"You needing something?" He leaned, licked Len's lips too.

"Always. Always needing you. Come here." Yanking him right off the chair, Len pulled him down across thighs like tree trunks, getting him so he could rub away. He took one hard kiss after another, giving Galen all he had. Clamping both hands down on his ass, Galen pulled him closer, cock rubbing up under his balls, slipping and sliding. Wet-tipped. Hot. Damn.

"Want in, Len?" Galen's cock slid between his cheeks, and he squeezed, giving the man some friction.

"God, yes. I want to. So bad." Two fingers pushed against his lips, sliding, opening him. "Get me wet."

Shane sucked, licking and pulling, wetting those fingers. His cock was making a comeback, the heat against him enough to drive him crazy. Pulling free, Galen reached around and slipped two of those fingers right into him. That just opened him right up, the pressure of it making him bear down and let Len in.

"Fuck." He smiled, the heat and stretch just everything he wanted.

"Fixing to, darlin'. I promise." Panting, Galen rubbed against his balls, fingers moving inside him hard and deep. Yeah, he could feel how ready Galen was.

They moved together, foreheads pressed together, and Shane couldn't decide if he needed that thick cock or the constant push and press of those fingers. The decision was taken out of his hands, Galen's fingers sliding free, the head of that hard cock pushing right up. Right into him.

His spine went stiff, his hips bucking as he tried to get that pressure just where he needed it.

"Shane. Jesus. Hold still a minute...." Galen held him, hands on his hips, digging in. Then Len moved, hips swiveling, and boom, he was right where he needed to be.

Shane's eyes snapped open, his whole fucking body on fire. "There."

"Right there?" Muscles bunching, Galen moved, pushing up to hit that spot again and again.

"Right. Fucking. There." His cock throbbed, ready to go again.

"God, darlin'. You're so fucking pretty like this. So hot. I just can't get enough of you." Sweat beaded on Galen's skin, and that cock pegged him again and again, right where he needed it, and damn....

"Yours. Fuck." He fucking flew, every inch of his body shuddering, shaking.

"Mine. Oh God." Galen lost the rhythm, slamming into him, head falling back to show that tanned throat. Tendons stood out, muscles bunched, and Galen had to be the prettiest thing he'd ever seen. He watched, jacking himself in time, this orgasm sweet as fuck. Wheezing, Galen held on to him, shaking with the aftershocks, looking stunned. "Damn, darlin'."

"Uh-huh." Yes. Damn.

"Love you, darlin'. The steaks should be ready." Galen winked before leaning to kiss the corner of his mouth.

"If Khan didn't steal them, yeah." He reached up, stroked the lines beside Galen's eyes.

"I bet she didn't." Galen glanced over at the grill and started laughing. The Tupperware was gone, the steaks were on the ground, and the pups were feasting.

"Oh, you *fuckheads*!" He hooted, shaking his head.

"Looks like pizza, huh?"

"We could get dressed up and go out, if you want."

"You want to? We haven't done that in a bit." Relaxed, easy in his skin, Galen was still chuckling at the dogs.

"We could even go dancing. I'll wear my new jeans."

"Hell, yes. I like your new jeans." One hand patted his ass, showing how much Galen liked the parts that went into the jeans.

"Cool. Let's go hop in the shower, and then we'll go play."

"You got it." They moved, Galen lifting him right up, hauling him into the house. The pups could have the steaks.

He had what he needed, balls to bones.

Author's Note

HEY, Y'ALL! Galen and Shane had long been put to rest when, in 2015, I was challenged to write a bar-based story titled *Bartender Rescue*. I have to admit, I never even considered another pair to write about. Shane was happy to be the emotional one, and Galen loved the whole idea of being a hero.

Bartender Rescue (in which Shane isn't a bartender anymore, somehow) is set approximately eight years after the end of *Hurricane*. The guys surprised me with this look at their lives and how things had changed. I'm not sure the boys will have another story in them, but you never know. They always show up when they're not expected.

Much love, y'all.

BA

Bartender Rescue

"I swear to God, y'all. If you don't watch your pours, I'm going to start ripping faces off. I can't afford to run specials if you're pouring triples on every drink."

Christ on a sparkly crutch, Shane had a headache. He'd spent the last four days studying the books on his latest project, trying to figure out why the busiest club of five bars was the one losing fucking money.

"But boss...."

He shook his head at Greg, his so-called manager. "Don't. I don't care. Fix it, y'all. Now. Or you're all fired."

"I'd like to see *him* do it perfect every time," one of the little barbacks was muttering, and Shane saw red, right about the time Greg winced.

"Give me a bottle of Bacardi," he snapped, one hand held out. "And four glasses."

He poured the four shots—boom, boom, boom, boom—without even bothering to look. Each one of them perfect, right on, and he knew it. "Any questions?"

"Yes." The newest bartender, a shrewd little redhead with

bright green eyes, raised a hand. "Do you do it by count or with the bubble or what?"

"I used to count. Now I know it by heart. It's practice. Y'all have to get, if you're getting them fucked-up with two drinks, that's ten bucks to the till, what? Two bucks to you? Three if you're lucky? With four or five drinks? That's twenty-five bucks to the till and more than five in the tip jar."

"Can you show me one more time?" She was taking the initiative, at least. So he bit back his frustration and showed her.

Four pours. Four shots. Four perfect glasses.

Christ, his head hurt. Bad. And he still had to put out fires at Mickey's, run deposit at the Spotted Kitten, and approve proofs for the new menus at Bell.

The bar business was booming, even if other things were sliding, like the old bait shop. Galen could run that with one hand tied behind his back and still do all the weird financial shit the man was into. Hell, they'd had it for more than ten years.

He wasn't sure how he'd ended up like this—how he had ended up owning five clubs. He didn't even drink hardly anymore.

Hell, right now he was tired enough that he didn't want anything but caffeine and energy drinks by the case.

"Cool, boss. Thanks." What the heck was her name? Allie? She winked. Winked at him. Lord.

"I've got to go. Greg. Work on this, man."

"I will. I swear." Greg could do earnest. Shane just hoped there was follow-through.

He grabbed his laptop bag and headed out. Time for the next stop on his rounds....

Someone stood right in front of his new, sparkly blue Jeep. Leaning on the hood in fact.

He stopped, took a second to admire. Damn. Damn, his

Len was fine as frog's hair. Those long legs went on and on, the ripped jeans and tight polo shirt just right. Galen's shoulders still looked like they might block the light.

"Galen. Everything okay?"

Raising one hand, Galen crooked a finger at him. "C'mere, darlin'. I got this terrible problem."

He came over, like his soul was on a string. Nothing on earth was good as this. Galen straightened up when he got close, reached out with one long arm, and snagged his shirt. Quick as a wink, Galen had Shane backed up against the Jeep, pressing against him, all up and down.

"Remember this, darlin'?"

Oh sweet Jesus and all the choirs of angels. "Len."

He remembered. He so totally remembered. Their very first time, hot as fire and twice as dangerous, right out in the parking lot. Hard and fast and enough to blow his mind.

Galen leaned down, mouth an inch from his. "Wanna do it again?"

"Fuck yes." Over and over. "Please, Len."

"Boss? Boss, oh, I caught you. I need this signed, and Kitty from Mickey's called and needs you to pick up pineapple and celery on the way to her."

Fuck.

He closed his eyes, his head screaming at him. "What needs signing, Greg?"

Can't you see I'm getting laid?

Galen growled, the sound almost like an alligator warning off a Rottweiler. Too bad Greg didn't take the hint.

"Just this thing for the deposit tonight."

"Okay. Okay. Fine." He slid out and signed the paper. *Go away now. Damn it.*

"Pineapple and celery for Kitty."

He sighed, nodded. "I got it."

"Thanks, boss." Greg left.

Galen didn't. "Seriously? You have bar managers."

"I know." He rubbed the back of his neck, the tension there vicious.

"Well, you want me to call one of them?" That white smile flashed, making Shane relax a little.

"Yeah. No. No, this isn't your job. I'm being a whiny titty baby."

"No, you're not. I'm the one pulling the whiny card." Galen touched his cheek. "I miss you, darlin'."

He leaned into the touch, eyes closing for a second. He needed an upper. Bad. His head was going to... oh. Oh, Len massaging his neck was better than any pill.

"Jesus, darlin', you're like frozen rope. Come home."

"Can I do that?"

"Yes. You call Kitty and tell her to send someone for the fruit who's not you, and then we turn your phone off."

God, that sounded like heaven. No phone. No clubs. Just quiet and Galen.

Possibly naked Galen.

In the shower.

Or using the leather straps.

Then a nap.

"You make that call, darlin'. Then we'll go and get busy." Galen gave his neck one more rub.

"Promises, promises." He knew better. He'd call someone, and there'd be an emergency, and he'd be screwed. Except not.

Except then Galen took his phone and dialed Kitty, not giving it back when he reached for it. "Kitty? Yeah. Shane has a migraine. He can't drive, so I'm taking him home. Take a twenty out of petty cash and get your fruit. Uh-huh. Bye."

Then Galen turned his phone all the way off and shoved it in a back pocket, staring at him, daring him to say shit.

At least Galen hadn't fed it to an alligator.... Shane

grinned, the pounding in his head easing a little. He'd done that once, when Galen had been so busy with work.

"Come on, darlin'. Home. Hot tub."

Galen didn't wait for him to answer. The man just grabbed him and plopped him in Galen's truck, then shut the door. Bang.

They were tearing off at twice the speed limit in no time. Galen still took corners on two wheels.

He watched the sun go down over the water, like the ocean was swallowing it up. Gulp. He kinda wished a storm was coming in, because they would go to the beach and let it wash over them, but the hot tub sounded nice too.

Galen didn't talk, but the radio came on, Kenny Chesney singing, and that was okay. Comfortable.

By the time they got back to their little house out there by the water, he was half-asleep, his head nodding. God, please let him have a day, maybe two. Just a second. Maybe an orgasm.

"You awake, Shane?" Galen put the truck in Park and turned to face him, sliding one hand across the back of his seat.

"Mostly. Love when you drive."

"Well, I can keep on, figuratively at least." Len leaned over and kissed him, mouth hot, beard just a little scratchy.

Oh. Oh yes. Len still wanted him.

He grabbed the broad shoulders, dragged Len as close as he could. His lover blocked out the last of the sunset, that big body pushing against his.

His cock was full, pushing at his jeans, reminding him that it had been too long since he'd been touched. Galen was all about the touching too, pinching at his nipples, pulling the rings there through his shirt.

Oh, that made him want to wiggle and hump, made him a little stupid.

He couldn't catch his breath, and it got worse when Galen yanked him out of the truck and tugged him into the house.

"Len...." He stumbled along, his prick so hard.

"Need you now, darlin'. I had this grand seduction planned, but I can't wait." Galen dragged him into the bedroom, tugging at his clothes.

"Oh, thank God." He bit Galen's shoulder.

"Yes." Those hands... he could write odes to them if he did poetry. Galen lifted him, stripping off his jeans.

His prick pushed right out, wanting Galen's attention so bad.

"God, Shane, I can smell you." Len grabbed his cock, pulling nice and strong.

He braced himself, spread his thighs, and pushed into the touch. He humped, wanting nothing more than to come all over his lover's hand. "Don't stop, Galen. Please."

God knew, something was waiting to stop them, interrupt them. He tried to block everything else out, though. Len deserved his whole attention.

It got easier to focus when Galen rolled his palm over the head of Shane's cock, bringing him up on tiptoes. He was leaking, his ass muscles clenching. The denim of Galen's jeans rubbed him mercilessly.

"More. Hurry, Len." He was going to scream with it.

"Uh-huh. Want skin." Galen tossed him down on the bed before stripping down, baring that amazing body. The man was still as ripped as any professional athlete.

Fuck, Len made his mouth water, made his balls ache.

Then Galen was back with him, rubbing against him, covering him. Their cocks pushed together, making him grunt. He wrapped one leg around Galen's hard ass, dragging them even closer. God, that man made him crazy. He forgot, sometimes, how good it was.

"Stop thinking, darlin'." Galen kissed him, stealing his breath right away.

He wrapped around Galen as tight as he could, just

humping up. No thinking. He used to be good at that. He used to be happier.

"Shane." Galen bit his lower lip. "No frowning."

"I'm not." Was he?

"You were." Len spread his legs wider, pulling them up over those shoulders.

"Oh fuck." He spread, his toes curled.

"Better. Just need the slick." Galen leaned off to get the lube, stretching his thighs until they screamed. Fuck a duck sideways, he hadn't felt that in a while. His heels drummed on Galen's back when they returned to upright, and Len didn't let him slow down a bit.

"Need you. Come on." He rolled, rubbing, making a clear offer.

"God, darlin'. So hot." Galen gave him two wet fingers sliding right into his hole.

His body clenched, the pressure immediate and welcome. Perfect. Len was perfect. Amazing. "Miss you."

"Yes. I want inside, darlin'."

"All the way. Deep and hard."

"Now." Pulling those long fingers out, Galen pushed up against him, cock poking at him, demanding.

He pushed right on back, bore down, took that sweet cock in. Shane felt the burn deep; it had been too damned long. The sting made him breathe hard, made him rock back and forth.

Galen groaned. "Look at you."

Why on earth would he do that? Galen was right there. Broad shoulders, fuzzy chest, ripped abs—Galen was a feast for the eyes.

He reached up, fingers dragging on Galen's skin. Touching felt so good. The closeness... yeah, he'd been too busy too long. He stroked Galen's nipple ring, making the flesh go hard for him.

"Shane. Darlin'. Tight." Galen grimaced, but it was all pleasure.

"Uh-huh. So good."

"Fucking love this." Galen moved, hips rocking, that cock thrusting deep inside him.

Which was handy, because Shane needed it.

They moved together like a well-oiled machine, their skin slapping hard enough to make a heck of a racket. The bedsprings were screaming, the headboard whacking the wall. He loved that sound, loved how good they were when they got their shit together and stopped thinking. Thinking never got them anywhere.

"Soon." He reached between them, grabbed his prick and started jacking, sending them both higher.

"Yeah, darlin'. Soon. Fuck, you make me crazy." Len worked harder, hips like a piston.

Those hard muscles clenched, abs rippling. Fuck. Galen was like a fucking god, all sinew and flesh, sweat and musk.

He could worship at this altar forever, yessir.

"Now, Shane. Can't hold it." Galen smacked into him, hips grinding.

He worked the tip of his cock hard, making himself bear down. He bit his lip as he shot.

"Fuck!" Galen came for him, deep inside, filling him up.

Yeah. Yeah, better. That almost got his headache to back off.

Almost.

Galen flopped down on him, easing his legs down on the bed. "Oh damn, darlin'."

"Uh-huh." His muscles were jerking and jumping. Crazy.

"Love you, darlin'."

"Love." He nuzzled Galen's jaw, so happy. He hadn't felt this good in months.

"Mmm." Galen got heavy on him, weighing him down. "Rest, darlin'."

It was still early, but Len was sound asleep.

It was probably for the best, really. He had work to do, and he knew it.

At least now he could do it in a good mood.

WHEN GALEN woke up, he felt great. Loose in his skin, happy, his body thrumming with good feelings. He cracked an eye open to look at the clock—10:00 p.m. Woo. When he reached for Shane, though, the man was gone.

He knew Shane would be here somewhere—the man didn't have his Jeep, and Galen had hidden the keys to his truck. Still, he'd seen Shane's eyes. The man should be asleep.

Galen grumbled, climbing out of bed to pee and wash up before hunting his suddenly very busy lover. Shane the bar magnate.

It didn't bother him, really, except that Shane seemed so unhappy, so tired.

Maybe he needed to take a firmer hand.

"... some reds, man. I'm worn out. Yeah. Yeah, I ran the numbers. That's good." Shane barked out a laugh that didn't sound like him at all. "You know I don't do computers. I did it with the adding machine like a real boy."

Reds? Oh no. Galen had this knee-jerk thing about drugs. He didn't think they were immoral or anything. He just didn't think he or Shane needed them.

"No. No. I'm cool. Just tired, and I don't have but a couple days' worth left. Yeah, I know. I know. I need to replace Kitty if she can't do her job, but she's got kids and she cries. No, man, I can't come out tonight. I got a bitch of a headache, and I can't see well enough to drive. I'll just work 'til Len wakes up and then maybe get something to eat."

Galen frowned harder. He thought maybe Shane needed a vacation. Like a real one. And a general manager.

Hell, how had Shane gotten in this deep, working this hard? His laughing, relaxed lover?

He guessed it was easier than he'd thought, if Shane could get so wrapped up in it. Oh, that wasn't fair. Shane had proven a damned good businessman.

He waited until Shane clicked off the phone before wandering into the office.

Shane gave him a tired smile. "Good nap?"

"Been better if you were there."

"I had shit to do. I wanted to."

"Mmm. I think you need to take some time off." He moved close, pulled Shane up out of his chair. His lover needed some time off, a long nap, and about thirty orgasms.

Maybe to be tied to the bed.

Oh, he liked that idea. Shane naked and spread, riding a dildo, hard for him. Unable to get away. No phone, no worries, just feeling.

Just feeling him.

He kissed Shane's neck, holding the man right up against him, waiting to make his move.

Shane hummed, chin lifting. "Oh, that's good."

Shane's phone started ringing.

When Shane reached for it, Galen picked it up and tossed it across the room. "No."

"No?"

He might be making it up, but it looked like relief on Shane's face.

"No, darlin'. This is our night." He lifted Shane right off the floor, tickled he could still bench press the man.

"Careful now." Shane gasped, the sound tickling his lips.

"Nope. Careful time is over." He was going to love Shane into a puddle.

Then they were going to have a talk. Seriously. About Shane hiring a competent manager. About reds. About remembering what was important.

He dropped Shane back on the bed, feeling some serious déjà vu.

"Weren't you just here?"

"Uh-huh. So were you." He needed to find some ties.

"You noticed." Shane sat up, belly rippling over the thin sweats.

"I did. No moving." He went to the closet. Shit, when had it gotten where Shane had ties and he didn't? "You have suits."

"I know. It sucks. I hate them."

"Then we should feed them to Vic." They still teased about their resident alligator, even if they hadn't seen him in over a year.

"They would give him a bellyache, Len."

"They sure give me one." Galen came back to bed with four ties in his hands. Time to up the ante.

"Those are my ties." Shane reached for one, the silk sliding through his fingers.

"Uh-huh. I can use them, though." He watched, waiting for the moment that Shane figured it out.

He saw it first in the dull flush that clawed its way up Shane's belly, those pretty nipples going rock-hard.

"Yeah, darlin'. Gonna make you crazy."

"Something's got into you, Len. Something hungry."

Galen nodded. "I get it. How too much work makes us dull boys."

Too much work, not enough sunshine and water and wild monkey sex. Shane needed that stuff. Was made for it. His happy lover wasn't made to wear suits and ties.

Losing his brother a few years ago had altered something in Shane, bruised something deep. Like the "good" one was gone, and now that Shane had contact with his nephew, he had all this new pressure. It was time to start healing that. Maybe they'd go to the islands somewhere, somewhere quiet and slow.

The thought made him smile, made him hum as he wrapped a green tie around Shane's wrist. Water, sand, sun, hours in bed.... He could so do that. Galen tied Shane's hand to the bedpost.

"Perv."

Uh-huh. Shane's body was tight, eyes laughing at him. Someone protested too much.

"I like you at my mercy, darlin'." He got Shane's other hand tied up before pulling off the man's sweats.

Shane's cock was mostly hard, resting on one muscled thigh. Galen yanked the sweats away and bent to lick at it. Shane's legs drew up, a wild cry on the air. Oh, very good. That was pure abandon.

He nuzzled in, inhaling deep, filling himself with Shane's musk. Fuck, he loved that smell. He could just stay there, but Shane's heels dug into his back, reminding him he was making the man helpless. Right. Ties. Ankles. Spread wide.

Focus, man.

He slid back, grabbing one ankle.

"Len... where are you going?"

"Tying your feet, darlin'. I want you immobile." He wanted Shane thinking of him. Only him.

"Oh." Shane's cock slapped that flat belly, proving his interest.

"Uh-huh. Oh." He tied one leg out, ankle against the wood.

Shane curled his toes, calf muscle tightening. Galen would guarantee the man wasn't thinking about anyone but him.

Perfect.

He secured the other foot, sitting back on his heels to admire his handiwork.

Jesus, look at that man. Compact, lean, not an ounce of fat on him—Shane was a sun-soaked fantasy come to life. Galen grinned, contemplating where to start.

His fingers looped casually around Shane's ankles, the man's skin warm against his palms. He watched Shane's muscles tense up, one after the other, all the way up to the hips.

Fuck, that was pretty. "Do that again."

"Do what?"

Galen squeezed, and Shane tensed. "That."

"Okay." Those muscles rippled and tightened for him, making his mouth dry.

Fuck. Galen tried to swallow, but there was a hell of a lump in his throat.

He let his hands move north, tracing Shane's legs, feeling them. Every muscle quivered for him, and he dug his thumbs into Shane's calves, massaging.

"Oh Jesus." Shane arched, heels digging into the mattress.

"Love your skin, darlin'. You were made for me to touch."

"I was." Well, that was easy.

Galen just laughed, pushing his hands up Shane's thighs. Warm. Fuzzy.

He leaned in, nuzzled Shane's cock, tracing the big, throbbing vein with his nose. The scent there, oh, it was rich, hot, musky. He could so smell where Shane had come earlier.

Christ, this was an addiction. He let his tongue drag up along Shane's prick, gathering that salty bitterness. He loved that flavor, loved how the motion made Shane dance on the sheets.

"Smells like rain." Shane arched, tugging on the ties, toes curling.

"Mmm-hmm. We're gonna miss it. You're gonna be here." He licked again, swirling his tongue around the head.

"Fuck!" Shane went all tight, straining to push into his lips.

"Shh." He blew air on that tight, hot skin.

"Galen. Galen, love. Damn."

"That's it, darlin'. Just you and me." He moved to one side, nipping at Shane's hip bone.

"Uh-huh." The tanned skin marked so prettily, a little purple bruise popping up. He sucked at the mark, making it deeper.

He wanted to be able to see it through those gauzy loose pants Shane wore around the house. Maybe one more bite....

He groaned, let his teeth sink in a little, letting Shane feel it.

Shane shouted, body almost lifting up off the bed.

Oh hell yes. How much fun was this? He let his chin graze that hard cock.

"Stubbly!" Shane felt that.

"Too much?" He knew better. Shane wanted more.

Shane shook his head. "Not too much."

"Good." He sucked at the tip of Shane's cock for just a few seconds.

A string of curse words filled the air, Shane growling at him. He chuckled, which just made that poor skin vibrate against his lips. His impatient lover. His needy man.

Sexy son of a bitch.

Galen finally gave in and sucked Shane's dick in deep, letting his tongue run down the underside. The heavy shaft jerked, twitched on his tongue, Shane primed for it. Galen breathed deep through his nose and went all the way down, sucking as hard as he could.

His lover humped like a naughty puppy, fucking his lips, grunting and calling out for him. Shane was totally focused, pulling at the restraints. Galen wanted more.

Galen wanted fucking everything.

He pushed two fingers in Shane's ass, loving how his lover gripped him. Hot, tight—Shane was so ready for him. God, that was enough to make his balls hurt.

Shane's eyes were squeezed closed, lips open, focused on his touches. That flat belly was flushed deep red, the pierced nipples hard as little rocks.

God, he should have put the chain on. He could have tugged it. Maybe a little later in the night....

"Galen." Shane's arms tensed, fingers curling up.

"Mmm." He hummed, sucking, licking, just really going to town, and Shane was with him, pushing up and rocking into his mouth, over and over.

He worked that fine ass too, his fingers pushing in and out.

When he hit Shane's gland, a sharp, happy cry filled the air. That was the ticket. Now he just needed to get in there with his cock and hit it over and over.

"Galen! Galen, hurry. I need, man. Please."

"I got you, darlin'." He popped off that sweet cock and sat up on his knees, ready to slick up.

"Hurry." Shane watched him, hips bucking restlessly. "Come on."

"Shh. No topping from the bottom, Shane. That's why you're tied up."

"You keep talking and not fucking me."

He laughed out loud but dutifully grabbed the lube. He could always last longer the second time in a night, but even he was getting impatient.

"Jesus, man, you're the most beautiful son of a bitch."

Galen slowed down a little, flexing as he opened the lube. "Damned glad you think so."

"Know so. I'm so fucking lucky."

"Love you." He got his cock slicked up, got set to slide into Shane's hole.

"I know." Shane was damn near holding his breath.

"Breathe, darlin'. Just breathe." He'd never get inside if Shane didn't relax.

"Trying. I want you, Len."

"I want you too, Shane. All the time."

And that was it, wasn't it? He wanted Shane all the time, and Shane didn't have any time. Shane was always frickin' busy.

"Would you stop thinking so hard and fuck me?"

"Yes." He laughed. That was more like old times, Shane accusing him of overthinking everything.

"Thank God. Come on." That smile lit the room up.

"God, you're something." He held those lean hips in his hands and pushed inside that tiny hole.

"You're something. Love how this feels."

"Me too." He gritted his teeth and pushed his hips forward, then back. He felt that heat surround his cock, inch by inch. His balls drew up so tight he moaned. "Damn, darlin', you feel like heaven."

"I do. Harder."

"Fuck." That was what they were doing. Fucking. It was amazing.

His thighs slapped against Shane's ass as he drove in, over and over. The sound made him a little crazy, erotic as it was. He gave it up, fucking Shane furiously, driving them both as hard as he could.

All he could do was rock back and forth, his belly tight, his breath heaving in his chest.

The bed groaned and creaked, Shane pulling hard at the ties. That made every muscle in Shane's torso stand out. Shit, Galen was a lucky bastard. This was his.

He reached up with one hand, tugging at Shane's nipple, and Shane's ass clenched around his prick like a mother-fucking fist. He should have gotten the goddamned chain, really. Like really. He would next time. Which would be soon.

He tugged again, twisted that tiny ring.

Shane cried out, shaking, cock bouncing against the flat belly. The sound it made was almost a slap, and it made Shane cry out, shoot.

Look at that. Galen watched every moment of that orgasm, not wanting it to end. Until his started, that was.

Shane's body worked him, like that sweet hole needed his pleasure. Galen came so hard his teeth rattled, his pleasure shorting out his brain.

Oh fuck. Better. So much better.

"Mine," Galen murmured, resting down against Shane.

"You know it." Shane made a totally satisfied sound.

Galen let himself relax again, secure in the knowledge that Shane was tied down.

Lights flared in the bedroom window, a car pulling into the drive. He lifted his head, staring. "Are we expecting someone?"

"I'm sure as shit not. Untie me, man."

"Yeah." Damn it. He pulled back and untied Shane's hands. Shane could get his own feet while Galen got them clothes.

He had his jeans on when the knock came to the door. He hoped to God nothing was wrong with his mom. She would just call, right? The house phone was still on.

"Shane? Shane, man? I need you to come to the club, man. Kitty's walked out."

"What?" Shane came up behind Galen, reaching past him to open up. "Andy?"

"Kitty's walked out. I tried to call. We need you, man. You have to fix this."

Shane sighed. "Okay. Okay, give me five minutes and you can take me out there. My ride is in town."

"Seriously?" Galen hated that he sounded so petulant. He knew Shane had to go if a manager walked out, but damn, they'd been having a good night.

"I'm sorry. What else am I supposed to do?" Shane sounded fucking furious.

"I don't know!" He didn't. Shit. "I'll drive you back to your Jeep."

"Okay." Shane stormed back to the bedroom, tore on some clothes. "I fucking hate this shit."

"Me too." They both ignored the kid still in the living room. Until the dogs set up an unholy racket.

"Uh... boss? Are they mean?"

"Nope. You three get down, right now." Shit, Shane could snarl.

The dogs slunk away, the kid hit the door at a run, and Galen left with Shane, locking up, a habit he'd almost forgotten.

Shane was vibrating under his fingers, tight as a bowstring.

He had a million words hanging on his lips, but he didn't say them.

Shane met his eyes, the look beaten down, bruised. "You sure you don't want the kid to just drop me off? It'll save you an hour of being in the car."

"No, darlin'. Someone has to make sure you get home tonight."

"I hate this shit, man." Shane squeezed his hand, and then they were moving, heading out for the car.

Galen just nodded. Okay. Okay, Shane meant it. And if he hated it, then Galen just needed to set out to find a way to ease the pressure. He was good at business. He could do that.

There was no way he was letting his lover do this if it sucked.

No fucking way.

SHANE SLIPPED into the walk-in just to get away from the noise and the lights for a second.

He needed help, of the red pill kind, or he was going to scream.

Or fall down.

Or kill someone.

Kitty had walked and taken three bartenders with her, and things were so far out of control it was like a fucking *Hangover* movie. It had taken him and Galen and the other guys two hours to clean up messes. Fuckers.

Now he was waiting for one of his guys to help him out.

If Dylan didn't get there in the next ten minutes, he was going to be fired too. Damn it, Galen shouldn't have to be behind the bar, chopping lemons.

He caught his breath, headed back out, and got back to work, Dylan showing up with thirty seconds to spare. Good man. Heck, Dylan threw in and worked hard enough that Shane thought about promoting him on the spot.

Galen was finally sitting, and things were normal again, and Shane stopped, so fucking tired he couldn't cope.

"Hey, Dylan. You got this 'til closing?" That was Galen. Watching him closely.

"Sure. No sweat." Dylan looked at him, eyes narrowing. "Hey, boss. You want... to come to the break room?" His voice lowered. "I got stuff. You look pooped."

"Yeah." *God, yes.* He was so tired his toes hurt.

"No." Len popped up like a jack-in-the-box. "No reds."

"I...." He looked over, bit back a snarl. He needed some help. "Thanks, man. I'm cool."

"Well, if you need me to make a run later, holler." Dylan was a good guy.

Galen was about to be on his shit list.

He looked at Galen. "Can you come up to the office a second, man?" He was two breaths away from a meltdown.

"Sure, darlin'." Len followed him, right on his heels.

They headed in, and he closed the door, locked it. "I need help." He wasn't 100 percent sure that was what he had intended to say, but it's what he said. And he meant it.

"I know. What do you need me to do, darlin'?" Len didn't touch him but did reach out, leaving it up to him whether they had this conversation close or apart.

"I don't know. I hurt, Len. Everything hurts." He needed that pill, just one, just tonight. Or maybe he just needed a nap and a hug.

Hell, he didn't know.

Shane pushed into Galen's arms and held on tight.

"I got you, Shane. I do."

"Okay." Good. He needed Galen to have him, because he sure as shit didn't. He felt like he was going to fly apart, and he obviously wasn't going to get his reds.

"Oh, darlin', I should have paid better attention."

He didn't know what to say. "I'm sorry. I just... I'm tired."

"Of course you are." They rocked a little, side to side, Galen swaying.

Were they dancing? He liked dancing, but it had been so long. Every time he pulled back a little, Galen rumbled softly, hand stroking his back. This wasn't exactly talking, like he'd had in mind, but it felt amazing.

"I feel like I'm going to come apart at the seams."

"You're not. It's just been a while since you let yourself be tired."

"I want the pill. I don't do it often, but... I'm so fucking worn." He could tell Galen; Galen would help.

"I know, darlin'. We can do this. Without the pill." Galen kissed his temple.

"You promise?"

"I do. We're the kings of coping."

He wasn't sure that was true, but they sure did poke along and do their thing.

Besides, Kings of Coping would be a kickass band name. If they could bottle it, that would rock.

He kissed Galen's throat, loving the stubble there, the scent. This was his drug right now. Though he might need a cup of coffee.

GALEN GOT Shane home. Again. That was half the battle.

Then he had to call all the bars and threaten them with death if anyone came, called, or quit.

He'd misjudged how tired his lover was, how close to the edge Shane was. He had to figure something out now. As in right now.

Shane was sitting on the front porch, staring at nothing, hands on the pups. Poor baby was just wore out. Dogs helped. They always did.

Hannah was on Shane's lap, and Mookie was on his back, getting a belly rub. So cute. He hadn't been sure Shane would ever get over losing Goob at the ripe old age of ten, but the man had bounced back. Maybe he could get Shane to give him a belly rub too.

Shane's head was down, and Galen wasn't sure if the man was awake or asleep. Maybe dozing. Shit, he didn't know what to do.

He grinned, shook his head. Shane still got him all tied in knots like he was a teenager. He just needed to breathe and find a way to get Shane some rest. Then they would work on everything else. "Darlin'? You want to come on in?"

Shane lifted his head like it was a boulder. "Uh-huh."

"Come on, you lot," Galen said, nudging dogs so he could get to Shane.

He didn't ask again, just picked Shane up and carried him

in. It spoke volumes that Shane didn't bother to protest a bit. Not this time. Oh man, Shane was tense....

A massage might just put the man to sleep.

He put Shane on the bed and started stripping that tight little body down. There were a few bruises on Shane's hips, shaped like Galen's hands and a couple like his mouth, and he stopped to admire them.

They looked like heaven, like he'd painted them right on. "God, you're beautiful."

Shane stretched for him, muscles rippling, jerking under the tanned skin.

Galen grinned, bending to kiss one nipple, then the other. Then he flipped Shane over, reaching for the oil.

"Len?" Shane didn't actually sound worried.

"Gonna rub you down, darlin'. You're like a pile of rocks." The tension in Shane's shoulders was visible, muscles actually jumping.

"Things are hard these days."

"They are." He oiled up his hands and started working on Shane's shoulders. "We need to work on that."

"I don't know how. I'm not smart enough to work on one more thing, Len."

"Stop it." He pulled back just enough to pop Shane's right asscheek. "No putting yourself down."

"Hey!" Shane's leg jerked up, thighs spreading. "Be nice."

"Nope. Not when you're talking trash." That was working, so he popped Shane again.

"Galen! Stop it! I don't like this."

"You sure about that?" Shane's body was telling a whole other story. Oh, he wasn't going to spank the man like a child, but a few more slaps would prime the pump.

"I'm not talking about you."

"No?" He smacked again, wanting this confession. "Then what?"

"No!" Shane shook his head. "All of it! I was happy before!"

"Then we get back to happy, Shane." He laid a flurry of blows on Shane's ass before yanking his lover up for a kiss.

Shane pulled back, shook his head. "I don't remember how."

Galen snarled a little. "Neither do I, but you've always reeled me back in when I got too far away."

"Don't you snarl at me. I'm trying to be somebody good. I'm trying to be a grown-up when I'm a natural-born beach bum!"

"You're not a bum!" Shane worked hard. Always had. He just wasn't meant to be a mogul. Neither of them were. "We just need to be us, darlin'. Stop letting people push us."

Shane nodded, wrapped around him so, so tight. "I'm tired, Galen. So tired it hurts."

He stroked Shane's back, needing to soothe. "You need to sleep, darlin'. Really sleep, without the buzz keeping you up half the night. Then you need a week off." At least.

His fingers started rubbing, giving Shane the massage he needed, digging in enough that he got nearly pained moans. Poor baby. Galen hated that he'd forgotten to be there, that he'd given up a little. Him, not Shane. Shane had just gotten bogged down in a routine.

His lover tended to get stuck like that, and Galen knew it. Why he hadn't acted on it was a worry for another day. Right now they were in the relaxing stage. Those tense muscles hadn't even begun to let go. He dug his thumbs in, Shane jerking against him, almost flailing, before the muscles let loose.

"That's it. That's better." He did it again, letting Shane grunt and dance under his hands.

"Galen." Shane's legs drew up, relaxed, drew up again.

"Uh-huh. It has to get worse before it gets better, okay?" He dug in deep, putting all of his strength behind it.

By the time he'd spread Shane out on the bed again and was working on the mess that was Shane's lower back, he was 90 percent sure Shane was sound asleep. He worked on it, though, trying to ease the pain there even more.

The tension eased, Shane melting for him.

Perfect. He could do some more massaging tomorrow. For now, he thought it was cuddle time.

He spread out, covering Shane with his body, keeping his darlin' still and warm and close. Tomorrow they would start to deal with everything else. This touching was what was important now.

Shane took a deep, deep breath, muttered, "Love you, Galen," then started snoring.

"Love you too, darlin'." There was not a damned thing more certain than that.

Now he just had to get certain about everything else.

SHANE SLEPT forever. Every time he woke up, Galen was there to snuggle, and he slipped back under.

Over and over he woke himself up, only for the dreams to grab him again. Len felt like heaven, and at some point it became a three-dog night too.

When he cracked his eyes open again, it was either still dark or he'd slept an entire day.

Christ. He tried to pop up, but the dogs held him down.

"Y'all." Tails started wagging, beating on him, making him laugh. When Copper started licking his ears, he snorted hard.

"You guys suck!" Oh, was that food he smelled? He was starving.

"I grilled, darlin'." Len popped into the bedroom, those thin linen pants hanging on to his hip bones.

"I slept." Look at that. Look at that fine son of a bitch.

"You did. Hell, I did too. Hit the head, and I'll feed you."

"Sounds good." He stretched, did his business, and found a pair of light pants to lounge in. Galen wasn't in a shirt; they weren't dressing for dinner. Then he wandered out, dogs blocking him at every step. "Did you call me in today?"

"I did." Len was putting out plates. "I told them I would kill anyone who came here."

"Yeah? And it worked?" Huh. Len must have snarled.

"So far. Dylan is filling in again tonight. You might owe him a bonus."

"I'm considering making him the manager." God, he'd slept through a whole day.

"Cool. He's willing to talk." Len had been busy.

Oh, grilled corn. Yum. He grabbed glasses and forks. They settled in to eat, and Shane had to really push himself to remember the last time they'd done this.

They didn't talk about the bars, about the staff, about anything more serious than how good the steak was, how much they both liked Momma's pecan pie. Galen had attempted to make cookies, and the mangled shapes cracked him up. They tasted good, though, and he had lots.

Too many, maybe. But they were good. And Len had made them for him. Not the guys at the bar or the old farts at the bait shop.

"Oh God. Best supper ever." He was full as a tick.

"Yeah. I needed that." Len grinned at him, handing him another beer.

"Not going to be able to drive now." He took the beer, though.

"Oh, the horror." Grinning, Galen settled in next to him.

"Mmm-hmm." He leaned in, lazy and warm throughout. It felt so damned good to relax. Just sit. Breathe.

Galen's hand landed on his shoulder, heavy and solid. He

loved Len's hands. They could do so much, or just do nothing but hold him. He liked that idea.

He finished his beer and let his head rest. He knew he couldn't just sit too long, but he wanted right now. Just this moment.

Galen slipped an arm around him, leaning. "Not a bad night."

"Not at all. I'm sure an emergency is coming."

"Nope." Len shook his head. "Not tonight."

"You don't think so?" Len sounded damn sure.

"I know so. They can handle it."

He took Galen's fingers in his, tracing them, wishing his brain would calm down.

"Hey. You need to breathe, darlin'." Galen squeezed his hand, leaning a little more.

"Am I not?" He looked up into the darkest eyes he'd ever seen. Every little lash showed up, thick enough to almost distract him from those amazing laugh lines.

"You're thinking so loud I can hear it."

"Yeah. What's up with that? It's not like me." It didn't use to be like him.

"You just got caught up. It happens so damned easy. You think, oh, just one more job won't hurt." Len sounded so sure. He'd been there, Shane guessed.

He nodded. He'd been trying to make himself respectable, be something besides a beach bum. Maybe that was his issue, just like Galen's worry about getting puffy and all. Maybe he needed to be proud of what he'd done.

Shane snorted. God, he sounded like Galen.

"What's funny, darlin'?"

"Me. You're rubbing off on me." Except, not literally.

"Am I? That might be bad. You always say I think too much."

"You do. I just, oh fuck, Galen. You know me. I'm not smart enough to figure this out."

Galen pinched him. "I love you and I think you're fine."

"Well, I'd hope so." He knew better, though.

"Do I need to beat you again, darlin'?" Len sure looked serious.

"Sometimes I get tired of being the fuckup." Most of the time. Of course, not fucking up took all his attention, and then he didn't get any loving.

"You're not. Any more than I am. We're just who we are, huh?" Len took his hand, toying with his fingers. "I think our next big enterprise should be us."

"Yeah?" God, he was lost. Hurting, deep in his chest, like something there was sore.

"Uh-huh. Like a cruise. One of those gay ones out of Orlando."

Oh. Oh God. He could totally handle that. Sun. Surf. Laziness and fucking. *Yeah,* the little voice in the back of his head said, *but what about the clubs? It's tourist season. You think you'll have enough put back to keep all the staff employed during the lean season? You think you can trust those yahoos to book bands? Do inventory?*

"I think Dylan and maybe Ben can handle everything."

"Yeah? Maybe." Maybe by next year. Fuck, his head hurt. "Maybe I could work it out for Christmastime. Although we usually have Momma then, and...." God, he wanted out.

"Nope. I got a plan. I am the man with the plan, remember. I just didn't know you needed one."

"A man or a plan?"

"A plan. You always have my man parts at your disposal." That little chuckle slid right down Shane's spine.

He had to smile—had to. Galen had decided something, that was for sure, and that was that.

It would be nice if he could figure out what that was, though.

Or not.

Hell, he kinda liked just letting Galen drive a little. Those shoulders were broad enough to hold a lot of problems.

"You're all caught up in your head, darlin'."

"I know." He nodded, sighed. "I know."

"Come back to me." Len turned his cheek and kissed him, really letting him have something to think about.

He crawled into Galen's lap, wanting the comfort the man could give him. Those strong arms wrapped around him, Galen humming for him, tuneless and gravelly.

"Love you, old man."

"Old!" Galen laughed, goosing him. "I love you too."

"Ancient." He winked.

"Uh-huh. So much older than you."

"Hey, six months is six months." He settled, his ass finding a good spot on Galen's legs.

"Oh, it's an eternity." Len looked so good, smiling, relaxed.

"Finally, you understand." He rested, cheek on Galen's shoulder.

"I do, Shane. I really do."

He had a feeling Len wasn't talking age.

GALEN STARED at his phone.

Shane had hung up on him. Well, not on purpose, but the call dropped, and Shane wasn't calling back.

Damn it. They had supper plans. Dylan was a fine manager. Why the hell was Shane still at work? Things had been... better. But now he was seeing less of Shane every damned day.

It was fucking crazy—Shane was in his head, distant, gone. Hell, he couldn't even get the man to bed. That had to be the stupid pills, but Galen never found them in the house.

He was going to have to get serious about this, he could tell.

Shane just never could figure out how to say no, to anyone.

His phone rang, Dylan's face showing up.

Galen frowned but answered. "Hello?"

"Hey. It's Dylan. There was a fight, and some asshole broke the boss's phone. Shane got the baseball bat out, and now the cops are here."

"Oh shit. I'll bring his spare." And possibly pay the bail if Shane got mad.

"Yeah, thanks. I... I'm fairly sure he's gonna have to go with them. The asshole's already gone in the ambulance." Dylan's voice dropped. "Man, will they do a piss test on him? Because.... You know."

"Shit. He can refuse it for the time being. I'll see what I can do." Galen had a few friends.

"Okay. Okay, I'll see you soon." Dylan hung up, leaving him with dead air.

Goddamn it. How the hell was this still spinning out of control? He got keys, wallet, phones.

When he got there, the cops were leaving, and the lights were on up in Shane's office. Oh, thank God. No trips to jail tonight. He climbed the stairs, remembering how he and Shane had used this office back when it was Bev's bar.

He heard the music from the little iPod, heard the sound of Shane's pacing.

Galen took a deep breath before stepping in.

Shane turned around, one eye swelled near shut, lip split. "Hey."

"Christ, darlin'. What happened?" All his calm went out the window.

"There was a fight. Asshole broke my fucking phone. My phone, man! Fucking hate pricks that think they can fuck with me because I'm little. I ain't that fucking short." Jesus, Shane was wired for sound.

"I know. I, uh, brought your spare."

"Thank you." Shane looked at him, eyes twitching away. "Jesus, I hate assholes."

"Darlin', I think you need to back off the uppers." What the hell else could he say?

"You tell me how to do all this without them and I will. I can't sleep anymore."

"I told you that you didn't have to!" They'd made inroads too, which somehow hadn't worked.

"I tried! I'm trying!" Shane slammed his hand down on the desk, hard. "Just go home, Galen. I'll be fine."

"No. Look at you, Shane. You're so fucking wired you can't see. You're all beat up." Damn it, they weren't going to do this.

"I know! I know, man, and I'm scared."

No. No fear. He grabbed Shane, hugging the man tight.

Shane wrapped around him, the taut little body just thrumming like a tanned, musclely hummingbird. Hell, the way Shane's heart was beating, it was like he'd swallowed a hummingbird.

"Okay. We're going home. Now."

He didn't wait for Shane to answer. Hell, he just headed out, his better half's arm in hand. If he had to drag Shane home, he would.

Shane didn't argue, though, at least until they got to the parking lot and Galen didn't even pretend he wasn't putting Shane in the truck. "My Jeep?"

"Dylan can take it to his place. That will keep anyone from vandalizing it." He would text Dylan from home. He put Shane in the passenger seat, buckled him in, and shut the goddamn door, just daring Shane to say anything.

Thankfully, Shane just leaned his head back and closed his eyes. God, he looked pooped.

Galen drove, teeth clenched, body tight as hell. His brain went into overdrive, trying to think of what the hell to do to get Shane out of the hole he was in. He didn't understand where Shane's head was, what was driving the man.

He'd asked, more than once. Shane didn't seem to have an answer, so it was up to Galen to find one.

He pulled into the driveway, and they sat there, both of them, just in the truck cab. Galen clenched his hands on the wheel, his muscles aching.

"I'm sorry." Shane sounded diminished somehow.

"Oh, darlin'." He turned to Shane, hand on the back of the seat behind Shane's head. "I'm not mad at you. I just don't know what to do to help make it right again."

"I don't either. I keep looking for the answer, but I can't find it."

"There has to be a way." He'd suggested selling a few of the bars, but Shane had balked at that.

"Yeah." Shane didn't sound like he believed that, not for a second.

"Come on, darlin'. Let's go snuggle." They were still super good at that. The touching.

"Okay." Shane slipped out of the truck and headed for the house, stopping just to love on the dogs.

Galen followed, watching Shane, who looked a little like a ghost.

"Wade's back in town. He texted me."

Galen frowned. Wade had been a good friend of Shane's. Had wanted to be more. Had tried real hard. "That's nice."

Shane shrugged. "I guess, yeah. It's been a while."

"It has." Wade had sailed off on a yacht, and that had been

that. Galen put an arm around Shane, bypassing the couch and heading straight for bed.

"Do you remember, back in the beginning, when I was living in my Jeep?"

"I do." He pulled Shane down with him. "On the beach."

"I used to drive out here, park up on the ridge, and watch you."

"No shit?" He leaned back, staring into Shane's eyes.

"Yeah. No shit. I would sit on the hood of the old Jeep and watch you through the bedroom window. You pace a lot before you settle."

He chuckled. "I do. I reached for you a lot. In the night."

"Yeah. You did. I used to wish you could sleep good. You do now, right?"

"I do, darlin'. I love my life." He wanted Shane's life to be happy too.

"I don't, not right now. I love you."

"I love you too." He rubbed their noses together.

"Good." Shane's muscles twitched and jerked as the man relaxed. It was heartbreaking, how tense Shane was, how desperate his lover was to be coping-man.

Galen wanted nothing more than to get his laughing, beach-loving man back. He needed it.

He needed Shane.

Now he just had to figure out what to do to get back to good.

For now, all he could think was to hold on. Tight.

SHANE PULLED up to the marina, Wade's yacht right there, all shiny and sparkly. He could have just floated away on it. Wade had offered all those years ago. Fact was, though, he loved Galen.

Completely.

He couldn't walk away from that.

The rest he could leave in a heartbeat. Shane sighed, heading up the dock.

"Hey!" Wade came up from belowdecks, looking good. Healthy.

"Wade!" He had to smile. Wade was the closest thing to temptation ever and a great friend. "You're home!"

"I am. Home again, home again, jiggety jig." Wade came and hugged him, pounding him on the back. "You look like hell."

"Fuck you, man." He pinched Wade's ass. "Show off your boat, make me jealous."

"Sure. Come on." Wade rubbed shoulders with him, just chattering on about his trip around the globe.

Shane listened with half an ear, grateful when they could sit down, rest, let his heart stop slamming in his chest.

"You okay?" Wade asked, staring at him like he'd missed something.

"I'm fine." The words sounded like a lie.

Wade knew it too. "Come on, buddy. What is it? Is it Galen?"

"I don't think so. I think it's me. I.... You know how when you're on a merry-go-round and you're spinning so fast? If you get off, you're dizzy and jealous of the kids that are laughing, and if you stay on, you're going to lose your fucking mind."

"Or at least your lunch." Wade nodded, eyes hooded. "I get it. That just means you need to get off."

"Yeah? I don't know how. I keep trying, man, and I can't figure it out. I can't figure shit out anymore."

"You're stuck, huh?" Wade went to the little kitchen, got him a bottle of water.

"I guess? I don't even know how I got here, man." He didn't know shit.

"Hey, I hear you. What does Galen say?" Wade always said

Galen in a weird way. Not mean, but totally without inflection.

"He hates the uppers, hates that I'm not home, hates that I can't figure out how to do this right." He'd never felt so totally fucking out of control. Ever. Making money was supposed to make things easier, right?

"Is he being ugly?" Wade's brows went up. "He promised me he was all about making you happy."

"No. No, he's not. He's right there and good to me. Hell, he just looks at me like he's sad."

"Oh." If Wade seemed a little disappointed, Shane would ignore it.

"I'm sorry, man. You don't want to hear all this shit. Tell me about your life." This was just rubbing salt in a mostly healed wound.

"It's been good. I traveled a lot. Got a good, solid crew on the boat now if you ever want to take it out."

"Yeah? That sounds fun. Just to go away." Him, Galen, and the dogs.

"It's good for the soul, man. No phones to speak of, no worries."

"Yeah." No worries. He didn't have that anymore. He had more than a boatload.

"Well, you should think on it. Want some pretzels?" Wade had always been obsessed with pretzels.

"Sure. I could munch." He must make Wade nervous now.

"Cool." Wade bustled a little, getting Cokes and beer and pretzels and this super-stinky cheese.

"Dude. That smells like feet!" He took the beer. He could switch to Coke later.

"What, the beer?" Wade frowned, elaborately sniffing his bottle.

"The cheese, dingus." God, he'd missed Wade, honestly, and Shane told the man so. "You're a good friend."

"I try. It was hard when I left that first time, Shane." Wade gave him a smile, his eye lines deeper now. Not near as yummy as Len's. "I think I'm in a good place now, though."

"I'm glad. I didn't... I hope I didn't lead you on back then, man. I didn't want to."

"You didn't." Wade touched his leg, nothing sexual, just comforting. "I just had hopes, is all."

"If I didn't have Len, but...." He did.

"I know. I'm good."

"I'm glad. What's the neatest place you went this time?" Enough deep shit. It was time to visit and drink.

"Spain. Malaga is amazing."

"I've never been there." He bet Galen had been there, though.

"No? You ought to go."

"Maybe. One day." They didn't travel much anymore.

"It's got orange groves and an old Roman fort and shit." Wade's eyes lit up, that lean face animated.

"Yeah? You got pictures?"

"I do!" Wade tilted his head. "You sure you want to see?"

"Why wouldn't I? Are you jacking off in all of them?"

"What? No!" Laughing, Wade pulled out a tablet and brought up a raft of pictures.

After beer three, he was sprawled on the deck, laughing his ass off at pictures of Wade and ten thousand Spanish men. Lord, Wade had worked his way through them. He looked so happy too.

"Jesus Christ, buddy, that son of a bitch is eight times your size!"

"I know, right? He wanted to lock me in the hold and beat me." Shaking his head, Wade went to the next picture. "I sailed without him."

"I bet." He snorted. "I mean, I don't mind a little rough, but that man could lay down the smackdown."

"That's what I thought, huh?"

"Man, I better get back to work. I've done dick-all today." He stood, the whole world spinning in a circle.

"Whoa, man. Sit." Grabbing him, Wade pulled him back down.

"Sorry." His heart was going ninety to nothing.

"No problem, but I think—here, lie down on your left side."

"You gonna have me nap here?" His eyes were so heavy.

"I am. No worries." Wade patted his back, warm and reassuring.

"Let Len know where I'm at?" He didn't want Galen to worry.

"Of course, Buster. I'll holler at him."

"Thanks, buddy." He closed his eyes, his heart just all pattery pittery in his chest. Sleep. Sleep a little. Then Galen.

"Nice bait shop."

Galen looked up from cleaning the shelves, frowning when he saw his visitor. "I thought you were with Shane. Is something wrong?"

Wade was the all-American boy, and he looked better than ever—white-blond, tanned, buff. "He's at my yacht, sleeping."

Why did that sound ominous?

"What happened? Do I need to go get him?"

"I don't know. I mean, are you two still an item?"

"What?" He was going to punch the man. "You know we are."

"Well, if he was mine, he wouldn't look strung out." Wade stared him down. "He damn near passed out, just trying to stand up."

"Shit. I'll go get him. Why didn't you bring him home?"

Wade looked at him. "I wanted to talk to you. He needed to rest. What the fuck is wrong with you, that you'd let him get so bad?"

His immediate instinct was to scream. Maybe beat Wade down. Instead, he blew out a breath and scrubbed a hand over his stubbly face. "I'm afraid of taking this away from him."

"Huh? The man's miserable." Wade went to the cooler, grabbed a Coke, put two bucks on the counter.

"But he's worked so hard." Galen knew Shane was unhappy. They were working on it, right?

"Why?"

"What does that mean?" Why did anyone try to be a success?

"Why has he worked so hard? It's Shane. Buster. The man isn't—" Wade searched for a word. "—ambitious."

Galen blinked some more. Since when had he and Wade been able to chat about Shane in any sane way? "But he's been doing this thing. I thought it was what he wanted."

"And it didn't seem weird? That he became like this businessman? I mean, he didn't even like managing the club, much less running five." Wade stared right into his eyes, serious as a heart attack.

Galen pressed his lips together a moment. "Okay, Mr. Know-It-All, then why did he do it?"

"I'm not his lover, man. I just wanted to be. Why did he do it?"

Galen got a Coke too. And sat. He needed to get Shane, but it was important to figure this out first. "I don't know. He's—shit, since his brother died he's been working his ass off."

"I didn't even know he had a brother, man."

"Yeah. Yeah, his brother passed away." That had been a clusterfuck. The sister-in-law was nice, let Shane get to know the kids, help out. The bitch of a mother still didn't talk to

Shane, but.... But those kids did, and they thought Shane was a hero.

Not just a bartender.

"Oh God." He dropped his head into his hands.

Wade took a long swig. "Are you done now, or do you need a few more minutes for self-flagellation?"

"Oh fuck, will you shut up? You think it's easy to see this from the inside?"

"No. No, man, I don't. I just need you to see it now and fix it so that Shane is okay." Wade actually looked worried.

"Is it really that bad?" He meant Shane's health. You lived together all day every day, you missed things.

"He passed out from standing up. He's lost a good thirty pounds since the storm, and we're supposed to puff up and shit, not dissolve. Don't y'all... you know... I mean, Christ, he's like the neediest dude I ever saw."

"I—" What could he say? He and Shane were both addicts of a sort.

"Look, I'm going to lay it out for you, best I can. He loves you, more than anything. More than money, more than fucking anything. I'd give my fucking soul for someone to want me like that. He needs you, Frost, and you have to do your goddamn job, or I'm going to take him away and pray he'll go for second-best."

"No one's taking him away from me." Galen stood, pacing. "What the hell am I gonna do with those bars?"

"Let me have them for a while." Just like that. There was no way it could be that easy.

"You want to run things?"

"Sure. I've watched *Bar Rescue*, and God knows I drink a lot. Y'all have a manager, don't you?"

"Dylan." God, this couldn't work, could it? "We'd have to go away awhile."

"He's already on the yacht. I have a crew. You can bring the dogs, if you clean up after them."

"I'll get one of those grass boxes." He was going to do this. Kidnap Shane and sail around the world. "They still have their doggie passports from that trip to Aruba."

"Good deal. Go, Galen. Pack some shit and go. I'll hang here, take care of the clubs for a month. Two."

"If you really mean it, I will. Dylan has access to all of the deposits, and I'll leave you the passwords and the work laptop."

"I mean it. I love him, man. I know I can't have him, I got that, but... I want him to have what he needs."

"Thank you." For the first time, Galen allowed himself to like Wade without any reservations. And to feel a little sorry for him.

"Just do your job. Bring him back."

"I will. Then I'll actually bring him back here too. And your boat."

"That works. I'll keep you up-to-date. Let's get my information and introduce me to Dylan."

"You got it. I'll get you keys too. You can stay here." Now that he'd agreed, Galen couldn't wait to get started.

"Good deal. I let the old condo go when they stopped taking care of the landscaping. I got standards." Wade stood. "What do you need me to do?"

"Let me walk you through the house and show you how to turn everything on and off. The bait shop can stay closed unless Cooter Wilson wants to run it for you." He had a million things to do.

"I'll figure it out. You pack and talk. I'll make notes."

"You got it." He whistled up the dogs. "If Vic comes back, there's a whole freezer of chickens."

"The alligator? It's real?"

"Yep." Oh, look at that. Wade got all pale. Galen had to laugh a little.

"Hey, I'm from Texas, man. Central Texas. Not here."

"Uh-huh. Well, at least you don't have to worry about him eating the dogs."

"No. You have to worry about using them as shark bait."

He chuckled, patted Wade on the shoulder as he walked by. "True. But you will have custody of my couch."

"And you'll have to promise not to break my bed."

"I can promise to fix it if we do." He was smiling, really smiling, for the first time in weeks. God, this was going to be fun. And good for them.

"Take your own lube."

"I'll get all that on the way to the boat, man." Galen took Wade on the tour of the house, glad he'd just had Jada in to clean.

Wade helped gather the pups' bowls and food while he grabbed electronics and clothes and Shane's favorite dildo. He felt ten years younger and a hundred pounds lighter.

This might just work. And if it didn't, well, it was a start.

MOVEMENT WOKE him, Shane's eyes popping open as the wind blew over his face.

Fuck. Fuck, okay. Wake up. Focus.

Where the fuck was he? He couldn't even remember lying down. Not a bit. Wade. He'd gone to see Wade.

He looked out at the marina, stunned to see that it was not only dark, but that there were no lights, no boats. Just dark. Had the power gone out? Where was everyone?

"Hey, darlin'. You slept hard."

"Galen!" *Oh, thank God.* He surged up, reaching out. "Oh fuck. I was scared."

"I got you." Galen took his hand, coming to sit next to him. "I was looking into supper."

"Are.... This is Wade's boat. Are we going somewhere with him?"

"No. We kind of hijacked his crew. With his permission." Galen held his hand, and he heard the scrabbling of dog paws on the deck.

"Wait. What?" He opened his arms when he saw paws and ears and tails launching at him.

He got a chorus of barks and a flurry of licks. A blond head popped up from the galley, a man he didn't know glancing at the dogs, then going back under.

"We're cruising. Heading for the Bahamas first."

"We're what? The Bahamas? Can you drive a big boat?" Somehow he'd missed a conversation.

"I can, but I don't have to. I told you, we borrowed the crew. Wade has two backups in case he wants to sleep or go ashore."

"Why did we borrow the boat, Galen? I don't remember talking about borrowing it...."

"Wade talked me into it." Len pushed the dogs away, pulling him up on Galen's lap. "Said he'd always wanted to try running a bar."

"A bar." *Oh God. The bars.* He hadn't told anyone he wouldn't be checking in today, and if they didn't get back to the marina tonight, he couldn't do deposits.

"Shh." Galen kissed his temple. "Wade and Dylan are on it."

Galen didn't sound worried, not at all, just relaxed and easy in his skin, and that backed the worry off. Shane didn't know what to think, but he knew he trusted Galen.

He wasn't sure what Galen was thinking, but the man smiled like Shane had done something stunning and kissed him like Sharktopus was going to get the boat. It was hot as hell, and made sure he didn't think about anything else.

One hand was wrapped around the back of his head,

fingers digging in and holding him still. Galen was so fucking strong, so demanding. It felt like they were back in New Orleans, right after he got pierced the first time. His body burned, and he cried out when Galen found his rings, tugged one, hard.

His cock jumped, his body jerking. He panted, his need ramping up so hard.

"Good." Galen smiled and tugged again, then pulled him into another fiery kiss.

Good didn't even begin to describe it. This was like the sun licking at his skin, making him twist.

Galen tugged him up, lips wrapping around his nipple, teeth just sharp enough to make him sob. "Please."

"Mmm-hmm." Galen licked and bit, pulled and pushed. The man was like a demon or something.

His entire focus was on the ache, the sting, and Shane was fucking lost, hands in Galen's hair so he didn't fly away. He wrapped his legs around Galen and tugged the man closer, and Galen rewarded him by sucking up a bruise right next to his nipple.

"Don't stop." The wind was picking up, and he could smell the salt. It was fucking magic. Almost like watching a storm from the coast. "Galen, please. Don't let it stop."

"No, darlin'. Not stopping." Len was on fire, nipping at him all over, leaving marks.

His skin ached, and he went with it, trusting Galen's arms to hold him as he writhed. Better than dancing. Better than anything, his Len. The man pushed lower, licking at his belly.

He sat tall, giving that wet heat as much skin as Galen wanted. All he had to do was lift up and Galen's mouth found the tip of his cock.

"Yes." He loved that mouth with every fiber of his being. He wanted it, wanted to feel it all the way down to the root of his cock.

The boat was rocking, and he was holding on to his sanity by the skin of his teeth. He scrabbled at Len's shoulders, trying to get more, to get Galen to suck him.

"Greedy boy." Galen jerked him up higher, and he fucking dangled.

"Don't drop me!"

"No, darlin'. I got you." Len's muscles never even shook. That mouth closed around him, tongue flicking against the head.

A string of filthy words escaped him, his hips rolling, pushing into that heat. Galen had the best mouth ever, and the man could do obscene things. His balls pulled up. He sobbed and arched, humping restlessly as he emptied himself, pouring his soul into Galen's lips.

Galen popped off his cock when he was done, pulling him down for a kiss that rocked him to his toes. He dove right in, his entire body buzzing with the aftershocks of his orgasm.

Hard, hot, Len's cock pushed at him through the swim trunks his lover still wore.

Oh. Oh, that was his. Every inch.

He tugged at the drawstring, pushed at the waistband.

Len lifted up to help get them off, chest heaving. "Help me, darlin'."

"Anything." Everything. He wrapped both hands around Galen's cock, pulling hard and fast, just like Galen liked it. He knew all the sensitive spots, knew every place that made Len shiver and moan. Shane found them all, every one, stroking and caressing.

Galen growled, fingers gripping him hard enough to bruise. That was good; Shane loved the tiny bright flare of pain.

He used his thumbs, working the tip good and hard, making Galen feel it. He could tell how happy that made Len, could feel the tremor in those strong muscles.

"Gonna ride you, later, when you can last and last."

"Uh-huh. Want that. Let you get up on me, watch your belly, your cock."

Fuck, nothing was better than Galen's laser focus on him. "All night long. I swear."

"I can deal with that, darlin'. I need you so bad."

"Here." He slipped down, wrapping his lips around the tip of Galen's cock. Too much talking. If he talked, he would get to thinking.

That was bad. So he sucked and Len called out to him and petted him and loved on him so good.

"Gonna tear you up, darlin'. Gonna make you scream for me, like the first time."

He smiled. That first time had damn near killed him. He'd never wanted anyone else like that again, only Len. Always Galen.

Galen's hand landed on the small of his back, hips working, pushing up faster, cock spreading his lips. He could taste the salt and bitter of Galen's precome, drops of it on his tongue.

He pushed at the man's heavy ball sac, rolling, demanding that Galen give it up.

"Fuck!" Len came for him like a piano lid slamming, bang. Hot, wet seed filled his mouth. He swallowed, over and over, pulling Galen in.

"God, Shane. I needed that." Galen was laughing, breathless, joyful.

"Uh-huh." He kissed the tip of Galen's cock, the flat belly, the curve of his ribs. The way Galen's belly sucked in made him chuckle. Vain man.

He nibbled a little bit before ending up in Galen's lap. He had questions, he did, but more than that, he wanted more of that need. More of Galen wild for him, happy and free.

"Hey, you." Galen kissed him, trading their flavors back and forth.

"Hey." *Kiss me, Len. Let me not worry for a little longer.*

It worked. Galen never let up on him, stroking his back, his hips.

Those fingers pressed against him, leaving bruises behind them that ached, so good. He loved it when Len was so lost in it that he forgot how fucking strong he was. He bit Galen's shoulder, throat, leaving marks of his own.

"Fuck, yes." Len's muscles jumped for him.

"Mine." He sucked up a dark mark, wanting Galen to feel it in his bones.

"Yours, darlin'. Always yours."

That had been the one constant all these years, and Shane was grateful. Proud of that.

He pinched one nipple, touched the tattoo that matched his, petting. He couldn't seem to get enough of the connection, of Galen's skin. He wiggled, rubbed, cock making an amazing comeback.

Shane grinned. God, a twofer. When was the last time he'd had one without a nap? He rubbed, and Len started to come back up too.

"We're going to fuck now?" He could ride, right here.

"Hell, yes. Get up here, Shane, and I'll get you wet." Len yanked him up again so he was kneeling over Galen's thighs.

God, he was flying, shivering, he was so excited. His body was ready, but Len made things even better by slicking up two fingers and pushing them into Shane's hole.

Galen had lube, right there, on Wade's boat. If he thought about that too much, he'd crack up, so he just swallowed his chuckles. Galen rumbled softly, fingers pushing deep enough his toes curled. "Focus, darlin'."

"Here. I'm here." Right here.

"That's it. Ride my hand." Len pushed in, pulled out, really giving him a stretch.

"Uhn." His shoulders climbed up around his ears at the burn of it, the twinge.

"So pretty." Galen held him up with the other arm, giving him purchase.

"More." Three fingers made his ass burn.

"Yeah." Galen gave him everything he asked for, sliding three fingers in, his hole spreading hard.

"Fuck. Fuck!" He was going out of his fucking mind. Galen was just going to make him explode.

Galen's laugh tickled all through him. "There's my Shane."

"Right here."

"Damn straight. Ready for me, darlin'?"

"Always. Always." Forever. Also, now was good. He pushed up as far as he could, letting those fingers slide free so he could take Galen's cock, which was hard and ready for him.

He reached down, grabbed Galen's prick and rubbed it over his hole.

"Uhn." Len arched beneath him, pushing up, sliding in a tiny bit.

"Uh-huh." Just like that. He took more, sinking down.

"That's it, Shane. Jesus, you're hot. Tight. Still so tight."

He squeezed, wanting Galen crazy for it. His muscles clamped down, and Len grunted, cock pushing up and up.

"Harder." He arched, grinding down.

"How hard, darlin'? Like this?" Len slammed up into him, hips punching like mad.

"Galen!" He bit his tongue, it was so good.

"Kiss me." Len took his mouth and took his ass, really giving it to him.

He grabbed his cock, yanking furiously, pulling himself

toward the edge. Len's big hand wrapped around his, helping him out. Oh, that was what he wanted, just that. Just there. Hard, fast, full of Galen. Shane gritted his teeth. Yeah. More.

"Hot little motherfucker. Come on my cock, Shane." Galen popped his ass hard, and that was all she wrote, spunk spraying from him.

Len grunted, spilling right into him in return, hot and wet, letting him know his lover was right there with him.

Oh. Wow.

Also, yay.

Shane cuddled in, humming as the cool night air blew across his spine. They rested, Len sort of toppling them over and stretching out.

There would be questions. Lots of them. Possibly grumping. Tomorrow.

For now, they could just hang out in the salt air and hold each other. With the dogs, who clambered up on the bunk with them.

It was weird as fuck, but it worked for him.

GALEN HUMMED, rubbing sunscreen into Shane's skin. Shane had slept for eight hours, and Galen had moved them belowdecks, then back up. Maybe it was time to wake Shane up for lunch. Supper? Breakfast?

Hell, he had no idea what time, or day, it was.

It was perfect. Shane hadn't even asked about the bars, or Wade, or anything. The man had fucked and slept, one hand always touching him.

Galen owed Wade big-time, and it didn't even chafe him a tiny bit. He hadn't been this happy in years.

He trailed his fingers down Shane's ass, his lover chuckling softly.

Wade's crew was incredibly discreet. They all disappeared

at the right times, taking the dogs with them. He and Shane were alone.

"Good morning, Galen." Shane turned to kiss him, lips like fire on his shoulder. "You smell like sex. So good."

"Mornin', darlin'. I smell coffee and cinnamon rolls too."

"Coffee." Shane smiled for him, stretched. "Sun feels good."

"It does. You should have seen Mookie swimming."

"He went in the ocean?" Shane sat up, looked around. "Galen, there's just water, everywhere."

"It's okay, darlin'. Wade's steward, Jon? He went with him, and he was wearing a floatie."

"But... Galen, what are we doing out here?" Shane leaned and poured coffee, then handed him a mug.

He sipped at it, not really to give himself time to think, but just because it was Jamaican brew and deserved to be appreciated. "We're here to get away from it all, Shane," he finally said.

"Oh. For how long?"

"I don't know. We have the boat as long as we want it. We dock in Nassau tomorrow." He loved Nassau, so friendly and bright.

"Nassau? I love Nassau." Again, Shane didn't ask about the bars. Not a bit.

That was okay with him. He'd managed to check his email yesterday, and Wade was having the time of his life.

Shane looked better already, lazy and happy, like a lizard in the sun. Galen had to pet that sweet belly.

"Len. So warm." God, look at that smile.

"Love your skin." He so did. Loved every scar and mark.

"We're basking." Shane wasn't complaining.

"We are. That's what the deck of a boat is for." The dogs came running up, shaking water all over them.

Shane hooted, laughing and reaching for the pups. They

were beside themselves, having Shane's attention, Shane's joy. He totally got that. Galen was pretty stoked about that too. If he had his way, they'd stay on the boat for a year.

Hell, maybe they would. Just loving on each other and being together in the sun. It was an idea. They'd rent a place on land every few weeks, let the dogs run amok.

Shane would get nice and brown, and the smile lines would come back. They would explore crazy little towns and swim.

Another cup of coffee was handed to him. Then he had an armful of lover again, that tight little ass snuggling right into him. That was enough to make him hum, to make the crew on deck disappear.

Okay, the whole crew thing was amazing.

Truly.

He hugged Shane to him, kissing the back of Shane's neck. "Pretty day."

"Perfect. It's like a dream."

"Is it weird?" He didn't think so, but he didn't want Shane to be wigged out.

"Weird? It's magic. I haven't felt so good since Colorado."

"Oh, good." He kissed Shane's shoulder, licking at the sweat. Colorado had been a long time ago. A damn long time ago.

"Do you think it's okay, Len? To just float away like this?"

"If I hadn't made a plan, I'd be worried, but Wade is having a ball running the business, darlin'. We owe him one."

That and Dylan needed a raise, but Wade had said he'd deal with that.

"I don't get it. I hate it, running them."

"Well, then, you don't have to anymore." God, he wished he'd known that. Oh, he knew Shane hated the stress, but if he'd known how much his lover really despised the whole bar-mogul thing, he would have sold those clubs in a hot minute.

"No? You promise?" Shane searched his eyes for God knew what.

"I swear. They're gone." He meant it too. They were set for retirement, really. No more bars.

"Okay. Okay, cool." Shane's smile was like the sun breaking through the clouds, and there weren't any clouds out here.

That smile was worth any effort. Anything. He kissed it, turning Shane to face him all the way.

Shane's cock nudged his belly, hands wrapped around his shoulders. That was far better than chatting about bars. Far better.

His hand cupped Shane's head, the soft short hair tickling his palm. All they had to do today was luxuriate in each other's company.

Then tomorrow, all they had to do was go play in Nassau, drink and goof off.

Life was pretty damned good.

SHANE WAS bouncing at the bottom of the best margarita he'd tasted in days. There was a beautiful man dancing in the corner, black skin shining in the sun, his drummers giving him a beat. It was hot as hell.

Almost as hot as Galen.

Shane glanced at his lover, who wore loose white pants and a tight gray T-shirt, skin tanned and smooth, gimme cap not hiding those dark eyes a bit. No, nothing was as fine as that.

They'd wandered and shopped, goofed off and played. And now there was tequila. And seafood on the way. Fried. With hot bread on the side. Nassau had the best food, sort of like a cross between New Orleans and Florida.

His phone rang, buzzing in his pants, making him jump. He grabbed it, grinning when he saw Wade's name. He'd almost forgotten the sound of his phone. Weird.

"Hey, Wade."

"Hey, Buster! Galen said it was okay to call." Wade sounded as chipper as he felt.

"It is. We're in Nassau. We took your boat!"

"The crew likes you way more than me." Wade chuckled. "How do you like it?"

"The boat? I love it. I sleep on the deck. We eat. I'm having tequila."

"Good on you! Hey, can I ask you a question?"

Shane braced himself, hoping Wade wasn't going to ask him to come home. "Surely can."

"What do you know about Dylan? I mean, is he, uh, family?"

"Wade. Honey, I don't know any straight men." At least he was fairly sure he didn't. Certainly not the ones who worked in his bars.

"Oh. You think he just doesn't like me? Maybe I've lost my touch."

"Oh ho! Are you macking on my bar manager?" He waggled his eyebrows at Galen.

"My bar manager, Buster."

"Right. Yours." He laughed. "You think he's hot, huh?"

"He's stunning, man. I might want to eat him for lunch."

"If you eat him, he can't work for you."

"No. I know. I just think he's hot, okay? I need advice."

"Uh. He likes dancing and Cajun food?"

"Really? Like club dancing?" Wade sounded dubious, which Shane understood. He'd seen Wade dance. Flail.

"Tell him to take Dylan to the Gator Grill," Galen said, poking him on the arm.

"Len says the Gator Grill, man. You'll drink, get sweaty, dance. It'll end up okay."

Wade chuckled. "Thanks, Buster. He makes me stupid like you did."

"He's a good guy." Shane grinned. Dylan needed someone to spoil and love him. Shane was already taken.

"So am I." Wade cackled, the sound like a giant bird. It was good to hear his friend so happy.

"You are. Tell him you have my seal of approval."

Wade snorted. "He's just glad you're having fun, I think, and staying out of his hair. Little micromanager."

"Fuck off, ass hat."

"I intend to." Wade chuckled. "So it's good? The boat and your man and all?"

"Perfect. I owe you. This is amazing. I could float forever."

"Good deal. I was ready to be on dry land, and my crew was bored."

"You're a good friend, Wade. You know that, right?"

"Of course I do, Buster. It works both ways. Have a shot for me."

"I might have two. Talk to you in a few weeks, man." Maybe. Maybe he'd be busy.

"Later, Shane."

For the first time since he'd met Wade, the man didn't sound reluctant to say goodbye. Or wistful. Wade and Dylan. Huh. Pretty damned cool.

He shoved his phone in his pocket, grinning like a monkey. "He's going after Dylan."

"No shit?" Len looked unbelievably pleased. "Good."

"Yeah. It is." He lifted his glass. "To tequila."

"To you, darlin'." Len clinked glasses with him. "I love you smiling and happy."

"Yeah. I just love you."

"Well, same here, dork. I just want to be with you."

"Want to go walk on the sand, Len? Wander?" He could walk for miles in this sunshine.

"I do." Len tossed cash down on the table and stood.

He admired that long, fine line of stud, then got up, took Galen's hand. "I'm ready."

"Come on, then." Galen led him out toward the beach, toward the waves and sand and all of his favorite things. He wasn't gonna think about bartending again if he didn't have to.

He was just gonna float.

Interested in learning more about BA's cowboys? Want free fiction and news? Join my newsletter!

Galen Frost buys a house and a bait shop in a small Florida town to get away from his life as a semipro football player. When he meets good-time bartender Shane Barton, the heat between them is instant and intense—like the burn of good whiskey.

Galen and Shane don't have much in common beyond their healthy libidos and their love of a good time, but the intoxicating heat brings them together like rain on the ocean, whipping up a frenzy of weather... good and bad. When trouble blows ashore, they will have to ride out the storm that breaks between them as Galen's past rears its ugly head.

<u>Stormy Weather Book 1</u>

The weather in the Florida swamps is looking a little rocky for retired football player, Galen, his laid-back lover, Shane, and their gator, Vic.

When Galen buys into a football team, promoting and wheeling and dealing are the name of the game. He's so busy he hardly gets to see Shane anymore, which means a lot of lonely naps on the couch.

Shane is tied up with managing the bar, covering for unreliable bartenders, and serving drinks to good-time party boys. Used to be Galen couldn't get enough of him. Now he can hardly pry Galen away from the phone, and Shane starts to wonder where he stands in Galen's life. Will things ever be the way they were?

When Galen starts to forget their dates, the pressure builds, jealousy and hurt swirling into a tropical storm. Galen and Shane need to seek shelter in each other before everything they've built is washed away.

Stormy Weather Book 2

Galen and Shane are back in the final installment of the *Stormy Weather* series, and a tempest of epic proportions is brewing. Once they couldn't get enough of each other, but now Galen's long hours are driving a wedge between him and Shane. Lonely and starved for his lover's attention, bartender Shane falls in with a new crowd that doesn't have his best interests at heart, and Galen struggles with a workload he can't manage and an unscrupulous partner who wants to eliminate Shane. He can barely keep his head above water, let alone chart a course home to Shane.

While they're floundering and trying to hold their relationship together, a hurricane heads for the Florida coast—and they're directly in the path of the storm. It's a crisis that will either finally break them apart or remind them how much they stand to lose if they don't hold on to each other.

Also included is the free novella *Bartender Rescue*.

<u>Stormy Weather Book 3</u>

About BA

Western to the bone and an unrepentant Daddy's Girl, BA Tortuga spends her days with her hounds and her beloved wife, having mother-daughter dates, and eating Mexican food. When she's not doing that, she's writing. She spends her days off watching rodeo, knitting, and surfing Pinterest in the name of research. Following their own personal joys, BA and Julia heard the call of the high desert and they now live in the New Mexico mountains. BA's personal saviors include her wife, her best friends, and coffee. Lots of coffee. Really good coffee.

Having written everything from fist-fighting cowboys to rural single dads to werewolves, BA does her damnedest to tell the stories of her heart, which is committed to giving everyone their happily ever after. With books ranging from heart-warming stories of found families, to rodeo cowboys that are fighting to make a mark, to fiery passionate love affairs, BA refuses to be pigeon-holed by anyone but the voices in her head.

Bombs and Guacamole

Ammo and Enchiladas

The Cereus Series

Cereus: Building

Cereus: Opening

Cereus: Training

Cereus: Rescue

The Cowboy Wanted Series

Cowboy Healing

The Foster Ranch Series

The Cowboy Contract

The Cowboy Guardian

Leanin' N Ranch Series

Commitment Ranch

Finding Mr. Wright

Whiskey to Wine

Come Back Around

This Old Wind

Perfectly Seasoned

Love is Blind Series

Ever the Same

Real World

Midnight Rodeo Series

Welcome to the Pack

Tails and Whiskers

Above the Fold

Brownie's Sway

Thack's Angel

Here, Kitty Kitty

The Recovery Series

Refired

Slip

The Release Series

The Terms of Release

The Articles of Release

Catch and Release

The Road Trip Series

Racing the Moon • Steam and Sunshine

Under Pressure • Walking on the Sun

Roughstock Series

Blind Ride

And a Smile

File Gumbo

Back to Back

Pulled from All Sides

Coke's Clown

Leading the Blind

The Sanctuary Series

Just Like Cats and Dogs

What the Cat Dragged In

The Spirit Quest Series

Crossing the River

Chasing the Moon

Breaking the Ice

The Stormy Weather Series

Rain and Whiskey

Tropical Depression

Hurricane

Two is Never Enough Series

Claiming Their Mate

Needing to Breathe

Contemporary Standalones

Adding to the Collection

Back Forty

Best New Artist

Boys in the Band

Broken In

Elite Connections *(April 2024)*

Fighting Addiction

Latigo

Things that Go Bump in the Night

Unearthed

Wolf Run

Lesbian Romance

Summit Springs Series

Christmas Bizarre w/ Jodi Payne

Honeymoon in the Cards w/ Jodi Payne

Tipping the Barrel

Contemporary Standalones

Bright Lights and Boobjobs

Games Girls Play

Historical Standalones

Bustles and Doeskins

With Jodi Payne

The Collaborations Series

Refraction

Syncopation

The Cowboy and the Dom Series

First Rodeo

Razor's Edge

No Ghosts

The Soldier and the Angel

The East Meets Westerns Universe
Temptation Ranch

Les's Bar Series
Just Dex
Hide Bound
Wholly Trinity

Lone Star Series
Tending Tyler
Roped In

Merry Everything Series
Window Dressing
Cowboy Protection
Cowboy and Cupcakes

Wrecked Series
Wrecked
Flying Blind
Special Delivery
Seeds and Sunshine
Pick Up Man *(March 2024)*

The Higher Elevation Series
Land of Enchantment
Keeping Promises

Bigger than Us

Heart of a Cowboy

Home Free

The Sin Deep Series

Sin Deep

The Trouble with Cowboys

The Triskelion Series

Breaking the Rules

Making a Mark

Making the Rules

Hey, y'all!

Thank you for giving Hurricane a try. I hope you enjoyed the story, and will consider leaving a review at the eBook retailer website where you made your purchase.

Don't forget to "like" my BA Tortuga page on Facebook to keep up with new releases, author news, special discount codes and sale announcements. And if you're interested in sneak peeks, rodeo pictures, and general fun, please come see the BA's Cowboys on Facebook. We'd love to have all y'all!

Yeehaw!

BA